A Walk into Darkness

Jade Winters

A Walk Into Darkness

by Jade Winters

Copyright 2013 by Jade Winters

www.jade-winters.com

Other titles by Jade Winters

Novels

143

Novellas

Talk Me Down From The Edge

Short Stories

The Makeover
The Love Letter
Love On The Cards
Temptation

To Ali
For always making the impossible – possible.

Prologue

The delft blue sky of South-East England changed suddenly as formidable dark clouds pooled together over the ancient Epping Forest. A young woman sat on a fallen tree in a small holding off the beaten track, her knees tucked under her chin as her finger traced lines in the bark. Her shoes were damp from the trek through the leaves and moss into the dense area of trees that made her invisible to passersby. This was her refuge. She retreated here when she needed to clear her mind; today she needed to be there more than ever. She clenched her jaw to prevent her teeth from chattering as the temperature suddenly plunged, causing her to pull her light blue cardigan closer together. She was fast regretting her hasty decision to run out of her parents' home without a jacket, but she couldn't stand arguing with them anymore.

Her parents tried to control her decisions—about love, life, her career—as if she were a toddler about to run out into the street. She humoured them by studying law instead of art history and she kept the kind of company her parents would find fitting for someone of her breeding and stature, though it disgusted her. Their disapproval of her affection for Peter was an unbearable burden that she could not remove. She pleaded with her parents to be reasonable, to look beyond class status and instead to the character of the person. They wanted her to date men from families they approved of, sons of MPs and CEOs, not the son of a construction worker and a cleaner. But she only wanted Peter. He was tall and strong, with an aristocratic face and a mop of curly black hair. She thought he was beautiful but she had known many beautiful people. There was something else that made her desire him.

They had met when he was the DJ at her best friend's eighteenth birthday party. It was an immediate connection, like an electrical current that drew them together. They had dated exclusively for the past year. Everyone could see that they were in love—except for her judgmental parents. *So what if he wasn't born with a silver spoon in his mouth?* she thought angrily. He hadn't attended the right schools or been taught to navigate the social institutions of the upper classes. She thought he was the most loving, down-to-earth, compassionate person she had ever known. If her parents couldn't be happy for her, then damn them. She was old enough to make her own decisions and she had just made up her mind: she was going to India to join Peter and there was nothing anyone could do about it.

Lost in her daydream as she considered her newly laid plans, she didn't hear the sound of branches snapping behind her. Seconds later, the unmistakable bark of a human cough brought her back to reality. A sharp tickle ran along her spine, as if a cold finger were tracing the winding curvature. She attempted to turn around. In an instant, hands with thick calloused fingers and cracked yellowed fingernails were upon her, roughly gripping the sides of her face. They held her in place so she couldn't turn to face her assailant. She could hear her heart thumping in her ears as adrenaline rushed through every vein in her body, propelling her to claw and pound at the hands which held her prisoner, but it was to no avail—she was no match for a man with his strength. The muffled laughter of a passersby gave her hope for a chance to escape. She attempted to scream but her move was pre-empted by the man as he clamped his hand over her mouth.

"Shhhh," he said, hissing in her ear.

They were soon alone in an eerie silence. She closed her eyes and could feel the hardness of him as he flattened himself against her. His penetrating odour of sweat and tobacco repulsed her. A wave of nausea engulfed her as he leaned closer and placed the sharp tip of a steel blade against her throat. She whimpered, gulping down air, hyperventilating in sheer terror. Despite the cold air she felt perspiration trickle down her brow and into her eyes.

Oh God, please don't let me die like this! The sudden halt of pressure on her neck gave her fresh hope until she felt the knife begin to slide down her front. In one swift movement her T-shirt was torn open and a breeze of cold air caused goose pimples on her exposed chest. She managed to let out a scream as he moved his hand from her mouth and roughly cupped her small breast—but the scream went unheard, her only chance of being saved had already been lost. For a split second it crossed her mind that he would not kill her, no, he was going sexually assault her. She cursed herself for not paying attention to the news reports about the dangers women faced by being alone in isolated areas. But this sort of thing happened to other people, not the daughter of a prominent Member of Parliament. If only she could make eye contact with the man—maybe she could in some way make him see sense. Using all her strength she frantically squirmed left and right—finally managing to wriggle free from his arms—mistakenly turning to face him instead of running away.

"You!" she cried in disbelief, her heart still pumping from the rush of adrenaline. "But I thought. . ."

Before another word left her mouth, he lunged at her. Grabbing her roughly he threw her effortlessly to the ground. His large bulky body straddled her small frame, his thick set legs pinning her arms in place so she couldn't fight him.

"Please, don't do this!" Her pleas became ragged gasps as she lay helplessly under his weight. "Please. I don't know why you're doing this to me." Tears mingled with the soil on her face. He looked down at her with an expression that was hard to read. That was when she saw the chill in his blue eyes and knew her life was over. Her heart grieved for her family and the life she wanted with Peter. She closed her eyes and recited the Lord's Prayer. She heard the soft swoosh of the knife being swung in the air before it finally plunged into her neck—blood splurged from her like a fountain. She shrieked but the sound came out as a low gurgle. It had felt like someone had shoved and twisted a hot poker deep inside of her. She felt it being slowly withdrawn, and brought down again, several more times—invading her body in a mad frenzy. The sharpened blade carved into her chest and neck like a knife through butter. Above, she could see the branches and leaves of a silver birch tree and the grey sky. The scene flickered each time she blinked her blood covered eyes. She heard a loud crack but couldn't tell if it was inside her or the snapping of a branch nearby. It didn't matter anymore. All of her earthly concerns were slowly fading away as a sense of calmness washed over her. Death wasn't how she imagined—there were no bright lights, nor singing angels, nor visions of Jesus—just a descent into gradual darkness as she sucked in the air and took her final breath.

Chapter 1

The song *Spirit in the Sky* filled the auditorium as men and women of diverse backgrounds eagerly took their seats, fidgeting in anticipation. As the house lights dimmed, a large screen came to life at the back of the stage. Highlights of the modern-day Nostradamus relaying messages from the dead to visibly distressed audience members flashed across it. The energy in the room elevated when the man dressed in a snazzy, shiny black suit, made his way onto the stage. He stopped in the centre while applause thundered throughout the hall.

"Thank you," he said, briefly bowing his head. "Thank you." After a few seconds had passed, he placed his index finger over his lips and waited for the noise to descend into silence.

His diamond-shaped face revealed a sombre expression as the camera moved in for a close-up, beads of perspiration visible along his dark hairline. He opened his broad mouth and began to speak in an intimate tone. "I have a young girl here," he said, tilting his head to one side, his eyes closing as if he were straining to hear her voice. "She's sad, so sad." His brow scrunched in the middle. "Es . . . Esther. Her name is Esther," he said with finality. "She's telling me about her eyes . . . she's saying they were magic," he relayed, smiling fondly. Then, sadly shaking his head, he said dramatically, "Oh, my poor darling, Esther, she's cold, so very cold." He wrapped his arms around his torso. "She was taken so young, she never had time to say goodbye to her loved ones."

He opened his eyes and walked across the stage

with his arms outstretched, veins bulging at his temples. "The person she is trying to contact is here in this area. She said she went out one day and didn't—couldn't return. Can anyone here relate to Esther?" he called out to the audience.

After a moments silence, a faint female voice rose from the back row.

"What's that, love, I can't hear you," he said, scanning the seats in front of him.

"I can," she called out again, stronger and more certain this time. "I know Esther."

He brought his hand up to shield his eyes from the glaring lights. "Please, stand up. Someone, get a microphone to this lady," he said, as the woman stood and waited for it to be passed along.

"What's your name, love?"

"Hailey."

"Hello, Hailey. Was there something I said that made you think that Esther is contacting you?"

"Esther is my sister," she said, clutching the right side of her arm rest with a trembling hand.

"Has she passed over?"

"No. Well, I don't know. She's been missing for several years. Her eyes . . . they were vivid blue. She always said that she could put anyone under a magic spell by getting them to gaze into them. Her eyes were always the first thing people noticed about her."

The audience let out a collective gasp.

"I always hoped I would see her again someday. I thought there was a chance she was still alive." Tears threatened to spill from her eyes.

"She knows you've never forgotten her, she says she loves you," he said, raising his voice in a dramatic fashion.

Hailey wanted to cry out but the lump in her throat stopped her from doing so. The medium continued, "She didn't know it was coming. She wants you to know she didn't suffer."

His words hit her with the force of a sledge hammer as he revealed Esther's age and the clothes she was wearing. Then he dropped the bomb.

"She's showing me an ancient forest . . . a silver birch tree. She said you could always find her there. Does that make sense, my love?" His face contorted with a sadness that would have been hard to fake.

Hailey nodded her head vigorously as tears streamed from her eyes. "It's where she always went to think, to be alone. Does that mean she's"—she paused whilst she tried to compose herself—"she's dead?"

"Oh, Hailey, love, I'm sorry." He descended the small staircase leading to the floor, striding briskly up the aisle with quick steps. The medium motioned for Hailey to join him, embracing her in his arms. In a voice that sounded like it was fighting back tears, he delivered this message: "I'm afraid so and she wants you to find her. She wants to come home."

***

Sometime later, Hailey stood patiently in line—she had been waiting over an hour but wasn't complaining—her mind was still mulling over the evening's revelations.

"Next!" a male voice called from behind a desk.

She walked tentatively toward the middle-aged man with thick grey hair, his tanned face devoid of any expression.

"Sorry for keeping you waiting," he said, matter-of-factly.

"That's okay. I imagine Friday is a very busy night for you," she said, licking her dry lips.

"Indeed it is. So how can we help you?"

"I want to report my sister's suspicious death," she said quickly.

PC O'Donnell demonstrated little reaction to her statement as he reached for his pen and looked up at her.

"What was her name?"

"Esther Campbell."

His breathing suspended for a few seconds. "When did she die?"

"She was murdered in 1984."

Chapter 2

Sunlight pierced through the lone window, casting a golden glow against a fawn-coloured crushed velvet headboard.

"What are you doing?"

"I'm about to put the phone down and go back to sleep," Ashley said testily.

"Wrong answer," challenged the voice over the phone.

"No, I think you'll find it's the correct one. I've had about six hours sleep since working the late shift last night."

"Well, you're going to have to catch up on your beauty sleep later."

"No, I'd rather catch up on it now if it's all the same to you," she said, yawning.

"I'd like nothing better, Ash, but it was Colleen who asked me to call you."

"Why would she want you to call me on my day off?" Ashley asked, switching the mobile phone to her other hand. She rolled onto her back and stared at the ceiling, resting her spare hand against her stomach as she waited for the request she knew was coming.

"Because she wants you to come in today and you know what Colleen wants. . . "

"Colleen gets," she said in unison with Dale, her colleague of four years. Letting out a long exhale, Ashley turned her head to look at her chocolate brown Labrador, who was sleeping on the floor beside her, then glanced at her watch. "I'll be in by noon. I've got to take Muffin for a walk."

"But, Colleen said—"

"No buts, Dale," she said pushing the quilt aside and sitting up. "That's unless Colleen wants to pay for a cleaner, of course."

"Okay, okay. I'll tell her. See you at noon."

She could hear the smile in Dale's voice, as they both recalled the last occasion she had failed to return home in time to take Muffin out for his hour long walk. And the consequences—it had taken several days to remove the scent of Muffin's *accident* from her house.

She snapped her mobile phone shut and threw it on the bed. "My one day off in over two weeks and they still can't give me a break," she said to Muffin who had roused, his ears pricking as she spoke. "Not that you care, right? You're another one that wants his pound of flesh."

Tail wagging, Muffin bounded onto the bed, his big wet nose rubbed against her arm. "But I love you so it's alright," she said, laughing as she ruffled his head. "Let me take a quick shower and then we'll go."

Ashley stood and after stretching out the knotted muscles in her neck, headed to the bathroom and turned the shower on. Stepping under the spray, she succumbed to the feeling of relaxation as the water eased the tension from her slender body. She wanted to stay in there a little longer but she was aware that Muffin needed his walk. Quickly squeezing a small amount of shampoo onto her shoulder length champagne blonde hair, she massaged the sweet scented liquid into her scalp. Above the drumming of the water against the glass door she could hear Muffin barking. She laughed at his way of letting her know she had over-extended her stay in the shower by a minute. Finishing up quickly, she towelled herself dry, slipped into a black tracksuit and pulled her wet hair into a ponytail. Thankfully, it was the middle of summer so it would dry before she returned home. She didn't want to keep her colleagues waiting while she fiddled with a hair dryer. What could they possibly want from her today_that couldn't have waited until tomorrow? She found Muffin panting by the front door, his tongue dangling out the side of his mouth.

"Come on, then," she said, slipping his collar around his neck. "Let's go and find that beautiful Husky you've had your eye on for the past week

Chapter 3

"So what's with all the cloak and dagger secrecy?" Ashley asked Dale, as she settled herself down on her chair. She bit into a cream cheese and salmon bagel that she had picked up on her way to work, savouring every morsel.

The space she shared with Dale was called an office but it had more in common with a broom cupboard. There was barely enough room for one, let alone the two of them. The shelves along the wall were stacked with bulging case flies, which, despite her height of five foot seven, still required a ladder to reach the top.

Dale sat opposite her, his well-built body encased in a beige shirt. He shrugged his broad shoulders. "Don't ask me, but I do know something big is going down. There's been a lot—and I mean *a lot* of activity going on here all morning."

"And there hasn't been any gossiping at the water cooler? I'm shocked," Ashley said, as she used her napkin to mop the excess cream cheese from her lips.

The door to their office opened abruptly. Ashley swivelled sideways in her chair to face the slender red-haired woman with cat green eyes, who spoke directly to her.

"Glad you could make it," the woman said dryly.

"What on my day off and all?" Ashley shot back, smiling sweetly at her. "No problem, Colleen."

"Well, believe it or not, there are a few items on today's agenda that are more important than dog walking."

"Not to Muffin, there aren't," Ashley said defiantly.

The women's eyes locked in hostility until a small, reluctant smile spread across Colleen's lips.

"Okay, I'm sorry—I take it back," she said, holding her hands up in surrender. "Now, if you wouldn't mind, can you follow me to my office . . . please," she added, almost as an afterthought.

"Of course I can," Ashley said, pulling a face at Dale before swirling around in her chair and standing up. Dale stood to follow.

"Not you, Dale. I want to see Ashley alone."

"And they say women have a hard time," he muttered to himself.

"Did you say something, Dale?"

"Me? Nope. Not a word."

"I didn't think so."

Detective Chief Inspector Colleen Rees had been Ashley's boss and Senior Investigating Officer for the Major Investigation Team for five years. Although they often had a turbulent relationship, Ashley ultimately respected her and the way she ran the team—most of the time.

Colleen opened the door to her office and allowed Ashley to walk in ahead of her. The medium-sized room was sparsely furnished. It contained a desk four feet wide, which was noticeably devoid of any personal effects, two mesh orthopaedic office chairs and a row of grey filing cabinets along the back wall.

Closing the door gently behind them, Colleen leaned against it for a brief moment. "I am sorry I had to ask you to come in, Ashley. I had no choice." She pushed back a strand of long red hair from her forehead.

"I'm listening," Ashley said, resting her hands on her hips.

"I don't know if you've ever heard about the disappearance of Esther Campbell? The daughter of the MP Edward Campbell."

"I remember reading about it a few years ago. Her father was making an appeal for any new information—he was offering something like a hundred grand at the time I think. Why do you ask?"

Colleen moved swiftly to her desk, sat down on the edge and gestured for Ashley to sit.

"Well her sister supposedly knows where her body is buried. She came in to report it yesterday. The PC who took her statement remembered the case and brought it to my attention this morning."

Ashley looked up after hearing this information. "So, she's dead?"

Colleen winced. "We don't actually know for certain."

"I'm confused. You just said her sister knows where she's buried."

"Yes, but it's not quite that simple. Initially, Esther was considered a runaway. There was some talk of, shall we say, 'disharmony' in the family. But when her room was searched and all of her belongings were still there a full scale investigation took place. Eventually, the case went cold. That is, until yesterday, when. . ." She shook her head, a wry smile on her face.

"When what?" Ashley asked.

She hesitated for a split second. "When Hailey

went to see a psychic and he basically gave her enough information to convince her that Esther was dead and could be found in Epping Forest. The area he identified was apparently frequented by Esther."

Ashley's face acquired an expression of blank surprise. "Tell me you're joking."

"No, I'm not," Colleen replied.

Standing, Ashley straightened her shoulders and cleared her throat. "Are you seriously telling me that you dragged me in here today for hocus pocus? I thought as officers of the law we dealt with fact, not fiction."

"Look, it's not about what we believe is true. I received orders from the top that this case must be treated with sensitivity."

"Is there anything else?"

"Well, yes, there are two things—Hailey Campbell will be coming in tomorrow. I'd like you and Dale to conduct an interview with her, see if you can get a bit more information out of her about last night's show and—" She paused briefly. "Detective Chief Superintendent Ripley is here, he's come to brief us about the original case, as he was part of the team that first looked into Esther's disappearance."

"Oh, that's just great. Can my day get any worse?"

"Listen, I don't want the animosity between you two affecting this case. We're meeting in the briefing room in five minutes, bring Dale with you, please."

Ashley advanced toward the door. Upon reaching it, she made a movement to leave before stopping and turning around to Colleen, her eyes blazing with fury, but her tone under control. "This really is outrageous, you know. If any old Joe walked in off the street and claimed his deceased Aunt Mary had told him through a medium where a missing person was buried, he would be directed to the nearest mental institution. Yet for someone in a position of power, we'll entertain a superstitious idea induced by grief, not logic. Hell, we'll even roll out the red carpet for them."

"I would like to believe that we'd investigate any potential leads in a murder enquiry the same way—regardless of the social status of the people involved," Colleen insisted.

"Come on, Colleen, we both know that's not true. After seven years on the force, we're both aware of the double standards implemented by the police service on a daily basis."

"Isn't it time you let the past go, Ash?" Colleen asked, the colour deepening on her pale face.

Ashley looked away from her as her lips began to tremble. "How can I? When we're still doing the same bullshit, even now," she said in a low voice, brushing aside the single tear that spilled aimlessly from her aqua green eyes.

Chapter 4

"Come on then, golden girl. Tell all," Dale said teasingly, as Ashley entered their office. He leaned back with his fingers laced behind his head, tilting the chair until the legs hovered off the floor. The top of his desk was mayhem, as usual. There were strewn papers, empty take-away containers, disorganised mounds of case files and a chipped coffee cup he refused to get rid of, despite Ashley saying she would replace it with a new one. She shrugged off her black jacket and undid two buttons on her white blouse. Waving her hand to fan herself with futility, she took three steps to the small window and opened it. There was no respite, Harlow was in the middle of a June heat wave.

"You'll find out soon enough," Ashley said in monotone, carelessly throwing her jacket on top of a grey filing cabinet squashed in a corner.

"Man, you look well pissed. What happened in there?"

"Don't even ask. Come on, let's go. I've been told to bring you to the briefing," she said, as she walked back to her desk, picked up her mobile phone and silenced it.

"I've always dreamt of having a moody, sultry partner. Lo and behold, I have one," Dale said, chuckling.

"Let's see if you're still feeling amused after you hear what Colleen has in store for us."

The smile disappeared from his lips as he brought the chair back down to the floor. "That sounds ominous," he said, launching off his chair and jogging after her as she made her way along the windowless corridor and into the briefing room.

Colleen sat at the head of the table, already engrossed in a conversation with DCS Ripley, a thin wiry man with a tall forehead that gave the impression of mental prowess. Ashley and Dale nodded in acknowledgement to the rest of the team as they silently took a seat at the table.

A few seconds later DCS Ripley addressed them all. "Good morning," he began, speaking in a strong, confident tone. "For those of you whom I've never met before, I'm DCS Ripley. I was one of the serving officers on the case when Esther Campbell was reported as missing back in '84. I know only a couple of you have been brought up to speed by DCI Rees about this unpleasant business." He spoke as if he were talking about the weather and not an actual missing person. "So, I'll go over it again for those who haven't yet been briefed. The facts are these," he said as he began to give the officers a rundown of events from a file he held in his hands. "Esther Campbell was eighteen years old. She was reported missing by her father, the MP Edward Campbell when she failed to return home on the evening of 21st August 1984. He'd informed the investigating officers that at first he'd thought she'd run away with her boyfriend, Peter Holmes, after a family argument. However, Mr Holmes was soon eliminated from our enquiries as we tracked him down to India. He was alone and had left before Esther disappeared. The case was quickly moved up from a missing persons case to suspected abduction and probable murder. We searched an area of Epping Forest because her sister told us Esther had said she was going there to think after an argument with her parents but we found nothing. We had no leads and no firm suspects and after two years of intensive enquiries the case was scaled down . . . until now," he said with dramatic flair as he glanced around the table. "Hailey Campbell—Esther's sister, attended the O2 centre yesterday evening to see a psychic show. During this event, the entertainer, Aaron Davies, stated that he had a message from her sister and gave details of where she could be found."

Ashley saw the muscle twitching in Dale's jaw from the corner of her eye and suppressed a smile.

"Now for all we know this *psychic* could simply be a quack. Nevertheless, we have to remain open minded as to the information provided to us in any investigation."

His words were met with silence. Heads moved, eyes darted, disbelief was visible in every face, but nobody said a word.

"Any questions?" Ripley asked, the point of his tongue slowly moistening his bottom lip.

"Isn't it a fact, that in court, hearsay isn't accepted as evidence so why should we accept the word of someone who said he heard it from a spirit?" Ashley spoke up as she didn't see anyone else in a rush to challenge the ridiculousness of the whole situation.

"We have our orders, McCoy, and unlike some people, I follow them—perhaps you'd like to have a personal meeting with the Commissioner to discuss any *issues* you have with the way he wants this investigation run," he said smirking at her.

"Maybe that would be a good idea, he could help me clear up some questions I have."

"And what would those be?"

"Up until now, and correct me if I'm wrong, the police service have always been sceptical of psychics. What's changed? Has new evidence come to light that I'm unaware of? Have I missed a case where a psychic has actually solved something? Has the scientific view that psychics are bogus been overturned?"

Ripley's face began to darken in colour. "Have you quite finished DS McCoy?"

"For now, yes."

Flustered, he glanced at Colleen. "DCI Rees, if you would like to continue."

Colleen picked up the papers in front of her. "Hailey Campbell will be coming in tomorrow to be interviewed, a task which has been assigned to DS McCoy and DC Taylor. I have also arranged with Phil Hopkins, our Police Search Adviser, to start coordinating a search of the area today. I am going there later this afternoon. I have also requested Esther Campbell's cold case files from archives and they will be split between you all to go over. Even if nothing is found, this case is now top priority."

"So did someone travel to India to interview the boyfriend?" Steve asked, a new trainee DC on the team, having moved from uniform only days previously.

"No, he was spoken to over the phone and it was verified that his passport was used the day before she disappeared. They also found Esther's passport at her house, so it was clear she didn't travel anywhere."

"So do you think they're going to find something out there?" Dale asked.

DCS Ripley started before Colleen could reply, "I doubt it very much, we searched those grounds thoroughly back in '84," he said, looking him straight in the eyes. "We left no stone unturned."

"So why coordinate a search again, unless. . ." Ashley said letting her words trail off into thin air.

"Unless what?" he asked in a low rough voice, his mouth tightening as if he had just ingested something distasteful.

"Unless it wasn't searched as thoroughly as you thought."

"What are you trying to imply, McCoy?"

"I'm not trying to imply anything, just thinking out loud. I mean really, are we going to waste valuable police time on the deluded ramblings of an entertainer who believes he can talk to the dead?"

"If you hadn't gone over old files you would never have solved the Coleman case, would you?" he said with a cold, self-satisfied smile.

"I don't have any objection to going over the case files but a full scale search is a bit much. In the Coleman case there was reasonable cause to search, brought about by investigative analysis, not whispers from the dead. Are our resources so stretched that this is what it's come to?"

"Enough," Colleen said giving Ashley a warning glare. "Why don't we actually wait and see what comes up before we start getting ahead of ourselves."

"I wasn't aware we were—"

"Drop it, McCoy. I think I'll bring this meeting to an end. There's nothing more to be said until we know more," Colleen said standing.

Easing himself up from his chair DCS Ripley

said, "I don't want a word of this leaving these four walls. There will be serious repercussions if anything is leaked to the press. Is that understood?"

Eight heads nodded in union.

"Have you done a background check on this psychic?" Ashley asked as Colleen reached the door, DCS Ripley by her side.

"We've made a cursory check of Mr Davies but nothing glaringly obvious stands out about him." She paused. "Yet," she added and walked through the door.

"Is that why Colleen called you in her office first, to give you the heads up that Ripley was around?" Dale said as they left the briefing room and headed down the corridor.

"Yep."

"I wish you would have told me."

"I didn't see the point of winding you up before we got in there and know the full details."

"It's a first for me. I've never had to put aside other cases to look for a dead girl on the word of a psychic."

"I'm sure once they don't find anything it will be the last."

"I can't believe Colleen is going along with this."

"She has her orders just like the rest of us."

"Talking of which, I think you'd better tone down your attitude a bit with Ripley, you were really skating on thin ice in there."

Ashley's relaxed features quickly turned into a scowl. "Oh, he just pisses me off. The hierarchy pay us to think with our minds on the one hand, and on the other they want us to kiss arse and question nothing. The whole politics of this place is wearing me down."

As they reached their office, Dale stood by Ashley as they looked at the four large boxes that had been dumped in the doorway blocking their entrance. Each box contained the key files of Esther Campbell disappearance—a cold case, or an ice cold case in this instance. Although Ashley believed whole heartedly that each case held its own merit in the need to be solved, she disliked cold cases in particular, especially the really old ones. The chances of finding new clues or information nearly always turned out to be impossible. Key witnesses had either died, changed their stories or just couldn't remember details from such a long time ago. All in all they were much harder to solve. She liked the adrenaline rush of a live trail where there was a good chance of finding the perpetrator.

Shaking his head, Dale said with a touch of irritation, "Would it really have been too much for whoever brought these up to have put them on the desk?"

Ashley shoved the boxes into the office with her foot. "I'm sure they would have if your desk wasn't such a mess."

"So where we gonna put them?"

"Let's stack a couple of them up against the wall and keep one each under our desks. I'll call Debbie to collect them as and when we finish." Ashley hauled the boxes to their destination. The musty odour of old paper assaulted her nostrils as she put the final box on top of the other. They had been stored away in the basement for years, along with hundreds of other unsolved cases crying out to be re-examined.

"I like a woman who's not afraid of a bit of hard work," Dale said jokingly.

She raised her eyebrows. "So that's why you're still single, aye?"

"Nah, I'm single 'cause every woman I meet seems to want me to be their baby daddy."

"Then stop picking women up in the park."

His eyes grew openly amused. "It's not my fault women find me irresistible in my jogging shorts."

"I don't even want to imagine your hairy legs in tight shorts."

"Hey, I'll have you know hairy is the new black," he said, lifting up his trouser leg and displaying a shock of black coarse hair.

Ashley laughed. "You keep telling yourself that. You might even start to believe it if you say it enough times," she said, flipping the lid off a box she had put on her desk.

She had loved Dale's gentle camaraderie since the first day they had worked together— it was one of the things that made her job just that little bit easier.

"Different strokes for different folks," he said opening his own box. "So what exactly are we looking for?" He took out a wad of papers and slapped them down on top of a pile of paper already lying there.

"Anything and everything," she said, shuffling through her own stack of files.

"I don't suppose they filed the reports in any particular order."

She glanced through the sheets of paper in her hand. "Doesn't look like it does it? Let's do that now, then we can read through them tomorrow."

***

At the end of what seemed like a very long day, Ashley finally returned to her three bedroom house, situated along a tree-lined street in a tranquil part of North London. She had bought it with her then partner five years ago, before property prices rocketed sky high. Letting herself into the light and airy hallway, she stepped straight into a small puddle on the polished mahogany floor. Within seconds, the scraping of Muffin's nails could be heard as he rounded the corner and was instantly upon her, standing on his hind legs, his two front paws rested against her chest, his tongue reaching out for her face.

"I'm sorry, Muffin," she said, nestling her face into his neck. "I didn't realise I was going to be so late."

She put her Chinese takeaway on the hallway table and reached for Muffin's lead. She hadn't eaten anything except for the bagel she'd had in the afternoon, *but my rumbling belly is going to have to wait,* she thought as she slipped back into the humid night air with Muffin at her heel. Though her mind was preoccupied with the day's events as she walked along the empty street, it didn't stop her senses from picking up the sound of a car's heavy motor purring complacently as it moved at a snail's pace behind her. Before she could turn around to take a look, the car's engine revved and accelerated away into the darkness of the night. She made a mental note of the car being dark, but it had moved too quickly for her to notice the number plate.

As soon as Muffin had smelt every bark of every tree on her road, they turned back toward home. As they approached her door, the dark car drove slowly past them again then picked up speed and vanished around a corner. Maybe her imagination was playing tricks on her but something didn't feel right.

Ten minutes later, after changing into white frayed hemmed shorts and a black sleeveless T-shirt, she dished out spare ribs and noodles sparingly, before heading for the sofa to eat. Years ago she may have switched on the TV for company, but she had given it away—what she dealt with at work was quite enough, she didn't need any added drama in her life. Normally if she wasn't too tired she liked to read light-hearted fiction, which made her laugh at the end of a depressing day. Though she had been on the job for many years, she was still shocked at the cruelty humans bestowed on each other.

Finishing off her noodles, she collapsed back against the scattered cushions on the natural-coloured fabric sofa, with Muffin beside her, huddled up in a ball sleeping soundly. Something was going to have to give—she couldn't keep leaving him alone all day. It wasn't fair on him. It was fine when Melissa had been around—*but she isn't here anymore so get over it*. She knew what she would do— she'd make the call first thing in the morning.

Chapter 5

Ashley awoke to the sound of drilling machines demolishing the concrete outside her window. Bleary eyed, she grabbed two pillows and squashed them against her ears. She was convinced there was a conspiracy to cause her an early death—from late nights at work to early morning noise from workmen, she didn't know which one was going to finish her off first. Giving up on trying to get back to sleep, she sat up, threw the quilt to one side and headed for the bathroom. Still not fully awake, she flipped up the tap lever and shoved her toothbrush under it.

Within seconds Muffin was at the door. "Good morning, my sweetheart," she said, her heart skipping as it did every time she looked into his trusting eyes. "How did I get so lucky with you, eh?" She scratched him behind his ears as he rubbed up against her leg. She let out a sigh, guilt washed over her as she knew she would have to leave him alone.

"It will all be different from today, I promise," she said as Muffin looked up at her with his brown soulful eyes. Quickly brushing her teeth, she went back to her bedroom to retrieve her phone before walking downstairs to the living room. Looking up at the large silver clock that hung on the chimney breast, she was glad to see it was nine already. She opened a door on the glossy unit in the alcove, withdrew the yellow pages and flicked through it.

"Here we are . . . dogs," she said. Pressing the number into her phone she waited until her call was answered.

"Hi, good morning. I urgently need to hire a dog walker."

***

The representatives from Barking Mad rang the door bell at 10am on the dot. Ashley strode to the front door and upon opening it was greeted by a chubby, middle aged woman with a mass of frizzy ash blonde hair.

"Hello," the plump woman shrilled as if she was high on caffeine. "I'm Polly." She thrust her ID card in front of Ashley's face.

"And I'm Tasha." An exceptionally attractive woman dressed in white cropped trousers and a black V-neck T-shirt, stood beside Polly and offered her hand.

Taking an unsteady breath, Ashley assessed the lithe young woman quickly, a skill that was a prerequisite in a job like hers. Roughly the same height as herself with a blemish-free heart shaped face, slender eyebrows arched gracefully over piercing peacock green eyes which were shaded with long curling lashes. Her dark brown, sun glinted hair hung far below her shoulders and an ever so small beauty spot was on the left side of her high curved cheek bone.

"Ashley," she replied, shaking her hand and then Polly's. Her heart was knocking so hard against her ribcage she was surprised Tasha couldn't hear it. "Please, come in," she continued, pushing her hair back behind her ears.

As she stepped back to let them in, she couldn't keep from staring as Tasha walked past her. It had been a long time since she had felt such an attraction to someone.

"He's in here," Ashley said as she led them into

the living room. Muffin stayed put on the sofa, eyeing the strangers suspiciously.

"What a lovely home you have," Tasha said, looking around at the room which seemed like it had been ripped from Habitat. Modern sleek furnishings were surrounded by Jackson Pollock artwork that adorned the white walls.

"Thank you."

"Tasha is going to be your dog walker, Ms McCoy. I like to come along on the first visit so I can talk you through everything and fill in a few forms," Polly said as she watched Tasha approach Muffin.

"And you must be Muffin," Tasha said, kneeling in front of the dog. She put the back of her hand near his nose so he could pick up her scent. "Aren't you a beautiful boy." She cooed as if talking to a baby. Finally deciding he liked her, he moved forward an inch and licked her hand. Tasha's face broke into an infectious smile that Ashley immediately felt drawn in by.

"Ah, there's a good boy," Ashley said to a happy, tail wagging Muffin.

An hour later, Ashley closed the door behind them both with a wide smile on her face. She was ecstatic. They had taken Muffin for a short walk, spoken intensively about what she expected from the service and she had immediately signed the paperwork for the company to start the next day. She wasn't sure whether her elation was actually due to Muffin being exercised twice a day or the thought of seeing Tasha again.

Chapter 6

Ashley and Dale headed down four flights of concrete steps to the interview suite on the ground floor. Her daily walks with Muffin had improved her fitness which was a good thing because having to run up and down those stairs everyday was not for the faint hearted.

The room was a narrow enclosure with glass bricks for windows, a cheap wooden desk and three matching chairs. It was a no frills let's-get-straight-to-the-point-setting. As they entered the room, Ashley smiled at Hailey who was sat at the table looking poised and calm. She wore a two piece, pale pink Chanel suit and black high heels, her mousey brown hair cut into a bob fanning her round face.

Ashley spoke first as Dale sat down. "Ms Campbell, thank you for coming in," she said, extending a hand and receiving a weak handshake. "I'm Detective Sergeant McCoy and this is my colleague Detective Constable Taylor."

Though she wasn't one to judge people on their appearances, Hailey didn't strike her as the type of woman you would normally see at a psychic show, she looked too straight laced—a woman who only believed in black and white, never considering grey as an option.

Dale leaned forward to shake her hand briefly. "Sorry to be meeting under these circumstances, Ms Campbell."

"Are you both going to find Esther's killer?" she asked, turning from one to the other, her voice earnest and pleading.

Ashley looked down for a second before meeting her eyes. "We don't actually know if a crime has been committed yet, Ms Campbell, but should there be evidence of foul play then yes, we will be part of the team that will be looking for the perpetrator or perpetrators."

"Good, that's good," she said, nervously twisting her hands on her lap. "I've heard many good things about you, especially the Coleman case it—"

"I appreciate your kind words," Ashley said cutting her short and dropping a file she was holding onto the table. It landed with a muffled thud. She sat down opposite her, her hands resting on the table.

"So where do you want me to start?"

"How about at the beginning. Can you tell me why Esther went to the woods that day?" Ashley asked, kick starting the interview whilst Dale's hand hovered with a pen over a notepad.

"I already answered that question twenty five years ago," Hailey said, tight lipped with impatience.

Ashley moved back slightly into her chair. "Not to me you didn't. I know this may seem like a pointless exercise to you, Ms Campbell but I need to get a feel for what Esther is like." She was very careful about using her name in the present tense. Although she thought the chances of Esther still being alive were slim to none—there was always that glimmer of hope. "And who better to fill me in than someone who loves her and cares for her deeply."

Relenting, Hailey looked down at her hands. "She always went there but that day in particular she had fought with our parents about her boyfriend. They didn't think he was good enough for her. He was the son of a construction worker. He didn't fit into their dream of what her life should be like. Esther rebelled and made plans to travel to India to be with him."

"And your parents didn't like the idea of that?"

She shook her head.

"Did she normally go to the woods alone?"

"Yes, always, that was her special place where she found solace."

Ashley thought that a young woman Esther's age would think she was invincible—teenagers usually did. Given that she was also the daughter of a front bench politician, probably meant she had a false sense of security. Unfortunately Ashley had seen the end result of such thinking—normally in the morgue.

"Did you see"— she opened the file and quickly skimmed it—"Peter after her disappearance?"

"No. I don't believe I ever saw him again."

"Did Esther drink or take drugs?"

"No," Hailey said, squirming in her chair.

"Was there any chance she could have gotten mixed up with the wrong sort of people?"

"No, Esther wasn't like that," Hailey insisted.

"Did anyone have a grudge against her?"

"For Christ sake she was only eighteen!" Hailey cried out, looking angrily into Ashley's eyes.

Ignoring her outburst but changing to a softer tone, Ashley continued, "Maybe she spurned someone's advances and they didn't take too kindly to it?"

Hailey shook her head. "I'm telling you there was no one—everyone knew she only had eyes for Peter."

Dale glanced at Ashley and she gave a small nod.

"Was she in the habit of talking to strangers?" he asked.

"No, I mean yes, if they needed her help," she said, looking uncertain as she put her elbow on the table and rested her forehead in her hand.

"Had she mentioned anyone or anything out of the ordinary leading up to her disappearance?"

"No!" Hailey cried. She began to sob into her hands as her once calm facade crumbled.

"Would you like to take a break, Ms Campbell?" Ashley said as she leaned forward and placed a hand on her trembling shoulder.

Hailey raised her head and looked at her. Her tear stained skin was blotchy and marked with trails of mascara. Her eyes, red and swollen. Trying to compose herself, she wiped her face with the tips of her fingers and sat upright in the chair, breathing deeply in an effort to stem the tears. "No, no, carry on," she said firmly.

"Okay, so back to Peter. Did he know where her special place was?" Ashley asked. Although he had been cleared at the time by his alibi, it didn't mean he couldn't have gotten someone else to do his dirty work.

Her eyes widened. "Of course he knew where she went, he was her boyfriend but he never infringed on her privacy there and he would never have hurt her if that's what you're thinking."

"I have to ask these questions. I'm sure you can understand why," Ashley said, waiting for Hailey to respond.

"Yes I suppose you're right. Everyone's a suspect until they're not."

"That's right," Ashley said, wondering what cop show she'd heard that line from. "So what do your parents think about your encounter with Aaron Davies?"

"They think he's a fraud but like me they can't understand how he could have received such precise information about her favourite place—the last place she said she was going to. I know the police searched the area in 1984 but I just can't help believing there is truth in what Aaron Davies said—he just knew too much about her. Things he just couldn't have known."

"Yes, we did search there, but as there is new information it will be searched again. I don't want to get your hopes up though, Ms Campbell, *psychics* are often very good at telling people what they want to hear."

"I know, but all the same I'd rather make sure."

"We understand that. There are just a few more questions we'd like to ask. Had Esther ever run away from home before?" Dale asked, briefly looking up from his notepad.

Hailey's eye's swivelled towards him. "No, never. She had problems with my parents like any normal teenager but we were close—really close, even if she ran away she would have contacted me without a doubt."

"Do you remember the last day you saw your sister? Was there any reason to suspect that she had any real intention of going to India?" he asked.

"At the time, yes," Hailey's voice dropped.

"Because she disappeared the day after Peter left the country."

***

"So what's your take on things so far?" Dale asked Ashley as he heaped a spoonful of coffee into three mugs. They stood in a small kitchenette area, having taken a break from the interview when Hailey had become overcome with emotion again and wanted to step outside for air.

"Not much at the moment—I think Hailey is being honest and forthright with us."

"That's what I was thinking. She answered you quite well until you mentioned drink and drugs."

"Yeah, but it's understandable. Nobody wants their loved ones under scrutiny, especially by the police. I'm sure by her reaction, Esther dabbled in a bit of both but I don't think that had anything to do with her going missing."

Dale turned and handed Ashley her mug. "You've got that look in your eye. Come on spill the beans."

Ashley leaned back against the wall, tilting her head upwards. "I don't know—Esther's disappearance just doesn't make sense. I mean, she was the daughter of a prominent politician, there wasn't a ransom note, no demands were made—how could she vanish off the face of the earth? And if she was murdered, why risk involving someone whose family connections are so public?"

"Maybe he didn't know who she was," Dale remarked.

"It's possible—but you and I know too well that in these situations it's usually someone the victim knows that's involved."

"You never know, Aaron Davies may be right and she really is buried near a Silver Birch tree in Epping Forest," he said with a wide grin.

"Oh no, not you as well. Am I the only sane one around here?" she said pushing herself off the wall and opening the fridge to take out a pint of milk.

"It's not like you to not consider all avenues."

She handed him the bottle and he nodded his thanks. "Dale, normally I believe in each to their own but this is just crazy; a psychic talking to a dead woman who just happens to tell him where she's buried. Hey, I've got a good idea, the next time there's a burglary we'll just use a psychic to tell us who the perpetrator is. I mean why even have police stations, let's just set up psychic hotlines. I'll tell you, Dale, if this prediction has any truth in it I'll eat my proverbial hat." Ashley took a sip of her black coffee.

"Ash, she's back." A uniformed officer poked his head around the door.

"Thanks, Adam," she said and then turned back to Dale. "Do you want to finish up making the coffees? I'll restart the interview."

***

"Are you sure you're ready to resume?" Ashley asked, leaning forward and folding her hands on the table.

"Yes, sorry about that," Hailey said apologetically.

"It's okay. I can't even begin to imagine how hard this is for you."

"I wouldn't wish this situation on my worst enemy. My mum and dad need closure, we all do—

this is the closest we've ever been to finding out what really happened to her."

"So other than the contention with your parents about Peter, was there anything else bothering her?"

"No, all she talked about was Peter."

"And you never suspected Peter had something to do with her disappearance?"

"Oh no, never, not once, they were so in love. It was like a romance out of the movies. He gave her a beautiful silver pendant which she adored. He had it engraved with a quote from Midsummer Night's Dream: 'Love looks not with the eyes, but with the mind'," she said, suddenly sounding like a star struck teenager.

"Which brings us up to the other night. Had you told anyone you would be attending?"

Hailey thought for a moment. "No."

"Have you now or at any other time subscribed to Aaron Davies' mailing list?"

"No."

"Have any of your friends or acquaintances?"

"Not that I'm aware of."

"When did you decide to attend his show?"

"Actually it was just on a whim. A flyer came through the door, so I thought. . ." She shrugged her shoulders. "Why not?"

"Were you expecting to hear" —she struggled to say the words— "a message from your sister?"

"I've always hoped that she's still alive but in my heart I think I know she's dead. So yes, isn't that the whole point of going? We all live in the hope of knowing our loved ones are okay. Have you ever lost anyone close to you?"

"I—" Before she could finish her sentence Dale reappeared with two steaming mugs on a tray. She was grateful for the interruption.

He placed the mugs on the table. "I'm going to take the tray back," he said, retreating through the door.

"Who booked your ticket to the event, Ms Campbell?" Ashley asked, getting the interview back on track. She hated it when people tried to pull her into revealing personal information about herself.

"I did, with my credit card on Aaron Davies' website."

Before she could proceed any further, the door swung open again. "McCoy, can I have a word please," Dale asked, tray still in hand.

Ashley stood up. "Excuse me one moment," she said to Hailey as she left the room. "What is it?" she asked impatiently as she closed the door behind her.

He held his hand out to her, as if he was giving something to her.

Looking puzzled she asked, "What are you doing, Dale?"

He grinned sheepishly. "Handing you your proverbial hat. Colleen just called me, they've just found a body. She wants us to meet her at the crime scene."

Chapter 7

...ey peered out of the passenger window as
...ed their unmarked car through the winding
...s. Despite the bright summer's day, the
...ad, weakening the sun's rays

...me into view ahead and Dale
...front of it onto a gravel track, then
slowed to a stop. He wound down his window as a
uniformed officer with a deeply lined face approached.

"Hi, Brian, is it far up?" Dale asked.

"Yeah, about half a mile up on the left."

"Cheers, mate," Dale replied, putting the car into
gear and driving through an open barrier, usually
accessed only by forestry commission vehicles.

The gravel surface tested the car's suspension as
they travelled deeper into the forest. Eventually they
saw the scientific support van parked to the left and
pulled up behind it.

Ashley immediately noticed the sharp drop in
temperature as she exited the car and walked towards
the police officer guarding the crime scene. Clipboard
in hand, the big stubble bearded man signed them
both in and directed them to the protective wear.

Putting on the oversuit, Ashley's senses were
alert as she absorbed her immediate surroundings; a
densely wooded area—it was an isolated and well
hidden patch, away from where a lone person would
normally venture. She figured it was a place that even
if you screamed, there wouldn't be anyone about to
hear you. Did the person buried here cry out and have
their plea for help fall on deaf ears? *If this is where*

Esther used to come, why did she feel so safe here? So self assured that there wasn't any danger lurking about? Even as a trained police officer with a range of self defence skills, it was not the sort of place she would visit alone.

Clad in white oversuits and blue protective feet covers, they headed towards a white tent which had been erected over the site where the remains had been found. The section outside the tent was a hive of activity with a number of Scenes of Crime Officers, scouring the area in a line looking for any evidence that could be of any importance to the case.

"White suits you, Dale," a jowly young officer standing at the entrance said smirking, as he opened the flap of the tent to let them enter.

"Funny," Dale replied, with sour humour.

Inside the tent the air was hot and humid, with an odour of rich earthy soil. Dale stopped a few feet in, giving the exposed skeleton a wide berth.

Colleen was leant over the shallow grave along with Joan Blackburn, both studying it with clinical detachment. Essex police normally called the forensic archaeologist when skeletal remains were found. Joan was a pleasant looking woman in her mid to late fifties with hair more grey than black. She worked in silent concentration as she searched the loose soil inch by inch, looking for any scrap of evidence that might have been buried with the victim. Ashley eyed the exposed skeletal bones and the large metallic box next to them which contained all of her equipment.

Joan looked up as Ashley neared. "Hey, Ashley, Dale. How's it going?"

Dale nodded at her before turning his attention

to anything but the open site. Despite being an experienced DC, he had a weak stomach when it came to crime scenes. This was partly the reason he had never gone for a promotion. Ashley, on the other hand could face anything if it meant solving the case as her superior rank reflected.

"As well as can be expected," Ashley said.

Colleen stood up. "The pathologist should be here soon and we'll see about having the remains removed. Joan has recovered some items I'd like you to take to forensics."

"No problem. Any idea of the sex?"

Joan pushed herself back onto her knees and brushed a bead of sweat from her brow.

"If you look here, Ashley," Joan said, drawing her finger across the pelvic area, "the female pelvis is broader and has a wider subpubic angle—this is the angle between the two sides of hip bone in the front. The opening in the centre of the pelvis is wider than a man's too, to allow a baby's head to pass through."

Ashley crouched down beside her as her eyes followed her fingers.

"As for her age, all I can tell you at the moment is she is older than fifteen because her knee bone has fused onto the thigh bone. I'll be able to give you a more accurate estimate once we get her back to the mortuary."

"How about the cause of death?"

"Going by a quick assessment, it was quite brutal. Look, you can see marks where a sharp object has cut the bone," Joan said, pointing to different areas on the skeletal remains. "As well as this, a leather belt was still around the neck area and the hyoid bone broken, which is a clear indication of strangulation. I don't know whether she was strangled first but looking at the knife impressions, I hope for her sake she was."

Ashley gave the remains another long searching glance and briefly closed her eyes as she thought about a young girl who, at one time had been full of life with everything to look forward to but had been cut down in her prime. To make matters worse, the person that had launched the fatal blow was still out there walking about free. She wondered if they ever thought of her or her family—did they feel any kind of remorse? If the remains were Esther's, she'd been laying here for all those years whilst her family had been looking for her in vain. Ashley's heart always went out to victims of crime. She knew she couldn't bring their loved ones back but she always tried to bring their families closure and more importantly, justice.

"What kind of belt was it? Was there anything distinctive about it?" Ashley asked rising to her feet and addressing Colleen.

"No, It's a generic man's belt but we will know more once forensics have checked it."

"Was there any ID?" she asked briskly.

"No, but there was a pendant and some pieces of blue clothing," she replied retrieving the evidence bags and handing them to her.

"A pendant?" She studied the muddy belt through the plastic bag first, wondering whether forensics could lift any fingerprints or any other organic matter from the less soiled, internal surface. Then she turned her attention to the pendant. Squinting her eyes she could just about make out writing on the back. "Shit."

"Something wrong?" Colleen asked.

"That all depends on how you look at it."

***

Dale furrowed his brow. "It's her isn't it?" His hazel eyes opened wide in wonder, making his long, lean face look softer than usual. When people first met Dale many thought he was an uncaring person, who did his job just to pick up the pay cheque— but that couldn't be further from the truth. His feelings ran deep, as had been attested to in the Coleman case they had recently closed the file on. He cared— maybe a little too much for their line of work.

"Yes, I think so," Ashley replied, trying her hardest to concentrate on the road ahead and not the million questions that were demanding she find an answer to.

"It's quite eerie if you think about it."

"Uh huh," she said as she swerved the car into the middle lane to overtake a van that had been travelling at a snail's pace for the past ten minutes.

"You've got to wonder, though haven't you, about the psychic I mean, how he knew she was there?" Dale stroked his chin in thought.

"This actually reminds me of a case I read about years ago," Ashley said, staring out into the road. " I think it was sometime in the '80s; a nurse went missing in L.A. and a member of the public came forward claiming to have had a vision that she was dead. Like our guy, she pinpointed exactly where the body was. Anyway, to cut a long story short, she took a lie detector test which she failed and when questioned further she gave the detectives conflicting versions of what she saw. Turns out the killers were eventually caught because one of them had gone around boasting about the crime he committed."

Dale scratched his head. "So is that what you think happened? Aaron overheard someone talking about it?"

"Once we get confirmation that it actually is Esther's body, that's exactly what I intend to find out."

Chapter 8

Ashley poured boiling water into her mug and stirred it quickly. Briefly checking her watch she glanced around the kitchen—dirty cups and plates littered the work surfaces. Yesterday had been a long day. By the time she'd arrived home she was so exhausted she had collapsed onto the sofa and that is where she had found herself when she opened her eyes the following morning.

I can't leave the place like this, Ashley thought. Just at that moment the doorbell rang.

"Shit," she said as she scurried around the kitchen in a desperate attempt to make it look more presentable. When it chimed for the second time she realised her efforts were futile. With a sigh, she grabbed her coffee and headed to the front door.

"Hi, Tasha." Ashley welcomed Tasha with a broad grin as she pulled the door open.

"Hi, Ashley," she replied, the warmth of her smile echoing in her voice.

"Come in." Ashley opened the door wider so she could enter and led her into the kitchen.

Muffin bounded in from the garden, his tail wagging furiously. Tasha bent down on her knees as he ran directly to her, sat down and handed her his paw.

"Well, hello to you too, handsome."

Ashley quietly watched.

"Have I caught you in the middle of breakfast?" she asked, looking around the kitchen.

"This is my breakfast," Ashley answered, raising her cup of coffee in mid air. "I'm a bit behind with my house keeping duties." A sudden feeling of self-consciousness washed over her.

"I can clear them away when I get back from walking Muffin if you like?" Tasha offered as she rose to her feet.

"Thanks, but that won't be necessary." Ashley put her coffee cup down and opened the dishwasher. "The convenience of modern day technology." She began to stack the plates into the white tray.

A bright hectic flush appeared on Tasha's cheeks. "Sorry, I didn't mean—"

Ashley looked up and said with a laugh, "Don't worry, you haven't offended me. I'm normally quite tidy but the past couple of days have been really busy."

Relief showed on Tasha's face.

"So, how long have you been dog walking?" Ashley asked, slamming the dishwasher door shut and straightening up.

"Oh, around three years."

"Must be tough in the winter."

"Not really, I love to be outside despite the cold, and as I'm walking most of the time, I don't really feel it," she said, bending down briefly to rub Muffin's chest.

"How many dogs do you walk?"

"Five or six."

"At the same time?"

Tasha laughed. "Yes, sometimes."

"I can't imagine how hard that must be."

"They're normally well behaved. Polly is very particular about which dogs she walks, especially after. . ." Tasha stopped mid-sentence.

"After?" Ashley prompted her.

"Well, it's not normally a good idea to tell clients."

"You can trust me, I'm a cop."

"Are you kidding?" Tasha said her hand flying to her chest.

"Nope." Ashley slipped her ID from her jacket and showed it to her.

"Oh, my God and there you are saying how hard my job must be, yours must take nerves of steel."

"Nah, it's not at all like you see on the TV. The majority of people tend to hurt people they know, not police officers," Ashley said in a casual tone.

"All the same."

"Anyway, you were about to tell me about . . . ?"

"I was? Well, erm, some of the dogs we used to walk, were, you could say, a little boisterous."

"How boisterous?"

"Let's just say one of them mauled another dog to death."

"Urgh." Ashley frowned.

"I won't tell you which breed because I don't want to give them a bad name but ever since then we only walk dogs that have had some training."

"It's a pity we can't have a system like that for humans," Ashley said with some cynicism.

"Do you mind me asking how you cope with seeing all the bad things people do to each other?" Tasha asked, looking at her intently.

"Who said I did?" Ashley replied quietly.

"I'm sorry, I didn't mean to pry."

"It's alright you're not. I get asked that question more times than I care to remember, especially from my mother."

Muffin let out a bark, then rolled onto his back in front of her.

"Okay, so he's obviously smitten with you already," Ashley said draining her coffee and putting the mug on the granite island. "The house keys and the list of what to do, is on the counter. Help yourself to tea or coffee or whatever."

Tasha looked at Ashley with a stare that unnerved her. "Thank you."

Feeling heat rise to her face, Ashley turned to leave. "Okay then, I'll be off. Have a good day."

As she left the house and opened her car door, she looked back towards the house. She was unable to contain the grin that spread across her face.

***

Tasha knelt down on the floor so she was level with Muffin. "Your mummy is lovely isn't she," she said, stroking his cheeks. She hadn't been expecting Ashley to be so attractive—though she was far from judgemental, most of her clients were getting on in years and none were as stunning as Ashley. She liked the way she held her eye contact when she spoke to her—a sign of a confident person her friend Charlotte would have said. Her best friend from childhood knew her stuff, considering she devoured all the books she could find on body language in her quest to find love.

Muffin stood and circled her, seemingly less concerned with what she thought about his owner and more interested in when he was going for his walk.

"Okay then." She laughed as he nudged her

several times. "I get the message. Let's see what we've got here." Tasha stood up and picked up the sheet of paper from the worktop.

"Don't feed you before your walk; keep you on a short lead as you like to be in control." *Hmm, that sounds like someone I know,* she thought as memories of her father flooded her mind. "Be careful of you trying to lick Ivy—it all seems simple enough. Shall we go then?"

Muffin barked and ran into the hallway. As she passed the living room she poked her head through the door and took another look at what she had seen briefly the day before. *Not bad, not bad at all,* she thought, admiring the artwork on the wall. Looking around the rest of the room, she realised that somehow it didn't seem to reflect Ashley—it was cold, depersonalised even. The walls were stark in colour, the furniture looked modern but stiff. She much preferred sofa's that were soft and plentiful, where she could curl up and read a good book. But it wasn't her house so it was irrelevant.

Strapping the collar around Muffin's neck she opened the front door and let him lead her out. She strolled along the pavement while Muffin stopped every few yards to sniff at a wall or tree and her thoughts returned to Ashley again. She had taken an instant liking to the woman, although she was shocked to find out that she was a detective. She thought she was a business executive by the way she wore her expensive looking blue suit and white shirt—if she wasn't wrong, the suit looked custom made. The fabric clung to her like a second skin.

It wasn't long before she found the small green

area where Ashley normally walked Muffin herself. A few people milled about with their little dogs yapping at their feet for attention. Tasha let him off his lead and sat on a bench while he went off exploring.

She wondered to herself about Ashley's status— she hadn't noticed a wedding ring on her finger and her house just didn't have the feel of a man living there. Was she single and if so, why?

Chapter 9

By the time Ashley pulled up to the large metal gates the temperature was pushing thirty degrees. Harlow police station was a dismal brick building with white cladding, characteristic of fifties architecture. The town itself was a 'new town' established in the forties to relieve overcrowding in London and as such was a cluster of identical houses and concrete tower blocks. Despite this, she loved the place. Spending two years on the beat here, she knew it inside out.

Ashley turned up the air conditioning, giving herself a cool blast before opening the window to scan her ID card in the silver slot and waited for the steel frame to grind its way open. She scowled as she noticed the entrance was overrun by men and women with video cameras. Several minutes later she was on the second floor heading towards her office when she heard Colleen's voice behind her.

"Ashley."

She turned and waited for Colleen to reach her. "Good morning," she said brightly, as Colleen fell into step with her. "I take it you didn't sleep well last night." Ashley noticed the dark circles under her bloodshot eyes.

"These are self-inflicted wounds. I went out. Never again, I tell you. I'm getting too old for late nights. How was your evening?"

"Same as usual. I see the vultures have arrived at the front entrance sensing blood."

"I know it's like a bloody circus out there," Colleen said, plucking a small strand of white cotton that had attached itself to the skirt of the black two piece suit she wore.

"Any idea who tipped them off?"

Colleen shook her head. "I just hope it wasn't one of our lot, because if it was there'll be hell to pay. Ripley isn't happy."

"I bet he isn't—has he called in his damage control team?" Ashley asked with an innocent expression on her face.

"This really isn't the time, Ashley." Colleen looked at her sharply.

"I'm sorry."

Colleen brushed aside Ashley's apology with a faint smile. "Did you manage to get a start on the files yesterday?"

"Yes, but we didn't get very far, there're four boxes. I'm sure if anything has been missed we'll find it."

"Okay, whatever you need it's yours."

"Thanks." She decided against telling Colleen about the black car that she had seen the other night, putting it down to just feeling on edge due to the long day she'd had.

By late afternoon they were no further to finding any leads and the oppressive heat in the office wasn't making things any easier.

"I'm going to get Steve to track down the witnesses tomorrow, see if they can shed any new light on the investigation," Ashley said.

"I'm done for the day, Ash. I think I'm going to make a move," Dale said as he stood up and put his jacket over his shoulder. He had spent the day going over files relating to information gathering, document management and internal communications with the families, and so far everything looked above board. Ashley, on the other hand, had been making slow progress on the laborious task of scouring record keeping and initial actions at the scene.

"Yeah, I don't think I'm going to be much longer. I just want to have one last look at this search report and then I'll be off too. See you tomorrow."

"Okay, see you in the morning."

As Dale left, Ashley spread the map of Epping Forest out on the table in front of her; red areas marked where the searches had taken. She picked up the written report and scanned each word possessively, re-reading sentences to make sure she had missed nothing out. By the end of a mind numbing hour of reading, everything seemed in order. Ripley had been right—they had done a thorough job, maybe she was chomping at the bit too much.

What to do next? Ashley thought as she stood and began to gather the papers together putting them back in the folder. As she started to close the map something caught her eye— the red area's that had been circled didn't tally up with the place she had gone today nor with the report. She double and treble checked her findings as her heart raced.

"What the hell have they done?" she said aloud. She picked up the phone and angrily punched in the numbers.

Colleen answered after one ring. "How's it going?"

"I've just gone over the report for the search in Epping Forest—"

She heard Colleen let out a deep breath. "I

thought we had agreed that they'd done a thorough search of the area?"

"They did that all right—but not in the area that Hailey had indicated, they conducted the search for Esther in the wrong place!"

Chapter 10

"Good find," Dale said as Ashley squeezed past him to open the window, wincing at the explosive heat in the room.

"Thanks. It's just a shame that a young woman and her family had to be the victims of their incompetency. If they had done the search properly and found Esther, there may have been more evidence and the killer might have been found. Now look where we are—twenty five years later and little more than a skeleton left and no leads." Ashley let out a sigh.

"I know and that prick, Ripley, giving all the attitude like he could do no wrong," Dale said rubbing his hand lightly over his short blonde spiky hair.

"It's always the ones that shout loudest who have the most to hide." Ashley settled down into her chair and switched on her computer. Despite feeling a little aggrieved she found herself smiling at the breath of fresh air who had walked through her door barely half an hour earlier. Tasha had arrived just as Ashley was leaving.

"What's got you all smiley this morning? I thought you'd be furious."

"Aye?"

"You're sitting there grinning like a Cheshire cat."

"Sorry, I was just reading a funny email."

"Want to share it?"

"No, it's a female thing," Ashley said, pushing

her chair away from the desk. "Anyway what's the point of getting angry now, it's over with, it just means we're going to have to be extra careful going over the files—God knows what else they've messed up on."

"So do you think this makes that psychic bloke more believable?"

"No, not necessarily. I checked out Aaron's biography yesterday on his website. When Esther went missing he would have been ten years old so it's looking more likely that he must have overheard someone talking about her murder."

"But why wait until now to alert anyone about it? And how would he have known Hailey was going to be in the audience to receive the message?" Dale said, looking unconvinced.

"McCoy." Colleen poked her head into the office and beckoned for her to follow.

"Someone doesn't look happy," Ashley said to Dale as she left the room.

"Take a seat," Colleen said with a sweeping gesture as she walked to stand by the window, her back to the room. Finally she let out a deep sigh. "We look like a bloody laughing stock."

Ashley remained silent, unsure what she should say— if anything.

"Over twenty bloody years that poor girl has been laying there due to our cock up."

"Come on, Colleen, you can't put yourself in the picture for this one."

She spun round. "Can't I? We're all representatives of the police service. The press will have a field day with us."

"So what's the plan?"

"I want you to drop by Mr Davies' house for a friendly talk. You need to find out exactly how he knew where she was," Colleen said, letting Ashley know she was dismissed by turning back to the window.

***

When they arrived at Aaron Davies' residence, it seemed as if it could belong to any middle-class Londoner. Nothing about his house suggested he dealt in matters outside of this world. It was surprisingly bourgeois. *What did I expect, a spaceship?* Ashley thought to herself as she admired the well maintained garden with its assortment of flowers in full bloom.

Dale pressed the doorbell.

Moments later a man's voice called from behind the door, "Who is it?"

Dale shouted back, "DC Taylor and DS McCoy. We need to speak with you regarding Esther Campbell."

"Lower your voice, Dale. I think they can hear you in the USA," Ashley said teasingly.

Aaron responded in a smooth tone, "Yes, of course."

The door was hastily opened and Aaron took a step forward as both Ashley and Dale held up their ID.

He peered at each of their badges. "Please, come in," he said stepping back.

Aaron Davies was not what Ashley had expected—there was nothing dark or nefarious about his presence, or at least not from first impressions. He had a trim, athletic body, with black hair clipped close to his head, military style. Smartly dressed in black trousers and a yellow shirt, his manner was easy and affable.

"Please, make yourselves at home," he said as he led them into a spacious living room. "Can I get you both a cold drink? I also have tea, if you prefer."

"A cup of tea would be nice. Thank you," Ashley said.

"I'll have one as well, thanks," Dale added.

The two looked around while Davies prepared their drinks. Book shelves sat in the alcoves either side of the chimney breast. The wood sagged under the weight of the tightly packed books. An African tribal mask took pride of place on the wall between them and fine furniture was positioned with precision around the room. Nothing was out of place, the house was clinically clean.

A gilt-framed degree certificate from Oak Hill Theological College caught Ashley's interest. She nudged Dale with her elbow and pointed at it.

"Tea is served," Aaron said, his voice reaching into the room ahead of him.

Ashley and Dale lowered themselves onto the silvery teak chairs as he entered and laid a silver tray down on a coffee table and sat down opposite them.

"You have a lovely home," Ashley said, while Davies poured tea. He paused over the Wedgewood sugar bowl and looked up, his blue eyes boring into hers. "One lump will be fine, thanks," Ashley said, nodding towards the certificate on the wall. "What's the story with that?"

Davies cleared his throat as he poured tea into

the other cups. "I went to theological college. My mother had this dream that I would become the vicar of a parish in the country. She fancied the idea that I would spend my afternoons having tea and cake with parishioners for the rest of my life, preaching sermons on Sunday. She was a religious woman and wanted me to serve the church she loved. It was not the career for me. I discovered through my experience there that I had a unique way of helping people deal with their grief. I connected with the eight year old daughter of a woman who felt her faith was threatened by her bereavement. She could not understand why God had allowed her child to die from cancer. It helped her immensely to know that her daughter was not simply lying in a grave. She had, in fact, moved on and she wanted to give her mother a message." Davies sipped his tea.

Dale inquired, "What was the message?"

"That she wasn't in pain anymore. She felt nothing but bliss. She wanted her mother to be happy for her."

"So you never actually became a priest?"

"No, I completed my degree in Theological and Pastoral Studies and started ordination training but as I said, I had a calling elsewhere."

Ashley jumped in. "So moving on to your *connection* with Esther. Can you explain exactly how you led us directly to the location of a dead body in Epping Forest?"

Aaron leaned back in his chair, crossing one leg over the other. "I did not choose the gift of sight. It was chosen for me by a higher power. When Esther contacted me, she gave me the image."

"The degree of specificity you provided is a concern for our department. You didn't say, 'You'll find Esther in Epping Forest'. Your information led us to the exact area where the body was buried. Lab reports haven't come back to us yet but the victim was female," Ashley challenged.

Davies said calmly, "I am willing to work with you and to do whatever I can to help you with your investigation. I have nothing to hide, detectives."

"We're glad to hear that," Dale offered.

Aaron smiled at Dale and then turned his attention to Ashley. Her face betrayed the frustration she felt inside. "You're not a believer are you, Detective McCoy?"

She frowned. "Depends what you mean by a believer. Do I believe that there are unscrupulous people out there who take advantage of grieving people for monetary gain? You're damn right I do. What I don't believe is that *mediums* are able to speak to the dead. But that's just my opinion."

She stared directly into his eyes, trying to look behind the persona but they revealed nothing. That didn't stop her from thinking *he either doesn't know anything about her death, or he's a really good liar*. In his line of work, he'd have to be a good liar she concluded. "So can you tell me why she told you this information now? Why not last year or even ten years ago?"

Aaron folded his hands in his lap. "You'd have to ask Esther that."

"And how do you propose I do that? I didn't realise skeletons could talk."

"Please don't mock me, detective. We're both

aware that they can't talk but a deceased person's spirit can."

Ashley suppressed a sigh. "And while she was telling you where she was, did she relay any other information to you, like for instance who put her there?"

"There you go again mocking me." He cocked his head to the side.

"Not at all, Mr Davies, I just find it incredulous that someone would go to all that effort to connect with a medium—that is what you call yourself?" He nodded before she continued. "And tell you in great detail of their whereabouts, yet they fail to mention the most important thing—who the perpetrator of the crime was."

"Maybe to her that wasn't the most important thing. Maybe letting her family know she is okay means far more to her. To be honest, I don't know what more I can say. I only tell people what I'm told, no more, no less."

"So that's all you can tell us? You know where she was because her spirit told you?"

"Yes, because it's the truth." Aaron retrieved his tea from the table and took a sip.

"So these dead people, sorry spirits, they just happen to turn up like magic as soon as you step onto a stage in front of hundreds of grieving people?"

"Yes, if they want to pass a message on to their loved ones."

"Are you normally so specific?"

"That all depends—"

"On the message," Ashley finished for him.

He nodded and placed his tea cup on its saucer.

"And there's nothing else you can add to this investigation?"

"I'm afraid not, Detective McCoy, as much as I'd like to help, I can't give you something I haven't got."

"Well we appreciate the time you've given us," Ashley said, putting her tea cup down.

"Is that everything then?" Aaron asked, watching them both as they got to their feet.

"For now," Dale said.

"If anything else comes to me, I'll let you know."

"You do that. Goodbye, Mr Davies, we'll see ourselves out."

As they neared the front door she heard Aaron address her from the living room doorway. "Ashley."

With a sudden stop, she stood riveted and faced him—wondering why he'd called her by her first name.

"I have a message for you."

"Oh yeah, and what's that?"

Aaron hesitated, slipping his hand into his trouser pocket. "A young woman is standing here, her hair is fair, she said to tell you . . . it's never goodbye, only see you later."

Ashley felt the blood drain from her face. Even the air seemed to be holding its breath as she stared at him dumbly, scarcely believing the words that had spilled so carelessly from his lips. As she stood wondering how to respond her eyes widened when she saw a disturbing glint in his eyes which vanished within seconds.

The sudden change in him unnerved her, though

she kept her features deceptively composed. "Don't try and play games with me," she said, stepping towards him.

A gleam of satisfaction crossed his face. "I told you, detective, I only pass on a message when it needs to be told."

"Come on, Ash, let's go," Dale said, placing a restraining hand on her arm. He looked at them both in bewilderment before coaxing Ashley out the front door and to their car.

"Are you alright?" Dale asked as he opened the passenger door for her.

"Yes, I'm fine," she said, lowering herself into the seat.

"What did he mean by that?" he asked, leaning into the car.

"It was nothing."

"It didn't look like nothing to me."

"Please, just drop it, Dale." She closed her eyes wearily as she pulled the seat belt across her chest.

"Okay, okay," he said backing up and slamming her door shut, before trotting around to the driver's side and getting in behind the steering wheel.

Memories of Melissa's face arose in her mind. *How the hell did he know?*

She forced herself back into the present moment. She couldn't afford to go back to that place in time.

"I'm sorry," Ashley said turning to Dale, placing her hand on his forearm. She hated herself for losing her patience with her colleague, her friend.

"It's alright, just don't make a habit of it," he said jokingly, putting on his seat belt before starting the engine and manoeuvring the car onto the road.

"Ash, you know I've always got your back right?"

She bent her head to study her hands. "I know—likewise."

"Good."

She was relieved when Dale turned on the radio and seemingly forgetting about her interaction with Aaron, began drumming his fingers on the steering wheel to the beat of a James Brown song.

Back at the station, in order to stop her mind replaying what Aaron had said, Ashley engrossed herself typing up her interview report only stopping when Steve knocked on their door.

"Hey, guys," he said, addressing them both as he strode in. "I've run a check on the list you gave me of all of those interviewed back in '84, and there's some good news and bad. Which do you want first?"

"The bad," Ashley and Dale said in unison. Better to get the worst over with first, then have bad shatter the good.

"Okay, out of the twenty key witnesses that were interviewed, eight are now deceased, five of them are women who have moved and I've been unable to trace them. Could be that they married and changed their surname."

"So what's the good news?" Dale said, shooting a scrunched up ball of paper at the wastepaper basket and missing.

"There are seven people who are ready and willing to go back over their statements with us, including Peter Holmes, Esther's boyfriend."

"Thanks, Steve, you're a treasure."

"I know, I know," he said handing her the file.

"What has Colleen asked you to do now?"

Ashley asked.

"She wants me to go over a list of known sex offenders who lived locally at the time. A couple of them were interviewed and are on your list but she wants me to make sure all of them were contacted."

"Okay, good luck with that. Let us know if anything pans out."

"Will do," Steve said as he left the room.

"So who shall we start with first?" Dale asked, leaning over his desk towards her.

"The boyfriend." Ashley opened the file and scanned the paper until she found what she was looking for. Grabbing the phone from its cradle she began pressing in the numbers. After a few seconds the call was answered.

"Hello, may I speak with Peter Holmes? You spoke to my colleague DC Bows earlier, would it be convenient if we came round to speak with you today? Okay, tomorrow will be fine. Thank you for your time, goodbye."

"How'd he sound," Dale asked when she hung up.

"A little shook up."

"Nerves?"

"Perhaps, I suppose it must be unsettling for your past to be dragged up after all these years."

"Unless, of course, it's because he's got something to hide."

Chapter 11

Ashley walked through her front door, briefly wondering why Muffin hadn't rushed to greet her, then realised he was out with Tasha. She was glad—she couldn't have faced taking him tonight, acting as if everything was normal when it was far from it. At work she had managed to put it to the back of her mind, but now she had no distractions.

His words kept turning over and over in her mind. How could Aaron have known? It was impossible but he'd said Melissa's last words to her before she died in her arms. 'It's not goodbye, it's see you later'. It was what they'd say to each other before they parted. Melissa had always lived in fear that Ashley wouldn't be coming home one day—she hated that she was a police officer and had begged her numerous times to quit or to even get a desk job.

Her mobile phone vibrated in her pocket, she snapped it open without looking at the caller ID. "Yep."

"Hello, big sis."

She smiled at her brother's pet name for her—though he was only a year younger than her and six inches taller he had always called her *big sis* from the time he could talk.

"Hey, Nathan what you up to?" she asked, walking through into her kitchen.

"This and that."

"That doesn't sound too good," she said, shrugging her jacket off and hanging it over the top of the door.

"You know how it is, sis, I'm always ducking and diving."

As much as her little brother liked to think of himself as a player out there in the big bad world, in reality he just finished law school and had managed to be accepted into a well-established criminal law firm.

"Where are you?"

"Getting ready to leave work. So are we still on for tonight?"

Her hand flew to her head. "Oh, crap!" Ashley said as the realisation hit her that her parents and Nathan were all meant to be coming over for dinner.

"You'd forgotten hadn't you?"

"No, no of course not," she said, opening each of the wall cupboards and not the slightest bit surprised by the fact that they were mostly bare.

"Ash, I know when you're lying and I'd say that's right about now."

"Okay, I forgot. What am I going to do? They're going to be here in a—"

The door bell rang.

"Now."

"Have you got beer?"

"I've got nothing," Ashley said, making her way to the door, pushing her hair back away from her face.

"Don't worry, I'll bring some."

"Thanks, Nat."

"No worries, see you in a hour." Nathan hung up.

She opened the door widely, trying to disguise her lapse in memory and failing miserably.

"I can tell from your face that you forgot we

were coming." Dressed in white jeans and a jade coloured vest top, her mother could have easily passed for her sister.

"I, uh, well. . ." Ashley said, tugging at the collar of her shirt.

"Don't worry, darling," her mother said soothingly, leaning inwards to peck her cheek.

"Where's Dad?"

"Getting the food out the boot. We thought a BBQ would be good seeing the weather's so nice."

"Ahh, thanks, Mum." Ashley smiled giving her a quick bear hug.

"That's what mother's are for," she replied as she stepped into the hallway.

Her dad appeared at the bottom of the path, wearing beige khaki trousers, a white shirt and brown sandals. At fifty five she thought he looked ten years younger. He still had a full head of dark hair and sharp features, not an ounce of fat could be seen on him anywhere. He had always joked he kept in good shape and health because he had the love of a good woman.

Ashley ran down to help him with the numerous bags he held.

"I swear your mother thinks she's feeding an army," he said, relinquishing some of the bags into her open hands and pecking her on the cheek. "How are you, love?"

"I'm fine, Dad, you're looking better than you did last week."

"It was only hay fever. You'd think I was on death's door the way your mother fussed."

"It's only because we love you so much."

"I know, love and believe me I'm grateful for that every day," he said as they walked into the house. "I just want to catch the news for a few minutes." He veered off into the living room.

Ashley took the bags into the kitchen and placed them on the floor.

"Where's Muffin?" her mother asked, pushing open the kitchen's double French doors that led into a garden aglow with a multitude of summer blooming shrubs. Long stemmed yellow and red roses clambered at will over a six foot wooden fence. "It's not like him not to come when I call."

"Don't worry he's with a walker I hired."

"A what?" she asked, moving back over to where Ashley stood.

"A dog walker. She walks him twice a day while I'm at work."

"Ashley you could have asked me, it would have been my pleasure."

"Mum, I don't want you taking on my responsibilities, you have enough on your plate with all the charity work you do."

"I wouldn't have minded," she said, lowering her head slightly before busying herself by unpacking the shopping and laying the food out on the counter.

"Well, I would have," she replied taking a seat. She pulled at her shirt as she felt a trace of sweat trickle down her back.

"So how long has this been going on, this dog walking lark?"

"Not long."

"And do you think Muffin's safe with a teenager?" she asked, raising her eyebrows.

"She's not a teenager, she's a grown woman and she, as well as the company, have been well vetted."

"Well, if you're sure."

"I'm positive," Ashley said reassuringly squeezing her mother's arm gently.

"Okay, then. Look why don't you go and get showered. I'll tell your dad to get the BBQ going and I'll start the salad."

"Okay, thanks."

Before she reached the door she turned. "I'm really glad you're both here today."

"Is something wrong, darling, are you still feeling down about—"

"Not at all, I'm just glad, that's all," Ashley said quickly, turning and running up the stairs before her mother could respond. The last thing she needed was yet another conversation about the emotional turmoil her life was in.

Half an hour later, her hair still wet from her shower, Ashley made her way down the stairs, wearing distressed denim shorts and a white vest. As she neared the kitchen door she heard unfamiliar laughter, then saw Muffin lapping up the water from his bowl. Tasha was perched on a stool in the centre of the kitchen, a glass of wine in her hand. She was bereft of speech as she stood at the doorway watching Tasha, dressed in a white sleeveless summer dress, conversing with her mother like they were old friends. It was impossible not to notice how beautiful she was as she brushed aside a strand of loose hair and tilted her head back slightly, letting out a laugh in response to something her mother had said.

Muffin was the first to see her and ran up

frantically wagging his tail.

"There you are, darling, Tasha just brought Muffin home. I've asked her to stay for the BBQ. We'll never get through the amount of food we brought," her mother said without stopping for a breath.

Tasha turned towards her, causing Ashley's abdominal muscles to contract and her pulse to quicken. "I hope you don't mind."

"Of course not, the more the merrier," Ashley answered clasping her hands together in front of her.

"Would you be a darling, Tasha and take the bread rolls out to Ray," her mother ordered, handing her a large bowl.

"Of course, Mrs McCoy."

"Please call me Sandra. Mrs makes me sound like someone's grandmother."

Tasha laughed. "Okay, Sandra."

"See, that sounds much better."

"What are you playing at?" Ashley whispered at her mother when Tasha walked out into the garden and was making small talk with her dad.

"What?" Sandra asked, raising her eyebrows innocently.

"Inviting her to stay—she's my dog walker," Ashley said unable to take her eyes off Tasha. She watched her as she took a seat in a garden chair, relaxing and soaking up the sun. Instinctively Tasha turned her face towards the kitchen as if she sensed her, causing Ashley to quickly look away.

"Oh, don't be so stuffy, you're not the CEO of a corporation and Tasha's not your subordinate," Sandra said, chopping up a red onion.

"You could have asked." Ashley had been in the company of some of the vilest people in her job but none of them made her as nervous as the woman who was sitting in her garden.

"You were in the shower and besides," Sandra said, drawing Ashley closer to her and whispering in a conspiratorial tone, "I think she'd be perfect for your brother, she's a lovely girl."

"He doesn't need you match making for him." Ashley crossed her arms in front of her chest. *How silly—as if Nat would ever be my love rival.*

"He's twenty six and still living at home—that speaks for itself."

"He still lives at home because you spoil him." Ashley picked out a slice of cucumber and popped it into her mouth.

"Well it's about time some other woman took him off my hands."

"She might already have a boyfriend or a husband."

"Nope, neither, I've asked." Sandra tossed the salad.

"You did what?"

"I asked, there's no point beating about the bush."

"Mum, sometimes you really are too much," Ashley said unable to resist a smile.

"Well touch wood," Sandra said tapping her head, "they'll hit it off tonight."

That's the last thing I need, Ashley thought as she followed her mother into the garden and tried her hardest to avoid Tasha's stare.

"The man with the beer is here, let the party begin," Nathan announced ten minutes later, jumping out onto the teak decking, startling everyone.

Tall and lean with dark short hair and brown eyes, he was the spitting image of their father.

"Oh gosh, sorry," he said bashfully, his cheeks reddening when he saw Tasha relaxing on a green and white striped recliner.

"This is my son, Nathan," Sandra said, rising gracefully from her chair and standing next to Nathan. "He isn't always this excitable," she added, trying to explain away his unconventional greeting.

"Nice to meet you." Nathan took Tasha's hand in his, bringing it to his lips.

Who said romance was dead, Ashley thought as she saw amusement register on Tasha's face. She had never seen such expressive eyes in her life.

"You too," Tasha replied laughing.

Ashley could tell straight away that Nathan was smitten with Tasha. Dread filled her—could she really cope seeing her little brother with a woman she herself fancied? Her heart rebelled at the thought. What on earth was she thinking—yes, Tasha was very attractive, yes she had caused her to have a physical reaction to her, one that she hadn't felt in years *but* and it was a big but, she was not looking for romance, especially not with a woman who may be straight.

"How long have you been friends with Ash? I haven't seen you before and believe me, I would have remembered if I had," Nathan said, flopping down on one of the loungers beside her.

Ashley bit her lip to stifle a laugh at her brother's cheesy chat up lines.

"We met a few days ago actually, I walk Muffin," Tasha said, looking over at Ashley as she answered his question.

"Ahh, a dog walker, I was thinking of getting a dog myself."

"Really?" Tasha asked.

"And who is going to care for this imaginary dog?" Sandra asked.

Nathan's face reddened. "I could always hire Tasha, couldn't I?" he said looking at her intensely.

"Well—"

"Nat, why don't you get yourself some food while Tasha helps me with the drinks," Ashley broke in.

His face fell. "Oh, okay, it's a shame we didn't bring our swimwear we could have relaxed in the hot tub, unless . . . Ashley can always lend you something." He carried on talking to Tasha as she rose from her seat.

"I think I'll pass on this occasion," Tasha said, looking down at him before joining Ashley in the kitchen.

"I'm really sorry about all this, it must feel like my brother is going to whack you over the head with a club and drag you back to his cave. I've never seen him so . . . intense, it must be the heat."

"It's okay, he seems like a nice guy."

"He is," Ashley said fondly.

"In fact, you're all really nice." Tasha gave Ashley's hand a quick caress and looked at her with a flirtatious glimmer in her eyes. Ashley felt lost in them, never wanting to be found.

"Can you bring me a beer, sis," Nathan called from the garden, breaking the moment between them.

"Won't be a minute," she yelled back, reluctantly

dragging her eyes away from Tasha's.

The rest of the evening flew by; her father fell asleep shortly after eating, Nathan monopolised Tasha with exaggerated tales about his work cases and Ashley and her mother played scrabble on the side table. From time to time she had met Tasha's eyes but had always been the first to look away. She didn't like how vulnerable she made her feel but she felt like a moth to a flame—she couldn't help looking at her.

Stirring from his sleep, Ray checked his watch. "Come on then, my love," he said to Sandra. "Let's be getting home, I'm sure Ashley has an early start in the morning."

Nathan's eyes widened at the thought of leaving. His expression was that of a fox caught in a car's headlights. "Ash is alright, it's not even that late," Nathan said reluctantly, his eyes pleading with his mother like a school boy.

"Yes it is, Nat, it's midnight and I do have an early start," Ashley said standing.

"Let me help you tidy up before we go," Sandra offered, as she began to collect the plates from the table.

"Don't worry about it, Mum, I'll do it tomorrow."

"Don't be silly it won't take me long."

"No honestly, Mum leave it," she said, putting her hand over hers and taking the plates from her.

"Okay." Sandra relented. "Would you like a lift home, Tasha?"

"It's no problem," Nathan chimed in.

"Erm, no, it's okay, thanks. I'll get a cab, I go in the opposite direction to you," Tasha said remaining seated.

"Don't be silly, a young girl like you travelling home this late," Sandra said.

"I'm sure I'll be fine. I use the same cab company all the time."

"Okay then, if you're sure. Come on, Nathan, get your stuff together."

"I don't want to go yet," he said solemnly.

"Well you have to, your sister needs to rest."

Nathan quickly scribbled his number down on a piece of paper before handing it discreetly to Tasha. "My number," he said, giving her a boyish grin.

"Thanks."

After Ashley finally managed to close the door behind her brother who had still been begging to stay the night, she turned to see Tasha in the hallway, her bag slung over her shoulder.

"I think I'd better make a move as well."

"Are you sure you don't want another drink?"

"I thought you wanted to go to bed."

"Even if I did, I wouldn't be able to sleep."

"Rough day?"

"You could say that."

"If that's the case I'd love another drink. I'm a bit of a night owl myself."

"Shall we stay in the garden? I can put more logs on the fire pit."

"That would be lovely."

Ashley turned off the kitchen light as they walked back into the garden, giving Tasha a glass of wine before lighting several candles and throwing more logs on the fire.

"It's so peaceful here and your garden is

beautiful," Tasha said breaking the silence.

"I would like to take credit for it, but the most I do is pay the gardener for its upkeep."

"Is that because you don't like gardening?"

"No, I just don't have the time. My work consumes most of my waking day. What about you?"

"What about me?"

"What do you do to unwind?"

"Walk dogs."

Ashley laughed. "And when you're not walking dogs?"

"I've just completed a degree in Hospitality Business Management," Tasha said, slowly running her fingers through her hair, a gesture Ashley couldn't help but think was extremely provocative.

"Really? That sounds interesting, so are you looking for a job in the hotel business?"

"Yep."

"Found anywhere yet?"

"Yep."

"That's good. In today's climate not many people are lucky enough to walk straight into a job from University. Which hotel is it?"

"Sunset Beach."

Ashley frowned. "Never heard of it. Where is it? Brighton or somewhere?"

"No, Australia."

"What! Are you kidding me?" Her heart sank at the thought.

"No." Tasha laughed. "It's family owned."

"I take it it's on the beach."

"Yep, it's in Cairns."

"Wow, that sounds amazing."

"Yes it is." The line of her mouth tightened a fraction.

"So when do you start?"

"After my Graduation in July." Tasha tilted her head to the side as she reached down and rubbed Muffin's belly.

Ashley's lips parted in surprise. "So how does dog walking and hotel management go together?" she asked, following the movement of Tasha's hand with great interest.

"I took a job dog walking to break up the monotony of being cooped up in a building all day." Tasha tipped her face to look up at the darkened sky, now peppered with twinkling lights.

"Are your parents Australian?"

"No, they're both British. Well were. My mum passed away five years ago it's just my dad now," she said, lowering her head and turning towards her.

"I'm sorry to hear that," Ashley replied in a gentle tone.

"It's okay. I'm over the worst now, they emigrated to Oz twenty five years ago to start the hotel." She crossed her arms and hugged herself tightly.

"And it's still going strong?"

"You could say that," was all she said on the matter.

"How come you don't have an Australian accent?"

Ashley could see her eyes squint, the candlelight casting over her features.

"I was a surprise conception. My parents were too old and uninterested in raising another child in their forties so I was packed off to boarding school in

England until I was sixteen. I went back to Oz for five years before coming back here to go to University."

"That must have been tough growing up without your parents."

She blew out a measured breath. "It was, but I was in the same boat as so many other girls—it just made us all wonder why they even bothered giving birth to us in the first place if we were such a burden."

"I think it's like so many things in life, people do things without thinking about the consequences."

"But surely that's really selfish to bring someone into the world that's not wanted."

"I totally agree with you but things are not so black and white—the unexpected happens and we don't always deal with them the way we should. Do you get on with your dad?"

"So, so. We don't have the sort of relationship you do with your family," Tasha said in a strained voice, looking back up at the sky.

"Oh, believe me, we have our moments," Ashley said, letting out a short laugh.

"I bet they don't try to force you to live a life *they've* planned out for you."

"I think they know better than to ever try and pull that on me," Ashley said playing with the ends of her hair.

"Exactly, you have boundaries and I can see they respect that, but my father . . . well, let's just say he doesn't know the meaning of the word."

"So I take it you're not looking forward to going back to work there?"

"How perceptive," Tasha said jokingly. "I am in

a way, but I'm really going to miss it here. I grew up here, it's my home."

"Well, that's going to dampen my brother's plans. You know he has an enormous crush on you."

Tasha brought her head down abruptly and snapped it towards Ashley. "Do you think so? I thought he was just playing around."

"Oh no, not Nat, he doesn't play around with things close to his heart. I think he's fallen hard."

"That's a shame."

Ashley looked at her with a probing gaze. "Why's that, don't you like him?"

"Of course I do. What's not to like? He's handsome, intelligent, funny, got a great smile but. . ."

"But?"

She rubbed the side of her temple with her fingers. "He's male."

It took a few seconds for the information to relay to her brain. "My mum isn't going to be happy when she hears that," Ashley finally said. A fluttery feeling in her stomach caused her to sit up.

"Oh?"

"Oh no, she's not anti-gay or anything but I think she already had visions of you down the aisle with my brother and two grandchildren to follow quite swiftly afterwards."

Tasha laughed. "And what about you? Does it bother you?"

"It'd be a bit hypocritical if it did."

They exchanged an understanding look.

"Oh, I didn't realise."

Ashley gave her a tentative smile. "I don't go round with it tattooed on my forehead. My sexuality is my business."

"That's pretty much the way I look at it as well. Will you let your brother down gently for me or shall I?"

"I think it's best I break the news. You don't want to see a grown man cry do you?"

"Surely he wouldn't be that upset."

"Nah, I'm only kidding he'll get over it . . . eventually."

By 2am crimson embers glowed in the fire pit, though they no longer emitted the forceful heat they once had.

"It's getting a bit chilly," Ashley said, moving towards the edge of her lounger.

"I hadn't noticed," Tasha said quietly, her eyes slowly blinking as they made eye contact.

Ashley glanced around uneasily. "We've run out of wood." She pushed herself onto her feet.

"It's a shame the evening has to end, I've really enjoyed myself." Tasha withdrew her mobile from her bag. "I think I'd better call a cab."

Biting her lip, Ashley moved awkwardly from one foot to the other. "Um, you can stay if you like. I have two spare rooms for you to choose from and a selection of toothbrushes, courtesy of my mother who believes you can never have too many."

Tasha laughed. "How can I refuse an offer like that?"

"Good, let's go in before I fall asleep here."

Ashley walked around the decking, blowing out the candles before leading Tasha up the stairs. "You can have the green room or the yellow room," she said, stopping in the wide hallway.

"Yellow— it's my favourite colour."

"That will be this room then." Ashley pushed open a door to a medium sized room, painted a light pastel yellow, with an oak wood wardrobe and chest of drawers.

"It's next door to mine. I hope you don't snore." She let out a small laugh. She now felt so relaxed in Tasha's company, as if they were roommates who had known each other for an age.

"There're toothbrushes and stuff in the cupboard in the en-suite and if you want to wear a top to bed, there are some in the drawers."

"That's okay, I always sleep in my birthday suit," Tasha said, staring intensely at Ashley.

"Okay." Ashley looked away, rubbing her neck briefly. "Well, thanks for staying for the BBQ and you know— this evening. I really enjoyed your company."

"Me too," Tasha said softly, taking a step towards her and clasping her hand loosely around her wrist.

Ashley swallowed hard and looked down the hallway as she heard Muffin making his way up the stairs. "You'd better make sure you keep your door shut otherwise you'll be sharing your bed with Muffin tonight." Ashley moved away slowly, causing Tasha's hand to drop away from her.

"I will do," she said, taking a slight step back as Ashley walked into her bedroom and gently closed the door behind her.

Within ten minutes, Tasha was laying naked on top of a crisp white sheet, her sun-kissed body enveloped in darkness. A much needed cool breeze drifted through an open window, gently caressing her skin. The day had certainly turned into something she hadn't expected— she would never have dreamt in a million years she would be sleeping under the same roof as Ashley. It was as if fate was playing a cruel trick on her. Though she had felt an instant attraction to her when she had first met her, it had now intensified into the danger zone category. She had been aware of Ashley staring at her for most of the night. She hadn't minded—she liked the feeling of being under the scrutiny of those aqua green eyes. It wasn't a total shock to find out Ashley was gay, although she wasn't at any point certain —Ashley was like a closed book, revealing nothing. Whatever she was feeling was irrelevant in the grand scheme of things because nothing could happen between them. She was going back to Australia in less than a month and if there was one thing she didn't want in her life, it was instability. That's all she could foresee if she started a long distance relationship with anyone who lived in any country but Australia. It seemed everything she wanted was always out of reach. Not so long ago her life had been set to go—her plans had been to study veterinary surgery and become a vet. All those dreams had to be abandoned when her eldest brother, Ken decided, one day, that he no longer wanted to be the head of the family business. Running off to Bali to become a surf instructor—not that she blamed him, at forty he had been doing his father's bidding for far too long. Now her father had gotten his claws into her and she couldn't see a way out.

Effortlessly she fell into slumber as she replayed the evening in her mind. Suddenly she awoke with a start at a sound coming from Ashley's bedroom—at first she thought it was Muffin whimpering until she realised it was Ashley crying. She sprang up quickly and grabbed her T-shirt from the floor, tiptoeing quietly towards Ashley's room. Tapping gently on the door several times, she tentatively opened it and peeped in. She could see the outline of Ashley's body in the silvery light of the moon, moving from side to side as though she was afloat on rough seas. Moving swiftly to the bed, she stood in front of her for a few moments waiting to see if she would wake.

"Ashley," she whispered gently, before sitting down beside her and resting her hand against her face. "Ashley," she repeated, raising her voice slightly as her crying became more intense. Suddenly, Ashley jerked awake, scrambling away from Tasha's touch to the other side of the bed.

"It's okay, it's me, Tasha. It looked like you were having a nightmare," she said, straightening up.

"I'm sorry," Ashley said rasping, evidently still shaken from her dream.

"Are you okay?"

"Yes, I'm fine. I must be overtired," she said, blinking sleepily as she lowered her body back onto the bed.

"Do you want me to stay with you?"

It was several seconds before Ashley replied so softly, Tasha could barely make out what she said. "No, it's okay, go back to bed."

Rising from the bed, Tasha stood and walked towards the door. She heard a rustling sound, as

Ashley settled herself between the sheets. Then all was still. She glanced back as she heard Ashley breathing softly and wondered what could have caused a woman who was seemingly so in control in her waking hours to be so vulnerable in her sleep.

Chapter 12

The next morning Tasha awoke to the contrasting sound of joyous mating birds and the loud clanging of construction work outside the window. She sighed when she looked at the digital clock on the bedside cabinet—*7:00am*. She pulled the quilt over her head with every intention of going back to sleep but reluctantly gave up after ten minutes as the noise seemed to be escalating. She yawned as she stretched lazily before getting up from the bed, slipping into her clothes and making her way downstairs. Ashley was already in the kitchen as she entered. Dressed in a dark grey trousers and a red shirt, she stood at the sink rinsing dishes, looking fresh and rested.

"Good morning," Tasha said as she thought how lucky Ashley was to be one of those fortunate people who woke up looking perfect.

"Morning," Ashley replied avoiding any eye contact. "You needn't have gotten up this early, I tried not to wake you," she said stacking the dishwasher.

"It's okay, you didn't—those workmen could raise the dead the amount of noise they make." Tasha sat down on a stool.

"I know, it's been going on for a week now. Something to do with a gas leak. Would you like a drink?" Ashley asked, finally looking up at her.

"Do you have hot chocolate?"

"No, only tea or coffee, I'm afraid."

Tasha shook her head. "I'm more of a hot chocolate fan in the morning."

"I would offer you breakfast but as you can see housekeeping isn't something I excel in," Ashley said, opening the door to the fridge, revealing only takeaway cartons inside.

"I can't believe I've actually met somebody who lives on a diet worse than me." Tasha laughed.

Ashley's face broke into a smile and Tasha felt the tension break. "How are you feeling this morning?"

"Fine . . . look I'm sorry about last night."

"Don't be silly you have nothing to apologise for."

"Yes I do. You must think I'm some kind of crazy lady."

"Not in the slightest, I actually think—"

Ashley's mobile vibrated on the counter. "Sorry." She scooped it up into her hand and rested it against her ear. "McCoy," she said with all the professionalism of a telemarketer. She listened intently for a few moments, the lines of concentration deepening along her brow. "It doesn't come as a surprise. No, don't worry, I'm leaving now." She snapped the phone shut.

"Work?" Tasha asked, noting Ashley's clamped mouth and fixed eyes.

"Yep, I've got to go. Sorry, what were you going to say before?"

"To say? Oh nothing, don't worry it wasn't important. I'll take Muffin out in a while. Is it okay if I take a shower first?"

"Of course," Ashley said as she headed for the door, stopping before she reached it and turning, "thanks for, you know, being there last night."

"Think nothing of it," Tasha replied to a retreating Ashley.

***

"What an idiot," Ashley said to herself as the memory of the previous night refused to go away. She put her foot on the accelerator a little too hard causing the car to lurch forward, narrowly missing the car in front. *How did I let that happen? Blubbering like a baby with a woman I've just met.* But she knew that she had no control over the nightmares that plagued her sleep. She was just going to have to face her demons the best she could. Her phone rang again and she put it on loud speaker.

"McCoy, it's Colleen. Have you heard the body has been identified?"

"Yes, Dale called me a minute ago."

"Her parents have been informed."

"How did they take it?"

"They weren't really that shocked. I think they were expecting it. At least now they've got a daughter to bury."

"That's true. Listen, Colleen, if it's okay I'd like to go and pay them a visit today."

"For what reason? We've got no new information to give them yet."

"I know, but I just want to talk to them and see if I can jog some memories."

"Ashley, if you think it will do some good, then go ahead. Now back to this psychic, how do you think he's connected to all of this?"

"I think he either knows the person who killed her or knows of him—either way I think Aaron Davies is the one that will lead us to her killer."

"Okay, this is what I want you and Dale to do. Find out about everything you can about Mr Davies. I want every inch of his life looked over with a magnify glass."

"Okay—I'll look into his family background, maybe he overheard a family member talking about it."

"Good idea. Oh, by the way, Hailey has been waiting at the front desk since the news was broken to the family this morning. She wants to talk to you."

"I know, Dale told me. I'll speak to her as soon as I get in. Shouldn't be more than ten minutes."

"Okay, but be warned, she's in a pretty bad state."

"Thanks for letting me know."

She pressed the end call button, relieved she had something else to think about until she got to the station.

As Ashley walked through the entrance, a stocky police officer manning the reception was regaling the previous night's events with great fervour to his fellow officers.

"So, I said to the guy, 'You need to put a skirt on with those fishnet stockings or I'm going to have to take you to the station and cite you for public indecency. You can't go around in holey fishnets with your business on display'. Do you know what he did? He called his mum and asked her to bring him a skirt. She did it, too!"

The officers let out a boisterous laugh.

"Hey, Ash, how's it going?" he said, noticing her for the first time.

"Good thanks, sounds like nothing changes then."

"Nope, we're still getting a few laughs," he said

still smiling at the memory. "I've put Ms Campbell in the interview suite out of public view. She was in a bad way."

"Thanks, Mark."

"No worries," he said before turning back to his colleagues who were eagerly awaiting to hear more of his tales.

Ashley looked through the rectangular glass in the door, as she geared herself up to face the grieving Hailey. It was the toughest part of her job. Yes, the murder scenes were awful but having to deal with relatives of the victims was far harder. It was something she would never get used to—and she never wanted to.

Hailey sat with her shoulders slouched down, her face blotchy and red, her hair which had been picture perfect the last time she had seen her, was scraped back into a ponytail and her face make-up free, revealing deep lines and dark bags under her eyes. When she pushed open the door Hailey barely looked up, as though the weight of her head was too heavy to lift.

She sat silently for a long time before finally saying, in almost a whisper, "I can't believe she's really gone." Abruptly she turned her head towards the wall and let out a wail, so heartbreaking that Ashley remained rooted to the spot, pushing her hands deep into her pockets—it was a sound she remembered well.

"Oh God, help me, please, please."

Ashley's feet began to move and within seconds she was knelt at Hailey's side, stroking the damp strands of hair away from her face.

"I can't believe this is true, I can't believe she is really gone."

Ashley said nothing—she knew there was nothing she could say that would ease the pain Hailey was going through. She recognised that finally knowing Esther was dead was going to be very hard for Hailey, like opening a wound that had been stitched up but had never healed. Her heart ached for her.

Blinking back the tears, Hailey looked imploringly at her. "Will you find whoever is responsible for her murder?"

"Yes I will," Ashley answered, her face set in determination. "If it's the last thing I do."

***

The vast grounds were surrounded by a high hedge and it wasn't until they reached the wrought iron gates that they could see the large detached Georgian house. Dale frowned and sighed deeply as he rubbed his hands together. "Ash, do you want to do all the talking. I kinda feel unprepared for this at the moment."

"Okay," Ashley said as she pulled up the latch and pushed the heavy gate open. Loath filled her chest while thinking of what she would say to the two grieving parents who were waiting behind the door of the three storey town house they were heading towards.

Taking a deep breath she reached up and brought down the brass knocker twice in quick succession, then stood back in line with Dale. While they waited in silence, she took in her surroundings. A rugged man, dressed in green overalls, stood on a small ladder snapping large shears together over the hedge. She glanced along the hedgerow that was yet to be cut and felt sorry for him, as she wondered how long it would take to finish the job in the searing heat.

The large oak door opened moments later by a small, middle-aged woman with a neat modest figure, her dark hair scraped back into a bun giving her features a severe look. Ashley and Dale flashed their IDs. "We're here to see Mr and Mrs Campbell."

"Yes they're expecting you. Please come in," she said in a soft tone which was at odds with her harsh appearance. She stood back to let them enter. As she did, Mr Campbell came into view, descending the elegant staircase with wrought iron balustrades, his large hand gripping the rail as though his life depended on it.

"It's okay, Hadria, I'll see to the detectives," he said in a rich flawless voice.

"Very good, sir," she replied before shutting the door and marching quickly down the long hallway.

They waited at the foot of the staircase until he reached them. Ashley looked up at the tall, well dressed, agile looking man whose thinning hair combed back over what seemed to be a bald patch. Though she took him to be in his early sixties his heavily wrinkled face made him look much older. She lifted her arm to shake his outreached hand in a firm grip. "Mr Campbell, I'm DS McCoy and this is my colleague, DC Taylor."

He moved his hand towards Dale to shake his briefly. His dull eyes looked everywhere but at either of their faces.

"May we offer you our deepest condolences," Ashley said to the side of his strong profile.

"Thank you. If you would like to come with me, my wife is waiting for you," he said, turning and motioning for them to follow him.

They entered the grand drawing room behind him. A large gold-glinted mirror hung on a pale wall above a cream two-seater sofa where Mrs Campbell was sat. A white bone china tea set was laid out on a glass coffee table in front of her.

She reached down and lifted the teapot and held it in mid air. "Can I offer you both a cup of tea?" she asked pleasantly, looking up at them. Her hair, silver in colour, was coiffed high on top of a thin drawn face, her frail body clothed in dark brown tweeds. Despite the sweltering temperatures she looked as cool as ice. The dark shadows under her eyes were the only tell tale signs of the strain she was under.

Both officers declined with a shake of their heads.

"Then please sit down," she said with a sweeping gesture towards a larger sofa that sat a few feet away, "and tell me." She paused while she rested the teapot on the table. "How are you going to find the bastard that killed Esther?"

***

"Well we never found out anything new from them," Dale said settling in his seat and strapping his seat belt in. "Everything they said was in the files we've got."

"I know but then again I didn't really think we would get any fresh information." Ashley started the engine, revving the accelerator, before pulling out onto the traffic free road.

"So why did you tell Colleen you wanted to see them in person?" Dale asked, turning to look at her.

"Because I needed to see them with my own two eyes, not through a written report."

He smiled knowingly. "So, Sherlock, what have you deduced?"

"That they had nothing to do with Esther's disappearance or her murder."

"Did you seriously ever think they had?"

"Dale, you should know better than anyone, I don't fall for that *he doesn't look the type* dogma. Murderers of both sexes don't exactly come with a label declaring their intentions. How many people have not been taken as a serious suspect because they didn't *look* the way we think they should?"

"Yeah, but come on, Ash, he's an MP and Mrs Campbell. . ." He let out a short laugh. "What a feisty woman she turned out to be."

"See, you've said it yourself," Ashley said, easing her foot on the brake pad before stopping at a red light and looking at him from the corner of her eye. "Admit it, you were totally taken in by her innocent demeanour until she opened her mouth."

He held his hands up in the air, palms facing front ways. "I know, I know—point taken."

The traffic lights changed and they moved on in silence. She suddenly felt very tired and emotionally drained. Her thoughts moved on to Tasha. Though she had barely known her for a week, there was something about her that drew her to her. It wasn't merely because she was so attractive—there was something else but she couldn't quite put her finger on it. Whatever it was, she was looking forward to getting to know her better. Maybe they could maintain their friendship when she went to Australia. *Australia*—the word caused a sudden stomach dropping sensation. She was going to be gone soon and she couldn't understand why she was filled with sadness at the thought of it.

"Hey, what's with the glum face?" Dale asked, breaking into her thoughts, his eyes weighing her up.

"Nothing," she answered with a lie, a fake smile lightly playing on her lips. "I was just wondering what to do next." She didn't tell him that she wasn't talking about the Campbell case, that it was all to do with Tasha, a woman who had come unexpectedly into her life and in a matter of months would be gone again. In a blink of an eye she felt like she had no control over her emotions and she didn't like that feeling one little bit.

Returning to her office, Ashley sat at her desk, the seventeen inch LCD computer screen before her a blank sterile white. She needed to write up the meeting with the Campbell's but her fingers failed to move. Her head throbbed as she felt like she was enveloped in a cloak of grief—that she had somehow been infected with Esther's parents' pain. On one hand, emotionally charged cases like this drained her but on the other it was what propelled her into solving cases—the need to find justice for the victims.

Every time she placed her fingers above the keyboard an image of Mr Campbell flashed through her mind; his desperate vacant eyes held the guilt of someone who blamed himself for his daughter's death. Ashley wondered how many times he had gone over that fateful day in his mind, wishing that he had done things differently or accepted her love for Peter. Perhaps he thought she would still be alive today if it weren't for his prejudiced attitude. He had said very little during the hour they had spent with them, just nodding in agreement with his wife when it was called for. Her mother seemed more pragmatic, she had let them know that she had accepted Esther was dead a long time ago—all that held interest for her now was finding the killer and making him pay. Ashley had noticed an icy cold hostility between the two of them and she wondered how their relationship had soldiered on despite being so irreconcilably damaged.

She forced herself to stop thinking and concentrate on the task in front of her. She began by just writing how the conversation went in chronological order and the rest seemed to flow. Fifteen minutes later, the report was written and she was standing in Colleen's over-heated office.

"Right," Colleen said in an upbeat tone after quickly reading through the report. "A reconstruction is taking place tomorrow, it will be aired on Crime Watch next week. Hopefully, it might jog someone's memory and we'll get a break in this case. A help line has been opened and I'm sure we'll get the usual crank calls coming in." She shook her head slightly.

"Do these people actually realise the harm they do to cases by clogging our system with useless information?"

"I don't think they really care—most of them are just lonely souls looking for attention. So what are your plans for the rest of the day?"

"I'm just waiting for Dale to come back from lunch then we're going to see Esther's ex-boyfriend. Then we've got an appointment with Principal Bradshaw at the college Aaron used to attend. We haven't told him who we want to talk to him about. I don't want to give him the heads up in case he's still in touch with him."

"Hmm, that should be interesting, keep me updated."

"Will do."

Chapter 13

Peter Holmes was a tall, heavy set man with a greying goatee beard, thick dark unruly hair flecked with grey and eyes the colour of a latte coffee. Bare footed and dressed in baggy shorts and a black rumpled David Bowie T-shirt, he looked as though he had just crawled out of bed.

He opened his front door wide, shielding his eyes from the sun rays with his hand. "Come in," he said, letting them step into his small cramped council flat, the stench of stale cigarette smoke overwhelming. "Sorry I couldn't see you yesterday. I bumped into an old friend. We had a lot of catching up to do." He led them into a living room where a fifty inch wide screen TV dominated the otherwise tiny room. An expensive brand DVD player sat underneath it and a slick music centre was positioned on a white shelf—they all looked new. Apart from one silver framed photograph propped up on the mantelpiece above a gas fire, there were no other personal effects to be seen.

"We all have our own priorities," Ashley said, looking around for somewhere to sit that didn't have piles of clothing or stacks of paper on it.

"Oh, sorry," Peter said, rushing to clear a couple of wooden chairs. "I don't have many visitors," he added, seemingly oblivious to the meaning behind her remark. "No one really has time for unemployed people."

Ashley shook her head as if genuinely concerned. "Must be tough."

"It is, this bloody Government doesn't care, though. Expecting us to live on a paltry seventy quid a week is a joke," he said, the lines in his forehead growing deeper.

As Ashley and Dale took their seats they exchanged a glance as they noted the expensive equipment. *Could be knock off gear,* Ashley thought. *But even then, how could he afford it?*

"Mr Holmes. . ." Dale began.

"Please call me, Peter. I can't be dealing with those types of formalities," he said, waving his hand in the air, as if swotting away a nuisance fly.

"Peter," Dale started again, straightening his shoulders. "Have you heard the latest regarding Esther Campbell?"

"No," he said, scratching at the left side of his nose as he leaned back into his tattered armchair, sprawling out his long legs casually in front of him.

"As you know, remains were found during a search in Epping Forest. Today those remains have been identified as Esther Campbell."

"I see." Peter reached for a packet of cigarettes from a small table beside him. "Do you mind if I smoke?" he asked, withdrawing one from the box and placing it between his yellow stained fingers.

"It's your home, feel free," Dale said, shifting in his seat whilst Peter put the cigarette between his lips and lit it.

He inhaled deeply before releasing a series of smoke-rings, watching them float up towards the ceiling before saying, "Yeah, but you know these health and safety fanatics, soon we won't be able to breathe in our own homes without being fined." He got to his feet and walked over to the window. Pushing it open, peelings of old discoloured white paint dropped away from it with ease. "I'll be the first to admit, it's a filthy habit but one I haven't been able to kick since I was sixteen," he said, looking at the white stick in his hand with disgust.

"So back to Ms Campbell," Dale said clearing his throat.

"Sorry, yeah that's very sad to hear if that's the case." He walked slowly back to his chair and dropping into it with a thud.

"You don't look that bothered, if you don't mind me saying."

He shrugged dismissively. "Give me a break, man, it was over twenty years ago. I was young. I didn't know anything about life. If you ask me she's better off dead than living with those freaky parents of hers." He took another drag of the cigarette, holding it in his lungs for several seconds before finally releasing it into a cloud of smoke.

"According to Esther's sister, Hailey, the pair of you were very much in love," Ashley interjected, leaning forward in her chair.

He turned to her. "Love! Don't make me laugh." He snorted. "We were just a couple of teenagers mucking around. I didn't even know what love was. Look, I was eighteen and still wet behind the ears. I liked her until she started getting. . ." He grappled for the right word. "Needy, wanting me to whisk her away from her miserable life like a knight in shining armour. She really thought I was going to marry her," he said, his square jaw visibly tense.

"Is that why you took off travelling? Were you

trying to get some distance between you both?" Dale asked, his facial expression remaining blank.

"Yeah," he said averting his gaze. "I didn't have the heart to tell her that I didn't really love her. I mean, regardless of everything, she was a good kid but we weren't exactly on the same social ladder, if you know what I mean."

"What about the pendant you gave her with the inscription on it?" Ashley asked, smoothing back her hair. It was all she could do not run to the window for some fresh air but she had to keep Peter in his comfort zone if he was going to talk openly with them.

His eyes widened. "How'd you know about that?"

"Her sister told us about it."

Dipping his head slightly he said, "I found that piece of junk in the ground when I was doing a building job for my old man, it wasn't even real silver." He looked up, his eyes darting from one face to the other. "I had my mum polish it up to give it a nice new look," he said, looking extremely pleased with himself as he brought the cigarette back to his lips, taking another drag.

"So how long did you end up in India for?" Ashley asked.

"Over a year," Peter replied, releasing the smoke and coughing into a closed fist.

"What parts did you go to?"

"Er . . . um . . . all over the place, it was a long time ago. The old grey matter isn't working as well as it used to." He crushed the cigarette into an overflowing ashtray.

"I went to India a few years back, it was one of

the most enriching experiences of my life. One that I'll never forget," Ashley said, staring directly into Peter's eyes.

He looked away. "Yeah, well good for you. Look—if there isn't anything else, I really have to be getting on."

"Busy?" Ashley asked still remaining seated.

"Yeah, something like that."

"Just a few more questions then we'll be on our way," she said smiling at him. "So what type of work were you in?"

"Construction, took over my old man's business when he died. I was doing alright until a few years ago—nice house, car the lot. Then the recession hit in 2007 and the rest is history. Nobody wants to hire a forty plus man with back problems," he said, raking his hand through his hair.

"Would you mind getting me a glass of water, please, my throat feels dry," Ashley asked, letting out a little cough.

"Sure, then you'll go?"

"Yes, I think we've heard enough."

When she heard the tap running in the kitchen, Ashley took his momentary absence to swiftly cross the room and pick up the framed photograph. Quickly removing the cardboard back she sneaked a quick glance behind the picture before replacing it.

"What are you looking for?" Dale whispered.

Before she had a chance to answer, Peter came back into the room with a cloudy glass, half filled with water.

"Is this your brother?" Ashley asked, raising the frame in the air and showing it to him.

"Yes," Peter answered, his face paling.

"You look so alike, you could be twins."

"So I've been told," he said, handing her the glass and taking the photograph from her.

"What's the age difference?"

"I dunno, why?"

"I can easily find out, Peter," she said letting out a sigh. "Look let's stop playing games shall we?"

"What are you talking about?"

"You didn't really go to India did you?"

"What! Of course I did, I have the passport stamp to prove it."

"I'm sure you do but you weren't the one using the passport were you?"

"Of course I was. Look, what are you trying to pull here?" he asked looking pleadingly at Dale for help.

"When was that photo taken?"

He remained absolutely motionless for a moment. "I don't know, I can't remember that long back."

"Shall I refresh your memory? How about 1985, it's written right on the back—me and Stuart 1985."

"So what if it was?" Peter said, clamping his fingers over his trembling chin.

"Don't you think it's a bit strange that it's your brother with the bronzed tan and henna tattoo on his arm, while you're looking somewhat . . . pasty. Unless of course you spent the whole year under an umbrella."

"This photo doesn't prove anything—now, I'd like you both to leave," he said, licking his lips nervously.

"Peter, it will take me less than an hour to prove that your brother was not in this country for a year. Do you want me to show you how?" Ashley took her mobile from her pocket.

He took a deep, pained breath. "Alright, alright, I didn't go to India—satisfied?" He turned and walked back to his chair, sitting down on the edge, resting his elbows on his knees.

"No, not really. I want you to tell me exactly what you know about Esther's murder."

He shook his head decisively. "I don't know anything. I swear, I had nothing to do with it."

"Why didn't you go to India?"

"It was all a bit of a prank. I told Esther that to let her down gently. My brother wanted to go but he didn't have a passport so I said he could use mine."

"Where were you on the day that Esther went missing?"

"I don't know. Can you remember that far back?"

"Don't play games with me, Peter. In a matter of minutes my colleague and I will be hauling your arse down the station."

Peter threw his hands up in the air and shook his head. "I'm telling you the truth. This is exactly why I've kept this a secret for all these years. I knew you lot would try and pin it on me. Did her father send you here? Is he still gunning for me after all these years?"

Dale stood up quickly causing the bones in his knees to crack. "No one sent us here, you were part of an ongoing investigation and after finding this out you've moved right up our list of suspects."

"You can think what you want," Peter said in a

challenging tone. "It's another thing trying to prove it, now I want you both to leave."

Moving towards the door, Ashley turned back towards him. "Rest assured, Mr Holmes, this is not the last of this matter, we'll be back . . . soon."

"What a cocky bastard," Dale said as they made their way down the concrete stairwell, the sour odour of urine filled their nostrils, causing them to hold their breath until they stepped out onto the forecourt. A bunch of pre-teen kids jumped off their car when they saw them approaching.

"Pigs," a freckled-faced ginger haired boy shouted as he stuck his middle finger up at them before rounding a corner with the rest of his friends, all laughing like hyenas.

"The little shits," Dale said sneering, noticing the scratch marks along the side panel of the car.

"Let it go, Dale, it's not worth it," Ashley said, opening the driver's door and getting in. On council estates like these the police were always considered the bad guys—that was until their help was needed in some sort of an emergency, then they were heroes. She knew there were some bad apples in the police service but they were the minority, it was the same in any work force but being a public servant meant you were an easy target.

"In my day, you'd get a slap round the head if you were caught damaging police property."

"Yes, Granddad and in your day, you wouldn't be hauled in front of a judge being charged with child abuse." Ashley let out a little dry laugh.

"That's why this country is in the state it is in today—all this bloody pandering to the criminals—

it's ludicrous," Dale said, adjusting his tall frame in his seat.

Ashley shared his sentiments. She would never have believed there would come a time when TV shows gave a platform to criminals to boast about crimes they had committed—not to mention some people who had the audacity to upload their abusive behaviour onto the internet. It was a sign of the times but she lived in hope that things could get better.

"We should have brought Peter in, Ash."

"For what reason? We need to build more of a case around him before we start jumping to conclusions."

"Are you saying you don't think he's responsible?"

"I'm saying, let's keep our options open. If he's the one that killed her, we'll get him but we have to do this the right way."

Dale's phone vibrated in his pocket. Snatching it out he listened for a few seconds before snapping it shut. "Principal Bradshaw just called the station to put the meeting back to tomorrow which means we get to go home early today."

Hallelujah, Ashley thought as she quickly glanced at the clock—if she could get back within half an hour she'd be able to see Tasha before she took Muffin for his afternoon walk.

Chapter 14

"Hey, Ashley I didn't expect to see you home so early," Tasha said as Ashley walked through the front door just as she was putting Muffin's lead on.

"I had an interview with someone that got put off until tomorrow."

Lucky me, Tasha thought. "If you're not too tired do you want to come for a walk with us?"

"I'd like nothing better, give me five minutes to get changed."

"I'll just take Muffin out front until you're ready."

"Okay."

Tasha couldn't help but smile to herself as she led Muffin outside. She was glad Ashley had come home early, not just because she thought she was overworked but she was happy to be able to spend more time with her.

"I'm ready," Ashley declared as she hurried down the path to join them. Dressed in faded jeans, a white and blue striped shirt and dark sunglasses, she couldn't have looked more different than when she came home from work.

"You look very nice," Tasha said as they began walking along the street.

"That doesn't say much for my usual dress sense."

"You know what I mean," she said playfully nudging her. It was times like this she felt she had known Ashley for a life time. They just fitted so well together.

"So how was your day?" Ashley asked as they

rounded the corner and the park came into view.

"Oh, boring."

"Why's that?"

"I had a load of stuff that needed sorting; clothes to the charity shop, booking my ticket, ordering my graduation gown, bah de bah. Absolutely not interesting things. How about you?"

"Spent the day chasing up leads, which is extremely difficult when you're working on a cold case that's twenty five years old. If I'm honest, it's a bit of a nightmare."

"I can imagine," Tasha said releasing Muffin from his lead and throwing his ball.

"Well, since we've both had such an unfulfilling day, what do you say I treat us to a tub of ice cream and a bottle of wine?" Ashley said enthusiastically.

"Even though the two of them together don't quite sound right, yes." Tasha's mobile phone began to ring. She looked down at the small display screen and pulled her face when she saw who it was. "Sorry, I won't be a minute, it's my dad."

"No problem, take your time I'll go and play with Muffin," Ashley said, walking over to where he was trying to dig a hole in the ground.

"Hello," Tasha said in a stilted voice.

"Have you booked your ticket?" her dad asked.

"Yes." *So much for hello, how are you?* Tasha thought as she kicked a stone along the path.

"Good. What about your graduation plans?"

"What about them?"

"Have you sorted your gown out?"

"Yes, Dad, I do have a brain, you know."

"Sometimes I wonder if you have. You know,

instead of wasting three months there, you could have flown home and began training for your role here. You could have easily gone back for your graduation nearer the date."

This is my home and if I had done what you wanted I would never have met Ashley, Tasha thought, turning to watch her play with Muffin. "It's too late to change anything now. I've booked my ticket for July."

"I spoke to Beryl, she said you're still doing this dog walking lark. Why you need to be doing that I will never know. It's not as if you need the money."

"I enjoy doing it, that's why. Look, Dad I'm going to have to run, I'm with a client's dog at the moment and he's getting pretty restless."

"Okay, fine, I'll see you in a few weeks."

As usual he disconnected the call without saying goodbye. Many years ago she thought he only did that with her, but she later found out he did it to everyone. He said it was because he found it unnecessary but to her it was just plain rude.

"Is everything okay?" Ashley asked as Tasha joined her on a bench.

"Yes, wonderful. If you think your father being thousands of miles away can still make you feel like a useless child."

As casually as she could, Ashley asked, "Why don't you just stand up to him?"

There was a pensive shimmer in the shadow of Tasha's eyes as she gave a small shrug. "If only it were that easy," she said as she picked up Muffin's ball and reaching back, flung it far into the distance. "Listen, I don't want to burden you with my dramas when you've come home to relax."

"You could never burden me," Ashley said in all seriousness.

"That's very kind of you to say, but the less I think about going back to Australia and all it entails, the better I feel. Come on, let's play piggy in the middle with Muffin," Tasha said, pulling Ashley up by her hands.

Forty five minutes later as the golden sunset was waning, the women were back at Ashley's, sitting side by side in the garden, with wine and ice cream just within their reach. She was pleased Tasha had relaxed a bit—she'd been in a tense, sombre mood following her conversation with her father despite her greatest effort to remain upbeat. She couldn't work out what was worse, having a parent care too much or too little—either way the end result seemed to undermine a child's confidence.

Turning to Ashley, Tasha spooned another heap of chocolate ice cream into her mouth. "Ummm, this is just heavenly."

"Here—you've got some on your chin," Ashley said leaning over and removing it with a napkin. Their eyes locked briefly and again she felt the familiar fluttering in her stomach.

Tasha's mood suddenly ebullient, smiled at her. "Thank you."

"Anytime," Ashley said, reluctantly leaning back against her chair. Every time she looked into her eyes she lost another part of herself. She didn't know how long she could go on like this—her feelings were growing deeper for her each day.

"Looks like Muffin has had his fill today," Tasha said, laughing lightly as she nodded toward Muffin.

"He's a lot happier since you've been walking him." *So am I,* Ashley thought, putting her bowl on the table and flopping back into her chair.

Looking down at him lying contently between the two chairs, Tasha lowered her hand onto his head. "He's such a beautiful boy and I feel lucky to have met him." She turned to Ashley. "And you," she said disarmingly.

Ashley felt a warm glow filter throughout her body as well as an unwelcome blush rushing to her cheeks. Whenever Tasha paid her compliments she didn't know what kind of reaction she would have. "We're both going to miss you when you leave," she said truthfully as she drew her feet underneath her.

Tasha sighed. "I wish I didn't have to go."

Ashley took a long sip of wine. "The way we're talking, anyone would think you'd been banished and could never return," she said, with assumed tranquilly, though her heart was heavy with an inexplicable sadness at the mere thought of Tasha not being a part of her life.

"I know," she replied, refilling their glasses and holding hers in midair. "This evening was meant to be a cheerful one so let's forget the future and concentrate on being in the now."

"I'll drink to that," Ashley said raising her glass and taking a mouthful whilst she thought how much easier her life would be if she could live in the present and forget about the past.

"So did you go to University?" Tasha asked,

licking the ice cream off the back of her spoon.

"Yep."

"What did you study?"

"Criminology."

"Wow, is that why you became a cop?" Tasha tipped her head to the side.

Ashley looked sideways at her, meeting her inquiring gaze. "No, and I've never told anyone this before so you are sworn to secrecy."

"On my life," Tasha said trying to maintain a serious expression.

"I became a cop," she started slowly, "because I wanted to be like . . . Christine Cagney," she said in a tone of admiration.

Tasha couldn't hold in her laughter. "No kidding? Wasn't that show from the '80s?"

Ashley joined in with the laughter. "Yep, I used to watch all the repeats. I was fanatical about her and becoming a detective. My parents thought I'd grow out of it but once I got accepted into University there was no stopping me."

"Why didn't you just join the police from school?"

"I wanted a good understanding of criminal behaviour before I joined. I always knew I was going to be a detective and thought it be useful—which it is."

"I would have thought you'd be more into Sherlock Holmes—you know, letting your intellect guide you through cases."

"Somehow I just couldn't picture him being in high speed car chases or getting right down and dirty with a villain."

"Oh, so that's how you really spend your days then?" Tasha asked, a shadow of alarm touching her face.

"Nah." Ashley laughed seeing her expression. "That's when I believed what I watched on TV. I was very impressionable as a kid."

"Somehow I can't quite believe that."

"I swear it's true. I didn't stop believing in Father Christmas until I was eleven."

"Aww that's so sweet," Tasha said leaning over and touching Ashley's cheek briefly.

Ashley brought the wine to her lips as yet again she struggled with the sensation Tasha's touch aroused in her.

They sat in an easy companionable silence until Tasha looked down at her watch.

"I've just realised you haven't had a meal since you came home. You must be starving."

"I ate something at work. We have a canteen there, the foods pretty good."

"Does your mum know about it?"

"Believe me, I've tried to tell her, but she won't listen." Ashley laughed.

"I really like your mum—well your whole family actually."

"And they like you," Ashley said placing her wine glass on the table and noticing Tasha wrap her arms around herself. "Are you feeling cold?" she asked.

"A little. Have you got any fire wood?"

Ashley swung round to face Tasha. "Yes, I had some delivered the other day. Do you want me to light a fire?"

"Would you mind?"

"Of course not."

Looking up towards the sky Tasha said wistfully, "I'd love to spend the night out here, with the fire and the stars."

"Well I'm not one to disappoint," Ashley said rising quickly. "I'll get some blankets. I hope you won't find a sun lounger uncomfortable."

"As long as I'm with you I can stand anything," Tasha said to herself as Ashley disappeared inside.

Chapter 15

Bright yellow shafts of sunlight flooded the conservatory. Tasha sneezed as she walked past a crystal vase bountifully bedecked with a dazzling display of stargazer lilies.

"I didn't hear you come in last night."

"That's because I didn't," Tasha said, bending over and kissing her Aunt Beryl on top of her silver fluffed hair.

"So where did you stay?" she asked, folding the Racing Post and resting it on her lap.

"Oh, at a client's house," she replied, kicking off her shoes and flopping down backwards onto a wide gold striped chair.

Aunt Beryl raised her eyebrows. "This is a first, who is she?"

Tasha laughed. "No, Aunt B, it's not what you're thinking."

"And what am I thinking, oh wise one?" she asked, looking every inch the elegant lady she was, in a plain white summer dress and silver sandals.

"That I've met someone who is more than just a friend."

"And have you?" Aunt Beryl asked, pulling down her glasses and looking over the rims.

"No, Ashley and I are *just* friends. She came home early from work just as I was about to walk her dog. We had a bottle of wine together that's all. As I walk the dog in the morning too, it just made sense to stay over." Tasha rubbed her back as she thought back to the previous night. Her body ached from sleeping on the lounger—but it had been worth it to watch Ashley sleep—to be so close to her.

"And nothing happened with *Ashley?*" Beryl asked, watching her closely.

"Aunt B, how could you ask such a thing?" Tasha flashed her a coy smile.

She chuckled softly. "Well, these days it's all about instant gratification isn't it? Nobody waits for that special one anymore."

"Well, I am," she replied, smiling warmly at her.

At seventy five, Tasha's Aunt Beryl had been a widow for thirty years, in that time she had never looked at another man—not that she didn't have the opportunities, but she'd always said when she took her wedding vows she meant every word of them. She would remain Uncle Bob's wife until the day she was finally reunited with him.

"I'm glad to hear it, young lady. I was only reading in the paper the other day about the rise of STI's. This is what you young people don't realise, viruses are very intelligent organisms, they keep mutating so they can't be cured."

"You don't have to worry about me, Aunt B."

"Well, I'm glad to hear it," Beryl said, picking her paper back up and flicking it open.

"Any tips for today?" Tasha asked with interest. One thing that was a surety about her aunt, was that she knew how to pick winners.

"Yes, I've got a few bankers for this evening's races," she said, her eyes alert and shiny as she leaned back against a large golden upholstered chair.

"I think I might have a small bet myself. Has anyone called for me?" Tasha asked, rolling onto her side and sneezing twice in a row. Her hay fever was playing havoc with her sinuses this year and it didn't help when her aunt kept displaying flowers as if it was the Chelsea flower show.

"Yes, Charlotte and. . ."

"And?"

"Your father."

"Oh," Tasha said, with a guarded look on her face. She hoisted herself forward.

"He's calling later in the week, he was surprised you weren't home at 7am."

"I only spoke to him yesterday! And why would he be surprised. Where should I be? Aren't I allowed to have a life?"

"You know he worries," Aunt Beryl said, as she poured herself a cup of tea from a delicate bone china teapot.

"I'm not a child, the sooner he realises that the better."

"I know, darling," Beryl said outstretching her hand to Tasha. "He just worries, like any parent does."

Tasha rose to her feet and walked over to her aunt, enveloping her small, liver-spotted hand into hers. "He smothers me, Aunt B, so much so. I feel like I can't breathe sometimes."

"I know, Tasha but he's an old man. He just wants his legacy to carry on."

"What about what I want? Or does that not count? I'll never measure up to what he wants, it's like he's punishing me for what Mark did."

Aunt Beryl squeezed her hand. "If I said I understood the dynamics of parenthood I'd be lying to you, dear child. I just know my brother and he thinks what he's doing is the best for you," she said in a quiet tone.

"More likely for him," Tasha said letting go of her hand and hurrying to the door, she didn't want to upset her aunt by dragging her into their tug-o-war.

"I'm going to call Charlotte back." The more Tasha thought about how her father had railroaded her into what *he* wanted, the angrier she became. She wheeled around before leaving. "I just want to be true to myself. Is that too much to ask?" Tasha asked looking earnestly at her aunt's sun-tinged oval face.

"No, darling, it's not," Beryl admitted, deep furrows forming in her otherwise smooth forehead. "Have you eaten yet?"

Tasha sighed, her anger slowly dissolving. "No." She didn't want to take her mood out on her aunt—she was her saviour. She didn't know what she was going to do without her when she went to Australia.

"I'll get Eloise to make you something," she called out to Tasha as she disappeared behind the door.

"Hey, gorgeous, I've been trying to get you since last night!" Charlotte said in a musical tone.

"My battery was dead. What's up?" Tasha lay back on her unmade bed and stared up at the ceiling.

"I've met this seriously fantastic woman and she has a friend who would be perfect for you!"

"Oh, please, not another one," Tasha said.

"No seriously this woman is *hot, and intelligent.*"

"How many times do I have to tell you, Lottie, I'm not interested." She didn't mention to her best friend that she had actually met someone who she had felt a deep connection with, whether the feeling was mutual, she didn't know.

"I swear this will be the last time, I promise."

"Hmm, I think I've heard that one before."

"I mean it. Have I ever lied to you?"

"That's a bit of an ambiguous question. Have you lied about important stuff—no. Have you been less than truthful when you're trying to set me up with countless women— that's a definite yes," she said slowly.

"Okay okay, I get your point, but please, Tash, for me, just this last time. I'm not asking you to get down on one knee and propose or anything, just sort of like, be there."

"What's in this for you? You sound overly eager."

"I fancy the pants off her best friend and she said she'd only go out on a date with me if I hook up her friend Louise."

"How old is she? Sixteen? God, it sounds like a right drag. I'm going to have to spend the evening watching you get off with. . ." Tasha hopped onto her feet and strode the short distance to the window, pushing it open. She stuck her head outside deeply inhaling the fragrance of freshly cut grass ignoring her hay fever.

"Claire," Charlotte said, filling in the name for her.

"While I'm playing second fiddle with Louise." She stifled a sigh as she fought the urge to sneeze again and brought her head back in.

"Come on, you know I'd do it for you," Charlotte said lowering her tone.

"That's the difference—I wouldn't ask you to."

"I know, because you're the best friend a girl could ever have. Oh, pretty please. And I'm not being funny, you haven't been out on a date in how long has it been? Oh, that's right—*forever.*"

Tasha released her sigh. "Okay, I'll come, but swear, Lottie, this is the last time." She pulled the band from her ponytail and shook her hair loose.

"I swear, I promise."

"Where shall I meet you?" She groaned, turning back towards her bed. She always gave into Charlotte, she couldn't help it. After hanging up, she put all thoughts of Charlotte out of her mind and wondered, not for the first time that day, what Ashley was doing.

***

Oak Hill College was an impressive white, mansion-like building, set in acres of parkland on the London and Hertfordshire border. Large oak trees lined the pea shingle path Ashley and Dale walked along as they made their way from the car park to the imposing college in front of them. Finally, they reached the grand entrance amidst a throng of students on the way to their next lecture. At the reception they were directed towards the Principal's office by a petite brunette, who gently tapped on his door, then pushed it open for them as a deep voice beckoned them in.

Principle Bradshaw sat behind a large desk in an oak panelled room. His portly body was short and his head was bald apart from a slight growth of moss-like curls around the edge of his scalp.

"Thank you for seeing us," Ashley said as they took a seat opposite him.

"Anything I can do to help. Now who is it you wish to speak with me about?" he asked raising his eyebrows inquiringly.

"Aaron Davies."

His eyes fluttered behind his gold rimmed glasses. "Well, that's a name I haven't heard in years," he said, a bemused smile on his face. "A lovely young man. I had high hopes for him—it was such a shame that he thought his destiny lay somewhere other than serving God. What would you like to know about him?"

"Everything really—what he was like, how he responded to others and more importantly why he left?" Ashley said studying the principle.

His expression stilled and grew serious. "To start with Aaron was a very presentable intelligent young man, who mixed well with the other students and staff alike. He seemed to be taking to the college like a duck to water and passed his degree with flying colours. But then when he started his ordination training he became, how shall we say—more distant. He would lock himself in his room for days on end, only coming out occasionally for food or water. His course work took a dramatic downward turn and he refused all of our help to reach him—to try and help him overcome what was obviously a very big obstacle in his life."

"Did he ever tell you what it was?"

"Yes, eventually."

"And what was that, if you don't mind me asking?"

"Of course not, it wasn't actually a secret in the end. He claimed he could talk to the dead."

"I suppose that didn't go down too well with the rest of the people here," Dale said with a smirk.

"You could say that. We gave him ample opportunity to rid himself of the devil he claimed he had inside. He gave the impression that he was a lost soul and nothing could save him."

"Did he have many friends here?" Ashley asked.

"By the time he left, no I'm afraid he didn't. What started out as sympathy for his plight soon turned to despondency. So many of us tried to reach him but you know it's impossible to help others who don't want your help." His faint smile held a hint of sadness.

"Did you ever meet any of his family members?"

"Just the once, if I recall—his mother Martha. I think she was quite unwell at the time, sad to say she died shortly afterwards."

"And how did Aaron take his mother's death?"

"Quite well we all thought. Being a young man left alone in the world, he adapted to his new status in life and just got on with things. He didn't ask for any time off to grieve. He was convinced she would contact him once she had passed over to the realm of peace and had adjusted."

"As far as you know did he say he ever managed to speak to her?"

"That, I can't tell you—I didn't feel comfortable broaching the subject."

"How about friends outside the college?" Dale asked.

"I don't think there were any. You've got to understand, coming from the background he did, he was a shattered individual. I know his mother did the best she could for him but she was no match for the brute of a man that called himself his father. It wasn't until he died—a freak accident I think it was, a car he was working underneath collapsed on him—that Aaron finally began to come out of his shell." He checked his watch. "I'm afraid that's all I really know about him. If there's nothing else, I really must be getting on."

Ashley and Dale rose together. "No, that's all. Thank you for your time," Ashley said.

"I hope I've been of help."

"Definitely, you've helped us to put some pieces of the puzzle together."

"Can I ask why you're so interested in Aaron?"

"He's still claiming to talk to the dead—only this time he's actually led us to a body!"

***

"That was quite sad," Ashley said as they exited the college. "Aaron doesn't sound like he had much of a childhood."

"Him and millions of others." Dale exhaled.

"I know, but that doesn't make it any less sad."

"Do you think he could be schizophrenic, you know with hearing voices and everything—he would have been about the right age to be getting the symptoms."

Ashley nodded thoughtfully. "Maybe we should check and see whether he's been institutionalised before. I know it's a long shot but he might have heard something about Esther's murder from one of the patients."

"I'll get Steve to do some digging, for now,

though, you have a press conference to conduct," Dale said withdrawing the car keys from his pocket.

Chapter 16

The clicking of heels on the laminate floor echoed through the hallway and into the small but neat living room.

"Did ya hear me?" the young woman in a black mini dress with fishnet tights asked a second time, bringing her hands to rest on her hips. The half naked man in the chair nodded without looking at her, his eyes remained glued to the TV screen. She followed his gaze. "Can you believe they found that poor girl after all this time? What her parents must be goin' through, God only knows." She adjusted the straps on her dress. "Well, I'll let me self out then," she said putting the money he had left on the table into her small silver bag. "Next time your wife's at her sister's, gimme a call." She fished into her bag and withdrew a bottle of perfume before spraying herself.

"Don't!" he yelled, jumping up and wrapping a fist around her slender wrist. "I don't want my house smelling like a brothel."

"You wasn't too concerned ten minutes ago," she said as she tried to yank her arm out of his vice like grip.

He smiled but there was little humour in it, his steel blue eyes glared at her. "That was then. Now get out of here!" he said glancing past her shoulder and shoving her towards the door.

"Alright, alright. I'll remember this next time you call. You bloody weirdo," she called out as she neared the front door, opened it and slammed it shut behind her. The man returned to his seat and turned the volume up. The parents had stopped talking, now it was the detective's turn. She was reiterating what they had said, but there was enough determination in her voice to make the man feel a little worried. *Sooner or later the chickens always come home to roost,* he thought rubbing the back of his neck. He had to keep his cool—if he didn't, the life he had built for himself these last twenty five years would all come crashing down and he was determined not to let that happen—whatever the cost.

***

The aroma of spicy chicken wafted through the air as she stepped into her hallway.

"Mum?" Ashley called out, throwing her keys onto the table. It seemed as though her mum had come around to cook dinner and she was eternally grateful. Sometimes she was convinced she had a sixth sense as she was exhausted—the day had been a draining and emotional one. Colleen had called a press conference in order to give Esther's parents a platform on which to speak about her as well as to encourage the public to come forward with new information. Since being promoted to Detective Sergeant a year ago, Colleen had given Ashley the job of dealing with the press. It was a stressful yet satisfying role. Many cases had been solved through the media's cooperation and widespread coverage of different crimes. She was hopeful that it would prove the same in this case.

The media were dubbing the murderer 'The Woodlands Killer'. She often wondered who came up with these buzz words—did they have a stock pile of them hoping for a match? The Campbell family had held up pretty well to the invasive questions being hurled at them from the press, eager to fill their pages the next day. During the summer, news was slow, or so she had been told. Mrs Campbell and Hailey fielded most of the questions. It wasn't until Mr Campbell spoke directly to the murderer, tears brimming in his eyes, did the press pack sit back and seem to listen. Taking on board that they were there because a young woman had died, in what seemed horrific circumstances.

She heard the creaking of the kitchen door opening, then seconds later Tasha appeared in her living room.

"Tasha!" she said, pleasantly surprised.

"Ashley, please don't think I'm stalking you," she said, obviously ill at ease. "I'm really sorry but I was here when your mum came round and she asked me to reheat the food she brought over before I left—I should have been gone already but it took me ages to work out how to use your oven."

"It's okay," she said, laughing as she bent down to ruffle Muffin's head.

"So," Tasha said, gathering up her bag from the floor. "The chicken and baked potatoes are in the oven, salad is already chopped up in the fridge and it should all be ready in about half an hour." She winced. "I'm really sorry I messed up, you must be starving."

"Please don't listen to what my mother tells you. I do actually eat during the day. She thinks I live on an island."

"That's mothers for you. Anyway enjoy your meal and you mister," she said looking down at

Muffin. "I'll see you in the morning."

Ashley walked her to the door. "Have you got plans for tonight?"

"Yes, I'm going on a date."

"Oh," Ashley said blinking—trying to ignore a sharp twinge of jealousy. "Who's the lucky lady?"

"I don't know yet, my friend has set me up on a blind date because she fancies her friend. She also thinks it's time I started dating."

"Why? What's been stopping you?"

"I just haven't seen the point in starting a relationship with someone when I'm going to be leaving the country soon. I still don't and I really don't believe in long distant relationships."

"I see your point."

"I wish my friends would! Anyway enjoy your meal."

"Will do and you try and enjoy your night. You never know, she might just be the one worth risking it all for."

"Somehow I doubt that very much."

Closing the door behind her, Ashley bent down to make a fuss of Muffin. "It's just you and me boy," she said, unable to shake the sadness inside her.

She made her way into the kitchen and opened the fridge, taking the lone beer left over from the night of the BBQ.

Thirty minutes later she sat alone at the granite island in her kitchen, reflecting over her day while she chewed on a piece of chicken. She tried to figure out if there could be a link between Aaron and Peter. Putting aside her plate, she grabbed a pen and paper from the side and drew a circle in the middle, writing

Aaron in the centre. In the circles around him, she wrote what she had learnt from Principal Bradshaw earlier that day; he was a loner, despite this he had good people skills and was always helping others out with their problems. His father had been abusive but was now deceased, as was the mother. He became 'paranoid' during his ordination training. She wondered if Aaron could have come into contact with Peter at any point in the last few years. Could he have unburdened himself on Aaron and told him about Esther's death and where he buried her? She tapped her fingers on the counter— her eyes narrowing as she looked at the list.

"How does this all fit in with you, Aaron?" Ashley asked out loud. *There has got to be a link, there's got to be.* She rested her face in her hands and instead of finding answers, all she came up with were questions about *Tasha.*

Chapter 17

"Quickly, come inside before somebody see's you," Peter said, roughly grabbing the man by his arm. "Are you crazy coming here? The police could be watching. What are you doing here at this time of night? It's after midnight."

"Just want to know what you've been telling them coppers that was here the other day."

"Have you been spying on me?"

"Let's just say I'm looking out for my best interests."

"Well, I didn't tell them anything—nothing. Do you think I'm stupid?"

"No, I don't. So this is what you've being buying with my hard earned money," the man said looking around the room at the electrical equipment.

"Well, I deserve something don't I. After all, I kept my mouth shut all these years after seeing you that day, especially after you did a runner when you said you would sort me out if I kept quiet. I knew if I was patient I'd bump into you again and it couldn't have happened at a better time."

The man put his hands in his pocket.

"So have the police got any leads?"

"No, they're as stumped about this case as they were all those years ago."

"So why did they come and see you?"

"Just following up on the incompetence of the officers' years ago."

"They were here for quite some time."

"Yeah, well they're nosey buggers aren't they."

"Didn't they ask where you got all this stuff

from?" he asked looking around the room.

"No."

"You didn't play by the rules, Peter."

"What do you mean?"

"I told you not to go splashing around your money, to remain inconspicuous."

"But they never asked anything."

"Which speaks volumes. How do they think a low life like you could afford all this stuff?"

"I told them my dad was loaded."

"Your dad is a washed out drunk. Don't you think they're going to check everything you said?"

"I don't know. What if they do? I'll just say it was knocked off."

"I don't know why but I just get the feeling that you're holding something back from me."

"Like what?"

"I don't know, you tell me—did those coppers suss anything out while they was here?"

"No, I just told them the truth about my relationship with Esther and that it wasn't the fairy tale romance her sister made it out to be."

"How did they take it?"

"They were really grateful for my honesty. They believed everything that I told them."

"Everything?" he asked narrowing his eyes.

"Well you know, about Esther."

"It's best you come clean now, Peter and lay all your cards on the table. It will be better for you if I don't have to pay you another visit."

Peter shifted indignantly on each foot. "Why is this about me all of a sudden? I didn't do anything wrong. It's not my fault that Detective McCoy figured out that I didn't go to India, it's only a matter of time before she connects all the dots." He turned to the window and looked down onto the communal gardens lit up by dim lights.

The man put his hand to his head—it was all unravelling around him, after all this time when he had thought he had got away with it scot free. He knew that DS McCoy was not going to stop until she found him and with idiots like Peter leaving a breadcrumb trail to him, it wouldn't be that long either. Maybe he would have to put an obstacle in her way—to take away the focus of this case. *But first things first,* he thought as he felt about in his pocket.

"What do you want me to do?" Peter asked, still staring ahead.

"I don't know," the man said. "Maybe you're going to have to go into hiding," he said, stealthily walking up behind him, looping a belt he'd withdrawn from the inside of his coat around his throat. "Permanently!"

Chapter 18

It's too late to back out now, Tasha thought with disdain, as the glass door swung open and Charlotte, a tall, well-built woman with short brown spiky hair, entered the bar flanked by two attractive women who could have passed for identical twins. Both were medium height with long Cinnamon hair, dressed in short black dresses and heels. Charlotte saw her immediately and waved excitedly, hurrying towards her.

"Tasha." Charlotte embraced her in a bear hug like they hadn't seen each other for years, though in reality it had only been a few days. "Please be good," she whispered quickly in her ear, before pulling back and introducing her to the women. "Louise, Claire, I'd like you to meet my friend, Tasha."

The women eyed her appreciatively. "Hi," one of them said in a low husky voice, who she presumed was her date for the night.

"Nice to meet to you," Tasha replied, extending her hand.

"Now the introductions are over we'll go and get the drinks in, ladies take a seat," Charlotte said motioning for Tasha to follow her to the bar.

"Well what do you think?" Charlotte asked when they were out of ear shot. "Didn't I tell you that they were hot?"

"Hmm," Tasha replied. Though she was the first to admit that she liked good looking women, it wasn't the be all and end all for her. What she looked for was a spark, and sadly she found that in neither woman. When she had met Ashley, before she had even opened her mouth it was there—that unspoken chemistry she would read about and yearn for as a teenager.

"Let's get the party started," Charlotte said, handing Tasha two of the four wine bottles she had just purchased.

Dread filled her, she knew what this signalled— a very long night.

They returned to the table and once the alcohol started flowing Tasha felt herself relax more. The company wasn't as bad as she first thought.

"There's one thing I'm curious about, if you don't mind me being a bit forward. I mean we're all friends now aren't we?" Louise laughed, followed by Claire and Charlotte in a dominos effect.

Tasha nodded and gave her full attention.

"I'm normally a good judge of character but you don't strike me as the sort of person who would be into swinging, you seem too prim and proper."

A puzzled look spread slowly across Tasha's face—at first she thought she must have misheard her until she glanced at Charlotte, who looked down and was toying with her glass. She narrowed her eyes at her—this was not the first time Charlotte had spawned a web of lies to get a date—her friend had always had the chameleon-like ability to adapt to others needs.

"Yes, well, at first it was very difficult you know, getting into the swing of things— excuse the pun," Tasha said playing along, "but um, now things are a lot easier."

Charlotte's face lit up with relief.

"It was quite easy for us wasn't it, darling,"

Claire said to Louise as her hand disappeared under the table causing her to squeal with delight. "It makes it all the more easier if you find the right people to get involved," she said, her eyes darting from Tasha to Charlotte and back again.

What the . . . ? Had Charlotte gone insane? She looked at her and decided she really had as she watched both women with bright vivacious eyes.

"Excuse me, I need to use the loo. Charlotte, I could do with some company," Tasha said as brightly as she could.

"Hurry back, we might as well take this party back to our place," Louise said, stroking Tasha's arm as she rose from her seat.

As they entered the toilets, Tasha did a quick sweep under the cubicles checking they were empty, then she turned to Charlotte who was rummaging in her pocket before bring out a small folded piece of paper.

"Did you hear that, they like us, we can go back to their place," Charlotte said, carefully opening it and dipping her finger onto the white powdery substance before rubbing it along the top of her gum.

"What the hell are you doing?" Tasha gasped in shock.

"Chill out, it's only a bit of speed," she said, repeating the process.

"Are you crazy? When did you start doing drugs?"

"Oh, don't start going all grown up on me, Tash. Claire gave it to me, to get me in the mood. Do you want some?" she asked, stretching out her hand.

"No, I bloody don't and please don't tell me you

think I'm going anywhere with those two."

"Why not? It'll be fun," Charlotte said, eyeing her through the mirror.

"My idea of fun is going to the beach in Bali or going skiing in the Alps. It is not fun, however, to be set upon by two red headed nymphet's who would eat me for dinner and still have room for dessert."

"That's a bit dramatic, Tasha," Charlotte said, smiling. "Gosh, when did you start becoming so straight laced?"

"Lottie, is this the kind of stuff you're into now? Drugs and free for all sex —you're worth so much more than this."

"That's easy for you to say, you're not the one who can't even get a proper date," she said, scrunching the paper in her hand and stuffing it in her jeans pocket.

"Charlotte, when was the last time I dated anyone?"

"That's because you don't want to, not because you can't. I'm sick of being alone all the time."

"You're not alone, you've got me."

Charlotte dropped her head. "Yeah, right, for how long? Once you go to Australia, I'll be a distant memory."

"How can you think that? We've been best friends for fourteen years."

"I know, I'm sorry I didn't mean that, but I'm so lonely, Tash. I'm not too ashamed to say it anymore. I'd rather have a pair of nymphomaniacs than nothing. I'm sick of being rejected all the time."

Tasha knew what she really meant was she was sick of being rejected by her parents. That's why they had bonded so closely at boarding school. Whilst all the other girls went home for summer holidays and the like, they were amongst the few whose parents left them there. It had been tough, living with the knowledge that your own parents didn't have time for you, but she had toughened to it—unfortunately Charlotte never had.

The door opened and Claire poked her head around it. "Our cab's waiting outside. Are you ladies coming?"

Charlotte spun round to the door. "Be out in a minute. Just finishing up," she said brightly.

"Okay," Claire replied before her head disappeared again.

Tasha reached out for her hands. "Please don't do this, Charlotte."

"What choice do I have?" she said, squeezing her hands before turning back to the mirror and giving herself one last glance before moving to the door. "I'll be seeing you then."

Choices, Tasha thought as the door closed behind Charlotte, *I'm a fine one to talk.*

Chapter 19

"I was thinking about Peter last night," Ashley said. "His story just doesn't add up. He's already lied to us and there is clearly more he's hiding."

"He just seems a dodgy character full stop. In one smoke filled breath he's telling us how hard it is for him to live on social security, while he's surrounded with top notch gear— stuff even I couldn't afford," Dale said.

"Exactly. Where'd he get it from and who's this old friend he just happened to bump into?"

Dale brought the car to a halt at a red light. "I think we need to go and pay him another visit. This time, though, if he starts his shit, I think we should bring him in."

"I agree."

They drove the short distance to Peter's flat in silence. As much as Ashley wanted to focus on the upcoming meeting she couldn't help thinking about Tasha.

"If those kids touch this car today, I'm going to nick every one of them," Dale said, bringing an end to her daydream.

"What? Yes, I don't blame you."

"You didn't even hear what I said, did you," Dale said.

"Sorry, my mind was elsewhere."

He pulled the car up on the forecourt and stepped out. Both made their way back up the stairs. As they reached the top of the landing they saw an elderly woman standing outside Peter's door. She turned when she heard their footsteps, relief flooding from her wrinkled features.

"Blimey, you came quick. I only called you lot a couple of minutes ago."

"Sorry, who are you?" Ashley asked.

"Mrs Baker from next door."

"Sorry, Mrs Baker, I'm confused. We're not here to respond to any calls, we're here to see Mr Holmes."

"Yes, that's what I was calling for," she said, looking at Ashley as though she was simple. "Last night I heard a loud thud, you know like when someone falls over, not long after I heard the front door shutting. The walls in these flats are paper thin. Anyway I thought he'd gone out to get some headache tablets from the twenty four hour shop up the road. Then, this morning I'm waiting for him to collect me to take me to the hospital and he doesn't knock for me."

"Couldn't he have just stayed out the night? He is an adult after all," Dale asked.

"He's not that kind of man."

"Regular boy scout is he?"

"You could say that. Not many people would give us oldies the time of day but Peter's different."

"What time did you say you heard this bang?"

"Oh, it was late, well after midnight, otherwise I would've knocked yesterday. It's not safe for the vulnerable 'round here after dark. I've tried so hard to get moved from here but my pleas fall on deaf ears, and now this. I think he might have banged his head and is now lying in there unconscious," she said, tears welling up in her grey eyes.

Ashley felt a lump rise in her throat. She hated

the fact that an elderly person, in fact—anyone didn't feel safe enough to leave their home at night.

"I'm sure there's nothing to worry about. Here, let me have a try," Dale said, opening the letter box. "Mr Holmes," he shouted several times but to no avail. He turned to Ashley. "A light's on in there and I can hear the faint sound of the TV."

"Maybe he just doesn't want to talk to us," Ashley suggested.

"He might not open it for you, but he's never let me down before," Mrs Baker answered, her eyes full of concern.

"What do you think, Ash, shall I break it down?"

"Yeah, he could be injured in there. Please step back, Mrs Baker, we're going to have to break the door down," Ashley said, gently taking her arm.

Dale waited until Mrs Baker had shuffled back a few feet before stepping back and brought his knee up to his waist. In one swift movement he kicked at the door using the bottom of his foot and it flew wide open banging hard again the hallway wall.

"You wait here with me, my colleague will let us know if there's anything wrong," Ashley said as Dale went into the flat.

"Mr Holmes," Dale called as he tapped on the living room door before pushing it open. "Shit, Ashley, get in here!" he shouted out loudly.

"What is it?" Ashley asked coming up behind him and following his gaze to the lifeless body of Peter Holmes.

***

Colleen waited until the room had quietened

before she spoke. "Whoever our murderer is, he must be getting nervous that we're closing the net. The crime lab lifted fingerprints from the belt and they match the partial prints found on the belt at Esther Campbell's crime scene. While this is some good news, the bad news is that the suspect's prints are not on the national database which pretty much renders them useless until we actually find him and can compare them. The pathologist, Dr Potter said Mr Holmes' death was caused by acute strangulation."

"Were there any signs of defensive wounds?" Ashley asked.

"No, there weren't any which led Dr Potter to believe he was caught by surprise."

"I checked the door for any kind of damage before I kicked it, there was none," Dale said.

"So it seems as though he let the person in because he knew them," Colleen remarked.

"Did anything lead you two to believe Mr Holmes had anything to do with this case?" DCS Ripley asked, addressing the question to Dale.

"Yes and no."

"What does that mean? Less ambiguity would be appreciated."

"No, as in there was nothing concrete, but he did lie about his alibi."

The door to the incident room opened. "Sorry to disturb you all," a female office said poking her head around the door. Catching Ashley's eye, she made her way towards her and handed her a file. "Sorry, I couldn't get it to you sooner, the computer's been down."

Ashley smiled at her. "Thanks, Kelly I appreciate

it," she said taking it from her.

"What's that about?" Ripley asked, eyeing the folder as the door closed behind Kelly.

"After we interviewed Peter on Friday I asked Kelly to run me a background check on Peter's parents."

"For what reason?"

She opened the file and scanned it quickly. "Just a hunch and it looks like I was right. Peter claimed to have run his father's business several years ago. According to this, his father was never the owner of any company. He worked for a construction firm as a builder until he was laid off with disability when he was fifty five."

"So what does that mean?"

"That Peter was a liar and he knew more than he was telling us. We were at his place today because we were going to bring him in for formal questioning, but we were obviously too late."

"So where does this all leave us now?" Colleen asked looking around the table and settling her eyes on Ashley.

"One of the things Peter was adamant about was that he had never met Aaron at any time in his life."

"And you believed him?" Colleen looked sceptical.

"I didn't believe anything he said."

"What about people coming and going from his flat?"

Dale shook his head. "Everyone we questioned said he kept himself to himself. No one saw anyone entering or leaving his flat last night."

"What about the possibility that he was the one

that got someone to harm Esther?" Colleen asked.

"For what reason? Why would he go to such drastic lengths?" Dale said.

"What if he came across the killer by accident at the time? When we first went to see him on Friday he mentioned that he had bumped into an old friend— that might explain all the new gear he had. Maybe he was blackmailing him," Ashley suggested.

"New gear?" DCS Ripley said.

"I take it you haven't read the report I left on your desk on Friday," Ashley replied. "Mr Holmes had a number of expensive looking items in his flat. Considering he was on seventy quid a week, they would have been out of his reach. Forensics found receipts for all of the items which showed he paid in cash."

"Well, it looks like we've reached a dead end," DCS Ripley said.

Ashley turned to look at Colleen. "I could always try and talk to Aaron again. Maybe I can put the frighteners up him as it looks like the killer is on a clean-up round."

"If you think it's worth a try by all means—give it another shot," Colleen replied.

Chapter 20

Bracing his feet against the wooden floor, clutching his head in both hands, Aaron fought the urge to scream at the images he saw in his mind's eye—blood streaming from gaping wounds onto golden leaves where the young girl writhed in agony, her face etched with terror—a tormenting wail leaving her lips.

"Oh, God," he whispered, "please make them go away." He bent down onto his knees assuming a prayer position. "I didn't ask for this," he cried with growing rage. "Why are you punishing me?" He put a trembling hand across his cheek to wipe away the tears. "Why are you doing this to me?" he asked the empty space.

He squeezed his eyes shut, as if that in itself would chase the nightmare away. The visions he kept having terrified him—they always came to him when he was most vulnerable—alone at night. As quickly as it had come upon him it passed and finally darkness closed in on his mind. He reached out for his phone. His index finger shook as he pressed each button slowly and deliberately.

"What is your emergency?" the operator asked.

"I . . . I want to report a murder."

***

Before snapping her phone open, Ashley looked blurry eyed at the illuminated clock— 4:00am.

"What's up, Colleen?" she said, leaning over and grabbing a bottle of water from the floor.

"We've had another call from our psychic."

Ashley groaned as she took a swig of water. "What now?"

"He's said he knows the location of another body."

"What!" Ashley said wide awake now. "How? Where?" she asked in quick succession.

"Epping Forest again, only a slightly different location. I'm here now with the search team. I'd like you to meet me down here."

"Does Dale know?"

"No, can you call him and bring him along."

"Yes, I'll do it now. It looks like we will definitely be paying Mr Davies another visit. I'm gonna take a quick shower first and I'll be there in an hour."

Despite the first rays of sunlight appearing over the horizon, the forest was still in darkness as their car pulled up by the search area. Ashley climbed out and saw a familiar white tent being erected amidst the glow of white light.

"Shit, they've found another body," she whispered to Dale.

Joan spotted them and made her way over. She shook her head in dismay. "Looks like the same MO; belt around the throat."

"What about knife marks?" Ashley asked, wrapping her arms around herself in an effort to keep warm. She had been in such a rush she hadn't brought a jacket.

"I haven't completely excavated the grave yet. They are erecting the tent now and then I can get to work. We did find a bag buried with her though, containing her college pass. And assuming it's hers—

she was only seventeen."

Ashley glanced at Dale. "It really does look like we may have a serial killer." Turning her attention back to Joan she said, "How long have you been here?"

"Only an half an hour. Colleen called as soon as they found the body—I only live five minutes away luckily."

"Is she about?"

"Yes, she's talking to the SOCOs."

"Okay, thanks," Dale said with a nod.

They walked over to the scientific services van. Ashley heard Colleen's voice as they neared.

"Dale, Ashley," Colleen said, breaking away from her conversation with two SOCOs. "As you've probably guessed, we found a body. Ashley, I'd like you to come back to the station with me and move the incident room to room ten. This is going to be a much bigger investigation than we initially thought. I've spoken to DCS Ripley and he wants to pool resources from the counties other Major Investigation Teams, so we will be having some visitors. Can you liaise with them and with Ripley?"

Ashley grimaced. "Yes, sure."

Colleen turned to Dale. "I'd like you to stay here and wait for any evidence Joan or the SOCOs turn up. I've arranged a briefing for 3pm, so get back to the station for then."

"No problem," he replied.

***

The briefing was no longer a Harlow affair. Senior investigating officers from the other major investigation team were seated around the oval desk under fluorescent lighting. A lone picture of Esther was prominently placed in the centre of a whiteboard charting what evidence had been collected so far. Photos of the belt that was recovered, the silver pendant and an aerial view of the location of the remains surrounded a picture of her. Next to this was who was thought to be the next victim—a pretty, curly haired young woman, with a beaming white smile. The photo had been blown up from the college pass which had been found in her bag. A belt found around her neck was similar to the one on Esther—a brand that was mass manufactured and it was therefore unlikely to be traced back to a specific shop. The contents of her bag gave away nothing more, only a lipstick, comb and a small mirror were found.

Colleen stood at the head of the table.

"The second victim found at the scene is believed to be Tracey Carver, aged seventeen. We've got a missing person's report filed on September 24th 1984. Her mother was the one who filed it. She said Tracey hadn't returned home from an evening out — there were no known boyfriends, but like Esther she was a frequent visitor to the woods. We've been trying to get in touch with her mother since this morning but to no avail, so DS McCoy and DC Taylor will be going there after this briefing to tell her the news.

Ashley was deep in thought. *It's as if the perpetrator just picked his victims out of thin air— he was an opportunist. That's why they couldn't move any further with the leads—there weren't any, they were random attacks. Unless . . . unless both victims met him by coincidence—but how would this link Aaron and Peter to him?*

"Right, Ashley, tell us what you've got on this Aaron Davies character." Colleen's voice brought her attention back to the room.

"Well," she said standing, unconsciously playing with the cuff of her shirt. "Mr Davies is an only child, no other siblings. He had an abusive father who died when he was a teenager as the result of an accident. His mother died ten years ago due to natural causes. He was born and brought up in Hertford. He's single, never married, no kids—can't find any previous girlfriends.

"We talked to the principal at the college he attended and he spoke of nothing but praise for him and said he was kind and helpful to the bereaved and that sort of thing." She cleared her throat. "He left the church when he had some sort of breakdown brought on by these so called visions. For the past eight years he's been touting himself as a medium. I did a background search on his shows, his popularity has been waning the last couple of years until recently. Well until his name was connected with this case. For the last few nights all of his shows have been sell outs."

"Were you able to track down any of his old neighbours?" Colleen asked.

"Most of them were elderly and have passed away. Two are in homes suffering from dementia, others I talked to couldn't remember Aaron or his parents," Steve interjected.

"Has he got a record?" Ripley asked.

"Nope, as clean as a whistle. He's not even been

issued with a speeding ticket. We also ran a check to see if he had ever been hospitalised with any mental health issues, all came back negative," Dale said.

"In my opinion this is nothing more than intelligent guess work. I want some of the DCs from your team, Tony to go and have another talk with him," DSC Ripley said, nodding towards the SIO of the Brentwood team.

Colleen shifted in her chair. "No, I think it's best if McCoy and Taylor speak to him again," she said firmly.

"They've already done that and nothing's come from it," DSC Ripley said gruffly.

"The last time they went there they interviewed him. This time they're going to interrogate him. I'm going to get uniforms to bring him in."

Ashley gave her a grateful smile. She'd had more than enough of Ripley. Not for the first time did she wish she could just stand up and tell him where to shove his opinions.

***

"She was crying out for help, begging me to save her," Aaron said in a choked whisper as he tilted his head back as if looking for answers in the air. "She was laying there covered in blood, so much blood—she didn't want to die she wanted to live."

"I can imagine," Ashley said dryly. She wasn't buying his spiritual act—he may have fooled hundreds, if not thousands of grieving people but she was not one of them.

Abruptly, Aaron turned towards her. "I thought you would have believed me by now, that you would have realised that the power I have has been given to me directly by a higher source."

"All I believe is that you know who has committed these crimes and for some reason you're protecting them." She admired his stamina more than anything else—they had been going at him for over an hour but he had remained resolute in his belief that the women who had been murdered had spoken to him.

"I'm not protecting anyone. I had a vision."

"Okay, let's say I believe you had a vision, why wouldn't you be able to give me more information so I can put the killer behind bars?" She felt a tightening in her throat, she had to be patient. He was trying to toy with her and she couldn't afford to let him win.

"This is not about that."

"Oh no, then what's it about?" she asked, swallowing hard.

"They want to be found, they want to be brought home."

"And they don't want justice? These dead women, they're quite happy to see a killer walk about free are they— free to kill again?" Ashley glared at him, the anger that was building up inside nearly choking her.

"No, they don't think he will."

"That is where you are wrong, Aaron. He has killed again. Do you know Peter Holmes?"

A puzzled look crossed his face. "No, never heard of him. Why?"

"He was Esther's boyfriend and was murdered yesterday—by the same killer."

"What! That can't be true."

"I'm afraid it is, Aaron. If you don't tell us the truth and we find a connection between the two of you, you are going to be in a lot of trouble."

"I'm telling you I never heard of the man."

"Then you won't mind submitting your fingerprints and a DNA swab will you."

"No, of course not. I had nothing to do with it."

"But you are still denying you know the person who did it? He's eluded capture for over twenty five years. Who knows how many other women he's murdered and you—with your *holier than thou attitude*—are complicit in his crimes as long as you are protecting him," Ashley said fighting to keep her voice steady.

"No, I'm not. I've told you, all I know is what the spirits tell me."

"You're right, Aaron, you've done the right thing but now you need to go that extra mile and tell us who harmed these people." Ashley reached over and opened a file on the desk and took out the pictures of Esther, Tracey and Peter.

"Look at them, Aaron. Don't you want to bring their families closure?" Rancour sharpened her tone.

"I have, they're reunited with their loved ones."

"And your killer gets away scot free. Is that how this works, Aaron?"

He remained tight lipped.

"What else did Tracey say to you?" Ashley changed tactic. "Did she tell you what it was like, having a knife plunged into her again and again as she felt the blood drain from her body? Did she show you the terror in her eyes? Or doesn't your spirit deal with the nitty gritty of their own murder," Ashley's accusing voice stabbed the air.

"I've told you once before."

"Tell me again," Ashley demanded, raising her voice even higher. "What did she tell you?"

"That she was lost and wanted to go home."

"Do you really think we're buying this bullshit, Aaron?" Dale spat out the words with contempt.

Aaron glanced towards him briefly before shifting his eyes down again. "I only did what I thought was for the best. I thought this could bring closure, isn't that enough?"

"No, it isn't, tell me who murdered them?" Ashley shouted in his face.

"I can't," Aaron yelled back, tears in his eyes as he stood up kicking the chair away from him. "I-I can't, now j-just leave me a-alone," he stammered, clutching at his head. Dale jumped up from his chair ready to restrain him.

"Why can't you?" Ashley moved closer to him, discreetly raising her hand to Dale to let him know she was okay. "Tell me, Aaron. What hold has this sadistic bastard got over you?" she said, her voice holding a softer tone. She'd pushed him as she far as she dared. She knew she wouldn't get any more from him at that moment.

"Nothing—no one has anything over me," Aaron said, sitting back down, trying to regain his composure.

Ashley flashed him a look of disdain. "Nothing you can say will convince me you're having visions. I think you're a liar and you're no better than the scum that you're protecting." She walked to the door. "I'm not going to waste any more of my energy on you.

Keep your secrets that are eating away at your soul. Whoever it is you're protecting, I hope they're worth it."

"DS McCoy, I really am sorry I couldn't be of much help," Aaron said as she reached the door.

She turned to him, suppressing her anger with a look of indifference. "You were more helpful than you'll ever know, Mr Davies." *You told me exactly what I needed to know,* Ashley thought as she and Dale left him alone in the windowless room. *Now we've got to go and tell her poor mother.*

***

Ashley and Dale made their way along the concrete balcony on the fifth floor of a decaying block of flats. It had long been in line for demolition but somehow the council had still not gotten around to it. Shelly Carver, a thin woman with protruding teeth and long greasy black hair, stood at the end of a row of discoloured doors talking to a younger woman. Her daughter most probably, Ashley presumed, due to the close resemblance, though her daughter was at least two stone heavier.

"Look who it is! What's the fuzz want 'round here now? I ain't done nothing wrong," the older woman said.

Ashley stopped when she stood a few feet in front of her. "Ms Shelly Carver?"

"Maybe, depends why you wanna know?"

"Ms Carver we're here to talk to you about your daughter, Tracey."

"What?"

"I've been trying to call you all morning to

arrange a convenient—"

"Come again? What about my Tracey?"

"Shall we step inside, Ms Carver?" Ashley said, gently touching her arm.

Brushing her hand away Shelly replied, "No, we won't step inside. You can tell me here and right now what you've got to say."

Ashley looked at Dale briefly. "Okay, I'm sorry to tell you but remains were found this morning."

"How do you know it's my Tracey?" Shelly cried, visibly shaken.

"It still needs to be confirmed by her dental records but her bag was found with her. It contained her ID."

"Come on, Mum, let's go inside," her daughter said as she led her over the threshold and directed her to a seat in the small kitchen. Reaching down into a fridge below a dirt stained white counter, she withdrew a can of cider and opened it, quickly pouring some of the contents into a glass tumbler and placing it between her mother's trembling hands. Shelly stared dumbly into the glass, which prompted her daughter, Melanie to guide it to her mouth, gently encouraging her to drink the fizzy liquid. She consumed the drink in one go and immediately outstretched her hand for more.

"Mel, get me fags from the other room," she demanded. Melanie quickly ran to do as she was told, bringing back a lit cigarette between her lips.

"Are you alright, Mum?"

"I'm alright darlin'," Shelly said. "The drinks helping with the shock." Her voice had an infinitely compassionate tone despite the harshness of her accent. "Where is she?" she asked, glancing up at Ashley.

"In the mortuary." Though it would have been obvious, she didn't want to actually tell her that there was nothing left of her daughter but bones. Looking at Melanie she could see what a beautiful girl Tracey would have been. What on earth had the poor girl done to deserve being treated no better than a piece of rubbish. "Would you mind answering some questions? If you prefer to do this another time—"

"No, you're alright, best do this now, get it over with. I don't want people seeing the fuzz 'round my door, might give them the wrong impression—mud sticks like glue 'round here. What d'ya wanna know?"

"The day Tracey disappeared, can you tell us what you remember about it," Dale asked, taking a small notepad and pen from the inside of his jacket.

"You must be jokin'. I can't remember last week let alone all those years ago. Anyway, shouldn't you have all that stuff I said written down somewhere?"

"Yes, it should be on Tracey's file. We'd just like to ask in case something new had come to mind," Ashley said.

"Well, I can't help you there, love," Shelly said, flicking her ash in the kitchen sink.

"What about boyfriends. Did Tracey have one?" Ashley asked.

"Bloody hell of course she did, quite a few, she weren't a nun." Shelly let out a harsh laugh. "She could have her pick of the bunch, like her ol' mum."

"Was there anyone in particular she liked?"

"No, she knew what men were like. I made sure

I taught my girls about them from a young age. What they're all after."

Dale shifted uncomfortably on his feet as Shelly gave him the once over. "The only decent blokes I ever met turned out to be gay."

"Have you still got any of Tracey's belongings?"

"Look around ya, does this place look like Buckingham Palace? You could barely swing a cat 'round here. Where d'ya think I'd keep it?"

"It was mostly clothes and make-up," Melanie piped up, causing her mother to swing around to look at her.

"No one's talking to you, missy now hop it."

Melanie's face fell and she turned to leave the kitchen.

"Before you go, Melanie. Are you both aware of the Esther Campbell case?"

"Yeah, been nothing but that in the paper lately. What about it?" Shelly asked.

"Do you know if Tracey ever had contact with her?"

"Yeah, course she did, they were best mates. Her parents were always 'round here having a cuppa." Shelly laughed harshly again. "You think people like them would mix with our sort?"

"I take it that's a no then, shall I," Ashley said, looking from mother to daughter. Melanie shook her head.

"Yeah, it's a no. Why you askin' anyway?" Shelly demanded.

"Your daughter's body was found buried yards away from her."

Shelly took a swig of her drink.

More to hide her emotions than the need to drink it, Ashley thought sadly. She looked as if she'd had a hard life where emotions made you seem weak—easy pickings.

"So there's nothing more you can add to our enquiries, Ms Carver?" Dale asked closing his notepad.

"Like I said, I can't remember anything. If I could, d'ya think I wouldn't tell ya? Do you think I want me daughter's killer walking the street? I might be many things but the first thing I am is a mother and I loved my Tracey, she was me first born." She used her cigarette to light another one.

"I sincerely believe you. Please if you have any questions you want to ask, get in touch," Ashley said handing her card to her.

"You ain't like the other lot that came 'round here when my Tracey went missing. Treated me like a piece of shit they did—ransacked this place." She cursed through a mouthful of smoke.

"I'm sorry they did that. I know some officers can be a bit overzealous in their approach sometimes but that doesn't make it right."

Simmering slightly Shelly said, "If I think of anything, I'll give you a bell. When can I bury her?"

"We'll let you know as soon as the post mortem is completed and her body is released. Just to give you a heads up, once Tracey has been identified we will be revealing her details to the press. We need to get as much coverage of this case as possible."

Shelly remained in the kitchen leaving Ashley and Dale to make their own way out.

"Detective," Melanie said quietly as they

stepped out onto the balcony.

Ashley leaned in towards her. "It wasn't just boys that were hanging 'round Tracey, it was grown men as well. Mum didn't want to tell the other coppers that came 'round at the time Tracey went missing 'cause she thought they'd say she was an unfit mum and take me into care."

"They should never have judged your mum, Melanie. I know she tries her best. Tell me, was Tracey ever intimate with any of the men she hung around with?"

Melanie shrugged her shoulders. "I'd say so, she used to spend a lot of time down Epping with . . . you know, men that would give her money. My mum knew all about it."

"Do you remember any of the men?"

"Nah, they'd come and go. She had her regulars as well, couldn't tell you who they were, though. She also had boyfriends but no one special when she disappeared."

"Thanks for sharing that with me, Melanie, I really appreciate it," Ashley said as she turned to walk away.

"Did my sister die quickly?" Melanie called out.

Ashley stopped and paused for a moment, before turning to look at her. "Yes, we think so," she said gently before heading back along the balcony to catch up with Dale as he made his way back to the car.

"What do you think of that then?" Dale asked once they were both seated in the car. "I get the impression the mother has turned a few tricks herself."

"Yeah, me too. It wouldn't surprise me if she got

Tracey into it."

Dale leaned back in his seat without starting the engine. "Let's think about this. So far then we have two dead girls. On the social ladder they are miles apart, never met but end up being buried literally side by side," he said, reaching up and snapping the sunroof open.

"Given that it was an area both girls hung out, this seems more and more like an opportunist killer. The question is, how many more people did he kill? Are there anymore graves we haven't found? And how are Aaron and Peter involved?" Ashley said, her mind racing.

"The profiler's report said the murderer knew the area well and most probably lived or worked in a ten mile radius. Maybe he was one of Tracey's clients and knowing the area had come across Esther one day."

"This still brings us back to Aaron, though. How did he know this information? And before you say anything, please don't mention spirits of any kind," Ashley said, looking at Dale questionably.

"I wasn't going to." He laughed. "What I was going to say is that I'm leaning more towards your theory, Ash. One body I could give him the benefit of the doubt, but two?" He shook his head. "That's even a bit too much for me. There has got to be a link somewhere." Dale sighed as he put the key in the ignition. "Do you fancy grabbing a few beers and chilling out? Today has done my head in."

"As tempting as it sounds I think I'm going to opt home and take a long soak and an early night. Another night, maybe?" Ashley replied feeling a touch of sympathy for her friend.

"Yeah, sure. Could you take the car and pick me up in the morning? I want to get legless tonight."

"Of course. Although getting drunk by yourself is never a good idea." Ashley smiled warmly as Dale turned the key and the car revved to life.

"It's okay, I think I'll make use of my little black book tonight. What are friends with benefits for if not for nights like this."

"Don't take all this to heart, Dale."

"I try not to but it's hard. These men, if I could find them I'd cut their balls off for taking advantage of young girl, regardless if she was a tom or not."

"Melanie looks like she's got her head screwed on."

"Let's hope so." Dale put his foot down on the accelerator and pulled away.

***

The man's veins bulged in his arms as he pushed the weights higher in the air above his head. He let out a short rasp of breath as he brought them down and pushed them back up again. The adrenaline rush was nearly as powerful as it was the first time he'd killed—but not quite. He needed to do something to calm his mind. That was the second body they'd found. What had he done to deserve this? After so many years of being on the straight and narrow, his past was coming back to haunt him—fast. For the first time in his life he felt at a loss what to do. He could have never foreseen this happening. He thought he had done the impossible—committed the perfect crimes. The same detective from the first press conference was talking, her eyes looking straight into his, promising she would bring him to justice. She was very attractive, a little old for his tastes but still, he wouldn't mind spending a few minutes with her, watching her face contort with fear. He felt a stirring below at the thought of it; her under his control, begging and pleading for her life.

"Do we have to watch the news," his wife said with a whine, entering the room with his protein shake in a tall glass, "it's so depressing."

He let out a short laugh as he laid his weights on the floor and grabbed her around the waist. "Bad things happen, sweetheart, you can't isolate yourself from reality."

She lifted her skirt up, revealing her nakedness as she climbed onto his lap. "You always told me I could do whatever I wanted."

"Yes," he said, releasing his erect manhood from his pants and quickly entering her, his eyes focused on Ashley's face the whole time. "And you know I'm always right."

Chapter 21

Wearily Ashley made her way up the path and into her house, she felt as though she had the weight of the world on her shoulders. Muffin greeted her excitedly for a few seconds at the door before going in search of his water bowl.

"You look exhausted," Tasha said, coming out into the hallway and noticing her demeanour.

She shrugged off her jacket. "More frustrated than anything else."

"Bad day at work?"

"You could say that. So how was your date?"

"It was okay."

"One of the first things we learn as cops is how to read body language and my antenna is telling me that it wasn't okay."

Tasha gave a wistful, embarrassed laugh. "Okay, you've got me. Turns out my date or should I say dates were interested in swinging and I'm not talking about from a tree type of thing, either."

Ashley giggled. "Wow, I wish I'd have been there."

"Is that your sort of thing then?" Tasha asked, teasing her.

"I can't knock it till I've tried it."

"You wouldn't, would you?"

"I doubt it. I'd hate the confusion of not knowing whose body bits belonged to who. Never mind, when you go back to Oz you might meet someone there."

"Maybe," Tasha said. She couldn't believe that Ashley had just spoken about reading body language

yet she had failed to pick up on how attracted she was
to her. Or was it because she just didn't feel the same
way? "Your mum was here again this morning. She's
left you more food. I was going to heat it up for you."

"Tasha, please don't let my mother turn you into
my housekeeper. I know her intentions are good but
you're not my servant."

"I don't mind. I like looking after people."

"I appreciate that but I'll be having stern words
with her."

"Oh, please don't say anything, she might think
I've complained."

"No, she won't, I promise."

Tasha was pleased when Sandra had asked her to
prepare Ashley's meals. She looked like she needed
looking after.

"So what are your plans for tonight? Going out
on anymore blind dates?"

"Nope, just an evening in watching the TV. I'm
not really in the mood for going out."

"Why don't you hang out here? I'm sure my
mum's provided enough food to keep two people
going for a week."

"Are you sure? I don't want to infringe on your
space."

"Don't be silly, I wouldn't have asked if I felt
that way," Ashley said smiling.

"Then yes, but only if you let me serve dinner.
You look like you're about to collapse."

"Deal—shall I pop out to the shop and get some
wine?"

"Sandra has already beaten you to it—she
brought two bottles round with dinner."

"Do you want to open a bottle whilst I go and change?"

"Sure." Tasha headed for fridge.

By the time Ashley had showered and changed into white cut downs and a black vest, Tasha had set the table in the garden.

"I thought it would be nice if we ate out here," she said, handing her a glass of chilled wine and discreetly admiring her toned body.

"Thanks, it looks great."

"Are you ready for dinner?"

"Yep, I'm actually starving."

"So your mum was right then."

"Yeah, but I'd never tell her, though."

"Go and take a seat and I'll bring the food out."

"Okay, boss," Ashley said touching her forehead slightly in a mock salute. It felt nice to be fussed over.

Over dinner they discussed their favourite holiday destinations, both laughing when they realised they preferred countries with a cooler climate. Eventually the topic got round to Ashley's work.

"I just saw you on the evening news," Tasha said putting down her knife and fork and taking a sip of wine.

Ashley rolled her eyes. "That's one thing I hate about working on high profile cases—press invasion and they always seem to get footage of me on my worst day."

"I thought you looked beautiful," Tasha said lowering her gaze.

Ashley's face turned crimson.

"You can't take a compliment, can you?"

"You don't get many compliments in my line of work."

"Have you ever thought of a career change?" Tasha asked, picking up her cutlery and resuming her meal.

"Nah, I mean what would I do?"

"I'm sure you've got many talents," Tasha said, smiling at her across the table.

"Is that another compliment?"

"How about calling it a truism."

"That sounds a lot better," Ashley said laughing.

"So how far are you in the case? I mean two bodies at one crime scene is pretty scary."

"Yes it is. Can you imagine what those poor girls went through?"

"Have you got any leads as to who it might be?"

"Nope, none what so ever."

"What about the psychic, Aaron Davies?"

"What about him?" Ashley sipped some wine.

"Isn't he the one that got the ball rolling on all of this, could he be connected in some way?"

"He was the one that alerted us to the bodies but unless he was a child serial killer I don't think he's the one that we're looking for."

"I see, so all you're left with is whether or not he's telling the truth about his visions. Do you believe him?"

"No," Ashley said matter-of-factly.

"Even though he directed you to two bodies?"

"Nope, I still don't buy it."

"You know, I have a friend who might be of help to you if you're interested."

"Who's that?" Ashley glanced up from her plate.

"His name is Michael Watts, you might have heard of him."

Ashley shook her head.

"Well, he's kind of an illusionist. Maybe he could give you an insight into Aaron Davies. He's in town for the week. I can always give him a call tomorrow and arrange to meet up with him."

"You know, I think that might be a good idea, thanks."

"You're welcome."

"So how's Muffin been treating you?"

"Like a true gent." Tasha laughed. "Oh boy, has he got a crush on Sky the husky."

"So you can see it too. I knew it wasn't my imagination."

"No definitely not," Tasha said as she used the paper napkin to dab at her face. "I wish it would rain and break this humid air."

"Do you want to get in the hot tub? I'll set the temperature low—it's a great way to cool down."

Tasha's eyebrows rose mischievously. "Really, Ms McCoy, are you trying to succeed where your brother failed?"

Ashley laughed. "No, I'd be a lot more subtle if I were."

"Oh, would you now? You're one of those quiet sneaky types are you?"

"That would be telling," Ashley answered, tapping the side of her nose.

"Well, if you don't mind me wearing just my underwear, I'd be more than happy to cool off in the hot tub."

"Good, I'll go and turn it on," she said, enjoying the harmless banter.

Fifteen minutes later, Tasha slipped into the warm water and sighed in pleasure as her whole body was enveloped by the forceful bubbles.

Ashley slid in beside her and rested her head against the back. "Oh, this is heaven."

"You can say that again. Do you want some more wine?"

"I'm good, thanks. One glass is more than enough for me."

"One just about gets me started," Tasha said, leaning past her to retrieve the bottle from the table. Ashley felt a stir of excitement as Tasha's arm accidently brushed against her breast.

"Sorry," Tasha said, stopping in mid air to look down on her.

Ashley smiled, letting the moment pass. She felt Tasha sit back down again, only this time nearer to her, their bare arms touching.

"So, do you mind me asking you why you're still single?" Tasha asked, sipping her wine.

"Who said I was?" Ashley opened her eyes and turned her head sideways to look at her.

"Oh, I thought—"

"I'm kidding," Ashley said sighing. "It's just one of those things—I work so many odd hours I never get the chance to meet anyone."

"That's a shame."

"Not really, I'm not the sort of person who needs a significant other to define me and I always have Muffin to come home to."

"Would you say you were a commitment-phobe?"

"No, but I wouldn't just enter into a relationship just for the sake of having one."

"You're nothing like my friend then." Tasha rolled her eyes.

"Are we talking about the one who set you up the other day?"

Tasha gave a forced smile and a tense nod of her head.

"Have you both fallen out over it?" Ashley turned to face her.

"Sort of. I don't know if I can talk about it with you, seeing as you work for the police."

"Tasha, as long as she hasn't harmed anyone you can tell me anything. When I'm with you, I'm your friend, I thought you knew that."

"I don't want to get her into any trouble."

"Well, rest assured my lips are sealed."

"It's just that these women she's got involved with. I think they've got a drug habit and seem intent on dragging my friend down with them."

"I think you've every right to be concerned, it's a slippery slope to be on. Have you told your friend you're worried about her?"

"Yes, but she won't answer my calls now. She said I was jealous that she was having fun."

"I'm sorry, Tasha, but when people get drawn in with drug users, it's hard to keep your own head, especially if you're easily led. Is there anyone in her family you could talk to?"

Tasha shook her head decisively. "I don't think she'd care what they'd say anyway, she barely sees them."

"Do you know how she's funding her habit? Maybe when she runs out of money and realises how hard things are it might give her something to think about."

"I'm afraid there's no chance of that happening, she has enough money to last her three lifetimes."

"Oh, well that is a problem then. If you like I can have a word with them—maybe put the frighteners up them a little bit."

"You'd do that for me?"

"Yes I would. Plus if they are dealing drugs it's a legitimate call. What're their names and where do they hang out?"

"Claire and Louise. Charlotte said they go to a grungy bar in Stoke Newington called Benders—they are there every weekend, apparently. But please don't mention my name."

"I won't, I promise—I would never let anything happen to you."

The shrill of Ashley's mobile pierced the air. "Sorry, I've got to take this, it might be an emergency," she said as she leaned over the edge of the tub and scooped up her phone. Snapping it open, she listened intently for a few moments, a dark frown covering her features. She closed it slowly, staring down at it.

"Is everything alright," Tasha asked concerned.

"That was my boss." Ashley climbed out of the tub and wrapped herself in a towel.

"They've . . . they've just found a third body a hundred yards away from the second one."

Twenty minutes later Dale was sat in Ashley's

living room, bottle of beer in hand, shaking his head in disbelief. "This is getting way out of hand now." He sighed. "How many more bodies are they going to find? Who found this one?"

"Some bloke walking his dog. He told officers he was interested in the area due to recent activities there. He let his German Shepherd off the lead. Five minutes later the dog comes back with an arm bone in his mouth."

"Jesus," Dale said.

"I know, but check this out, the remains didn't have a belt around the neck."

"So this murder might not be related to the other two?"

"Unless he changed his MO, no. They found a leather bag with her college pass. Her name was Amber Brooks. Her parents have been informed that the remains have been found although she still needs to be officially identified."

There was a gentle tap on the door and then Tasha poked her head around it. Dale jumped to his feet.

"Sorry to interrupt, I've tidied everything away," Tasha said looking at Ashley. "So I'll see you in the morning."

"Thanks, Tasha, sorry about—"

"Don't be silly, you have more important things to deal with."

"Tasha?" Dale said looking from Ashley to Tasha back to Ashley again.

"Sorry, Tasha, meet Dale."

"Hi, Dale," she said smiling. "It was nice to meet you."

"Likewise," Dale said grinning like a Cheshire cat.

"I'll walk you to the door," Ashley said standing and gave Dale a quick shake of the head.

"Thanks for dinner."

"No worries, Tasha. I'd like to do it again sometime."

"I'd like that too." Tasha gave a sweet smile.

"Listen, about your friend," Ashley said, "I'll sort it out in the next couple of days."

"Thank you. Well, I hope you have a productive evening," Tasha said, lingering at the door for a few moments before turning to leave.

Ashley watched her as she walked down the driveway and then slowly closed the door.

"I thought we didn't keep secrets from each other, Ash," Dale said as she entered the living room.

"We don't."

"Then who the hell was that? Oh wait, don't tell me, she was just a figment of my imagination. Because if you were dating someone that . . . hot, you would have told me about her."

"Dale, cool your jets. I'm not dating her, she walks Muffin for me."

"She's your dog walker?"

"Yes, Dale."

"First thing tomorrow I'm going to buy me a dog, is she single?"

"Yes, as far as I know."

"Has she got any kids?"

"Nope."

"Wow, this is great, oh, hold on a minute she isn't . . . no, please don't tell me she bats for the same side."

"I'm afraid so."

"No, no please don't say that," Dale said crumpling back into his seat. "Why would God make such a temptation out of my reach."

"That, you would have to ask him. Anyway, enough of the drooling, I thought you were here to talk about the case."

"I was, I am, oh damn," Dale said taking a long swig of his beer. "I suppose this is how it feels for lesbians when they fall for straight women."

"I wouldn't know."

"Are you serious? You've never, ever, ever fallen for a straight woman?"

"Never."

"Wow, that must be some strong gaydar thingy everyone talks about."

"Aren't I the lucky one. Anyway, getting back to the case. You know what this means, don't you?"

"No, what?"

"That we may be looking for two killers."

Chapter 22

"Dale, it's Ash. Listen, I'm going with Tasha to visit her friend, the one I told you about last night. I'll be late in," Ashley said, leaving a message on Dale's answer phone. Tasha had called her first thing that morning—she had spoken to her friend and the only time he was available was that very morning. After Muffin had been taken for his walk they were on their way to South London.

Ashley felt a slight shiver, despite the heat in the car being unbearably hot.

"Are you okay?" Tasha asked as Ashley ran a hand through her hair and let out a sigh.

"What? Oh, yes, sorry I was miles away."

"Anywhere nice?"

Ashley smiled. She had been daydreaming again—about Tasha. It seemed that's all she did lately when her mind wasn't on the Woodlands Killer case. She wished she could tell her how she had envisioned waking up beside her, where she could look at her until her heart was content. Instead she said, "Just thinking about the case."

"You'll get an ulcer if you're not careful. All work and no play makes Jackie a very ill girl," Tasha said changing the words of a familiar rhyme to fit her circumstances.

Ashley pushed her bottom lip forward in thought. "I'd have an ulcer over finding the killer any day."

"If I'm honest, I'm surprised you don't have one already—ever since I met you, all you seem to do is work."

"That's not true. If I recall correctly, you have been present at one BBQ and one meal at my house."

"Sorry, yes, you're right. I'll give you the BBQ but you're pushing it with the dinner night. Half way through last night you abandoned me to deal with your case."

"I would never abandon you intentionally," Ashley said before she could stop herself.

"I hope you wouldn't," Tasha said laying a hand over hers, causing Ashley's heart rate to spike.

"So, um, tell me about Michael. How do you know him?" Ashley asked changing the subject.

Tasha replaced her hand back on her lap. "He does quite a few shows in Australia. You know the type where he shows you how tricks and illusions are done."

"So does he do well?"

"Most of the time, but it's not really that hard. The world is full of theories that people can't prove—"

"I totally agree, it's crazy if you think about it."

"Yep, we live in a world full of illusions."

"What about love, is that an illusion?"

"In some cases, yes," Tasha answered. I don't know about you, but I've been under the illusion that I was in love only for it to blow up in my face when I realised that it was lust."

"So you've never been in love?"

"Nope, though saying that, recently I think I may be changing my mind."

"Oh, why's that?" Ashley's curiosity peaked.

"That's for me to know. Here, take your left at the lights and his flat is just on the right."

A great exultation filled Ashley's chest to breaking

point. *Could she possibly be talking about me?* she thought as she followed Tasha's instructions.

Minutes later they drew up outside a red bricked building. They quickly made their way up the path and Tasha pressed on a small silver button. Within seconds a voice called out and she heard the front door unlatch. Michael Watts, a young chubby faced man with a scruffy beard and large round glasses, led her into his ground floor apartment—spacious and sparsely decorated with furniture that she was sure cost a month of her salary.

"Tasha, baby," he said grabbing her in a bear hug, lifting her off her feet. "It's been too long."

"I know," Tasha said as he released her. "Michael, I'd like you to meet Ashley."

"You don't look like a detective," he said eyeing her.

"And you don't look like a sceptic," Ashley replied, smiling. There was no animosity between the two of them as they were both aware they didn't fit the stereotypes society placed on them.

"I like you very much," Michael said. "Please, both of you sit yourselves down and get comfortable." He dropped down onto a plush bean bag.

They both sat on a purple two-seater curved chair. "I'm really grateful that you could see me on such short notice," Ashley said warmly.

"No problem at all. If you're a friend of Tasha's, you're a friend of mine," he said, flashing Tasha a smile. "So, Tash tells me you're working on the case to do with Aaron Davies."

"Do you know him?"

"Not him in particular, but I know his type."

"Oh."

"The type that always throw the question back on you when you ask them to prove their validity. I cannot tell you the amount of psychics who have asked me to prove to them there isn't life after death. Just because I can't prove the spirit world doesn't exist, doesn't mean it does. In another sense it's like asking scientists to prove there aren't aliens. Does that mean there are? They're all mute questions with no way of possibly answering them. Unless you've seen it with your own eyes and I'm sorry to say, in my forty years on earth, I haven't."

"So how is it possible he knows so many things about people?" Ashley asked, captivated.

"It's just a simple observation of human nature. If you get a crowd of people in a room with a guy who claims he speaks to the dearly departed, you can bet your life on it that those attending have lost a loved one, friend or whatever. Once you've got your target audience nailed, you just have to tell them what's familiar. Throw in a list of generic names you'll be sure to get a hit with someone, then the reader can really amp it up and hone in on what they want to learn from you." Michael stood up and walked over to Ashley. "Let's talk about death," he said watching her closely. "Right, off the bat, if you walked in here and I didn't know anything about you I could tell straight away someone close to you has died and though it may not have been recent, it has been in the last few years."

"How did you know?"

"Quite easy, actually. It's called looking for

cues—I mention a word and all I have to do is study your reaction to know whether or not I'm hot or cold. Throw in a few generic comments here or there, maybe they'll be a hit maybe they won't, but it won't matter, you'll leave here remembering what *you* want to believe I said."

"I can understand all of those scenario's, what I can't get my head around is that he knew exactly where the victims' bodies were buried. Can you think of any way he would know only things the killer could?"

"I will bet my life on it that he's got inside information and it's not coming from beyond the grave."

***

Half an hour later, driving towards home so she could drop Tasha off, Ashley's mind was trying to connect the dots.

"So, what do you think?" Tasha asked, breaking into her thoughts.

"It was what I expected. Davies sounds like a fraud. But this isn't what this case is about—I can't police what people believe in, each to their own. It's about how he came across the knowledge of where the women were buried that concerns me."

She was going to have to try a different tactic with Aaron when they visited him later on that morning. It seemed he had his own way of garnering information and she had hers.

Chapter 23

Aaron's face looked tired and drawn when he swung open his front door.

"Ah, what now? Was it really necessary to wake me up so early? I had a show last night and I've hardly had any sleep." Aaron looked up at the clock in his hallway, which read 10:00am.

"I think so, don't you, Ash," Dale said, smiling at her then returned his gaze to Aaron.

"I don't know, I agree with Aaron, it is a bit early. I could have done with a lie in myself," she replied smiling briefly at Aaron. "Would you mind if we come in? We've got a few questions we need answering."

"Yes, I do really, look what's all this about? I've told you everything I know."

"Really? Have you had a falling out with the spirits?"

He stared at Ashley in bewilderment. "Can you stop talking in double Dutch and tell me what on earth you're on about, otherwise I'm going back to bed."

"We're just surprised that you didn't call in about Amber Brooks," Dale said, leaning in closer to Aaron.

The shock was evident on his face. "Who is Amber Brooks? I don't know anybody by that name," he said, his eyes darting between Ashley and Dale.

"Would you like us to give you a few minutes to open up your line of communication with the spirit world?" Ashley asked.

Aaron's cheeks reddened. "You may not have

anything productive to do with your time but I do," he said moving his hand swiftly to the door with every intention of closing it.

Prepared for the manoeuvre, Ashley stuck her foot in the gap, preventing it from shutting. "You don't know, do you? Oh gosh, he doesn't know, Dale?"

"Know what?" Aaron asked, frowning and opening the door slightly again.

Ashley gave a feigned expression of concern. "He didn't tell you, did he? The one you're protecting. We found another body yesterday, Aaron."

"No, you couldn't have." His face flushed as his hand felt about for the door handle.

"I'm afraid we did, barely a hundred yards from the other two."

"H-how do you know it's the same k-killer?" he said stammering.

"Same MO," Ashley lied.

"But I would have known, I would have known," he said as he bent his neck over, staring at the grey doorstep below him.

"'Fraid not," Ashley said gently, stepping towards him. "Can we come in? Aaron, I can see you're in shock, perhaps I can make you a tea."

He shook his head.

"Please, Aaron, this is the time to help us catch the man who did this and put him behind bars. He's obviously lied to you. Did he say he'd only killed two people? That he couldn't help himself? No one will blame you for telling us. Did someone tell you in confidence that they did these crimes? Is that how you knew where the bodies were?"

Waiting but not receiving a response she continued, "Did you meet him somewhere? At a show perhaps or was he a stranger. Can you at least give a description of what he looks like?"

Silence.

"How can you live with the knowledge that you're aiding and abetting a murderer?" Dale cut in.

Aaron gave no response.

"Principle Bradshaw said you were a kind and compassionate person—" she said.

A change took place in the neutral expression on his face. Involuntarily, his eyes rose to meet Ashley's.

"You spoke to my principle?" he said in a low murmur.

"We had to, Aaron, you can understand why can't you? You directed us straight to two bodies. We are in the middle of a murder investigation," Ashley said in a soothing tone.

"Am I under suspicion?"

"Of course not, we know you didn't have anything to do with it, Aaron, but we think you can lead us to who did."

"W-what did he say . . . Principle B-bradshaw?" He stammered again, bowing his head slightly to listen.

"That he was sad that you left the college—that you were one of his best students."

"He said I was one of his best students?" Aaron repeated raising his face to her again.

"Yes, he also said you liked to help people," Ashley said fixing her eyes on his.

"I do."

"Then help us to find the monster who's responsible

for ending the lives of these young women," Ashley said urging him.

"Was . . . was . . . she young?" Aaron's eyes took on a haunted look.

"Yes, Aaron, she was only sixteen, not more than a child. He cut short a young girl in her prime. Think about all the things she has missed out on— think about her grieving parents—"

"Did she have brothers and sisters?"

"No, she was the only child."

"I've always wanted siblings, someone to talk to."

"You can talk to me, Aaron, that's what I'm here for, to let you off load your pain onto me so you don't have to hurt anymore," she said.

"Have her parents been informed?"

Ashley nodded. "Yes, we told them yesterday and they begged us to help them to find the person that hurt their daughter so he couldn't ruin another family's life."

"I'm sorry to hear that."

"So sorry, that you'll help us?"

"I can't promise you anything."

"Whatever you can give me, will be a start."

"Okay, I promise. If her spirit talks to me I'll try and find out who hurt her," Aaron said, drawing himself up to full height before closing the door.

"I thought you had him there," Dale said as they strolled back to the car.

"He won't break that easy, his loyalty to the killer is obviously a strong one. What I do know now, is that it's not a stranger—it's someone he personally knows, I'm sure of it."

"But how are we going to get him to talk?"

"I don't think we're going to have to do anything—he looked genuinely shocked when he found out about Amber, which leads me to believe that he was only privy to Esther and Tracey. He's been kept out of the loop on the third victim for some reason, maybe this was the catalyst that we needed for him to lead us to the killer.

***

Dressed in a narrow striped tailored jacket and a knee length black pencil skirt, Colleen stood in front of the evidence board addressing the team. "So far, this is what we know. The third victim has now been identified as Amber Brooks. She wasn't known to frequent the woods by herself according to the original missing person's report. She didn't have a belt around her neck but did have marks indicative of stab wounds. The location of the body and approximate date of the murder are the only other things that link her to the two previous murders. We know the first two murders were definitely the same person as partial fingerprints were lifted from the belts. They didn't match anyone in the fingerprint database. We need to find out why Amber was in the woods and if she was taken there by force, or dumped there after being killed. If there is a connection between all three cases, we need to find it." Her normally attractive features looked tired and drawn.

"All the first two victims' friends and families are sticking to their original statements—none of them have anything new to add," Steve said tapping a pen against his clean shaven chin.

"So what's the next step, people, any ideas?" Colleen asked.

"This just might be the answer," an officer said, walking in holding a sheet of paper in the air. "We've just had a call from the hotline. One of the men who was originally interviewed for the Esther Campbell case, just lost his cast iron alibi."

***

They arrived at Mimi Collins' house just as a young girl with blonde streaked hair was leaving, flashing them a dirty look in the process.

"Something I said?" Dale asked her sarcastically as he exchanged a smile with Ashley. They made their way up the worn stone steps leading to a red front door. Before Dale's hand reached the bell, Mimi threw open the door and bustled them inside, smiling widely and shaking their hands as they passed by her. Adorable cat pictures lined the narrow hallway, a leopard skin cat bed hung from the radiator with a ginger occupant sleeping inside. Mimi showed them into a shabby but clean living room. Large colourful throws were strewn over the sofas and a small white cat curled up contently in an armchair.

"You'll have to forgive, Mr Chips," she said, nodding towards the cat who looked up as if sensing she was talking about him. "He doesn't have any social skills, he thinks he owns the house." Mimi smiled fondly at him. "Please, sit here," she said pointing towards a large three-seater sofa.

Ashley and Dale sat down and before they could utter a word Mimi began pacing the floor as she launched into a tirade about her ex-husband. "He was a self centred pig," she said, smoothing her hands over the long flowing skirt she wore. "How I put up with him for so long, God only knows, thirty years of pure hell it was. Always down the gym and he ate enough to feed a family of six but there was never enough money to buy me anything I wanted. . ."

Ashley waited patiently until Mimi came to a natural pause. "Can you tell us why you believe your ex-husband was responsible for Esther Campbell's death?"

"What? You mean apart from him asking me to lie about where he was and giving him a false alibi?" Mimi said rhetorically. "He became obsessed with the case, cutting out all the news clippings, recording press conferences off the telly."

"Okay, that does seem a little out of the ordinary but that's hardly enough to accuse the man of being a killer."

Stopping to face them, Mimi pushed her curly grey hair away from her face. "Oh yeah, so what if I was to tell you that he told me he saw her on the day she disappeared."

***

"What do you think?" Ashley asked Dale as they simultaneously opened a car door and climbed in.

"I can't tell if it's just a case of sour grapes or the info she's provided is kosher," Dale said buckling his seat belt.

"Well, there's only one way to find out." Ashley started engine.

Roger Collins lived on the second floor of a four storey block of flats. It was several minutes before heavy footsteps approached and the door was opened by a man with receding hair and a prematurely wrinkled face that looked out of place on his solidly built body.

"Roger Collins?" Dale asked.

"Yes?" he said, sizing them both up suspiciously.

"I'm DC Taylor and this is DS McCoy. Do you mind if we come in for a chat?"

"What's this about?"

"I think it would be better if we talked inside," Dale said, glancing towards his neighbour's door.

"Okay, come in, but can you remove your shoes. My girlfriend doesn't like people traipsing about with shoes on. She's afraid the laminate flooring will get damaged."

"It's a good thing I put on clean socks today," Dale whispered to Ashley as they removed their shoes and followed Roger into the living room.

"So how can I help you, detectives?" he asked, still standing, his arms crossed over his chest.

"We just have some questions we'd like to ask you," Dale said glancing round the well decorated room.

"Oh, yeah, about what?"

"Esther Campbell."

"What about her?"

"What, you haven't been watching the news recently?"

"No, believe it or not I have a life that doesn't revolve around the TV."

"Is that why you went to the expense of buying a top of the range TV?" Dale asked, pointing at the humongous TV in the corner of the room.

"That's for my missus. She likes to watch the soaps."

Though he spoke with a level tone, Ashley was under the impression that he was not altogether at ease. She knew most people felt like that in the presence of the police but maybe there was an underlying factor making him on edge.

"I would have thought someone would have mentioned it to you, seeing as you worked for the forestry commission in Epping Forest and were one of the people interviewed in '84," Ashley said.

"If you would have done your homework before coming here you would have also seen that I had an alibi back then."

"We checked and it seems you *did* have an alibi."

Rob looked startled. "What do you mean did? My ex-wife vouched for me that I was with her the day that girl disappeared."

"Now it seems she's recanting that alibi which leaves you up shit creek without a paddle."

"Jesus, now what is she accusing me of? Is she saying I had something to do with that young girl's death?"

"Did you?" Dale held his stare.

"Are you seriously going to take the word of that hag? Listen, she's been waiting to get back at me ever since I walked out on the nagging old cow."

"Where's your girlfriend, Mr Collins?" Ashley asked.

"Out."

"Will she be back any time soon?"

"I don't know, why?"

"How old is she?" Ashley studied Rob closely.

"She's legal if that's what you're driving at."

"How legal?"

"Eighteen."

"And you're what? In your late fifties?"

"So, what's age got to do with anything?"

"Do you like them young? Is that what it is? More easy to control?" Ashley's voice rose a decibel.

"Are you going to arrest me?"

"For what?"

"Then in that case, I'd like you both to leave, right now!"

"Why did you collect newspaper clippings to do with the Esther Campbell case?" Ashley held her ground.

"Is that what that lying bitch told you? And you believe her! First taking tips from a psychic, now from a woman driven by jealousy. You lot are a bloody laughing stock of the country," he said, moving towards the front door and opening it.

"So you do know about the case then. Why are you lying to us, Mr Collins?" Ashley asked as she walked out of the door.

"Just get out. If you lot hassle me again, I'll be straight on to my solicitor."

"You know there's a simple way to put an end to all of this," Ashley said, turning to face him.

"How's that?"

"Come to the station and let us take your prints."

"Piss off!" Rob said slamming the door in her face.

***

"Surely, he has to be moved to the top of our suspect list after that performance," Dale said as they walked along the corridor towards their office.

"Yes, definitely. I'm going to speak to Colleen about getting an arrest warrant so we can get his prints," Ashley replied.

"If it does turn out to be him, I hope Mimi Collins can sleep at night knowing she's protected a murderer all these years."

"It wouldn't be a first, though would it. The things people do for *love*."

"Well, if that's what love is, they can keep it. Are you coming for lunch, my treat?" Dale asked.

"Not today, I'm just popping out for a bit."

"Where to?" he asked, raising his eyebrows.

"Just out, I'll tell you when I get back." Without any further explanation she turned and hurried down the stairs.

A short time later, Ashley strolled in through their office door just as Dale was replacing the receiver in its cradle.

"Colleen just called and she's sorting the warrant and sending some uniforms to pick Collins up," Dale said.

"Great."

"Look what I've got," Ashley said holding up a pair of tickets.

"What's that for?"

"Front row tickets for the Aaron Davies show."

"You're kidding, right?"

"Nope, I thought it's time we go and see just exactly how Mr Davies struts his stuff."

"Don't tell me they're for tonight."

"Yep, is that a problem?"

"Why couldn't you have walked in five minutes ago. I've been summoned home for a family meal tonight—my mum no doubt wants to know why at thirty I'm still single and childfree."

"You would have thought by the amount of grandkids she has she wouldn't miss a couple of mini Dales running around the place."

"My thoughts exactly. I don't know what her obsession with kids are. She just can't accept that I'm not like my brothers and sisters. I don't need excess baggage to make me feel complete."

"Yeah, but some people just can't accept that you want something different to them. Once you don't follow the life script it makes people feel uncomfortable."

"You seem to be doing all right, Ash."

"That's because I don't care what people think about me. As long as my actions aren't hurting anyone, I don't give it a second thought."

"Maybe I should take you with me to meet mother and you could make her see it from your point of view," Dale said hopefully.

"Somehow I don't think my ideology on life would go down that well with her. It's time you had a serious talk with your mum and explain how you feel. She's had her life and she shouldn't now be trying to relive it through yours."

"Yeah, maybe I will—I mean she's constantly on at me about why I never go round, is it any wonder."

"Maybe you should tell her you're infertile."

"Well that wouldn't be a lie."

"What'd you mean?"

"I had the snip years ago."

"Not only is that a smart move it's also very responsible, Dale. I'm impressed."

"That's what I thought. Anyway who are you going to take tonight?"

"I don't know." For the past few months she knew that she had let her friendships slide. Every day had been consumed with her workload—she couldn't just call them out of the blue like she had just spoken to them yesterday. "I think I'll give Tasha a call and see if she's interested."

***

Finally managing to find somewhere to park in the crowded car park, they followed the swarm of people into the large majestic building. There was a buzz in the air as Ashley and Tasha handed in their tickets and made their way down the aisle and into their seats.

"Thanks for asking me to come," Tasha said as they settled back into the red velvet seats in the auditorium.

"I'm glad you were free."

"I can't believe how packed it is here." Tasha craned her neck to look around at the rows of people behind them.

"I know."

The house lights dimmed.

Here we go, Ashley thought as music began to blare around the hall. The loud sound in itself was enough to unnerve her. A tall thin man carrying a glass box made his way up the aisle and onto the stage, placing it at the back near a large screen which was showing images of Aaron. She already knew what was inside the box because she had already placed a message in there.

The music died down as a voice made an introduction over the tannoy. "Ladies and gentlemen, please put your hands together for the one, the only, Aaron Davies."

The crowd erupted into a crazed frenzy as Aaron made his way onto the stage looking like the Lone Ranger dressed in a black suit with a black shirt. He walked to the front of the stage and bowed his head modestly.

The camera zoomed in on him—his face filling the screen behind him.

"Thank you, thank you," he said, a broad grin revealing a perfect set of teeth. He took a step back then slowly closed his eyes. The crowd went quiet.

"I have someone beside me, his name is. . ." Aaron squinted his eyes. "James, but he's telling me he preferred to be called Jamie. He's very handsome . . . he's wearing shorts, the long type you see surfers wearing." His eyes darted from side to side. "He wants someone called Maureen. He just keeps repeating the name Maureen."

The camera left Aaron and scanned the crowd. Ashley felt sadness as she looked at all of the expectant faces—she didn't need to be a psychic to know they were in pain.

"Jamie's telling me he loved the water. Does this make sense to anyone?"

The camera caught the hand of a woman rising from the back row.

"We've got someone," Aaron said, turning to look at the screen. "Please stand up and wait until the microphone comes to you."

A woman in her early to late thirties with auburn hair stood up, tears already in her eyes as the camera zoomed in for a close up.

"Am I going crazy or is this a little bit ghoulish," Tasha whispered to Ashley.

"You're not going crazy, this is like watching a car crash," she replied, liking Tasha being so close to her.

"Hello, Aaron," the woman said in a soft tone as she gripped the cross around her neck tightly in her hand.

"The young man I have here, Jamie, does what I say about him make sense?"

"Yes, he was in Australia when he died."

Aaron turned to look at the screen, talking to her as if she were standing in front of him. "He wants you to know that he didn't suffer, it was very quick. Why is he showing me water, the sea?"

The woman broke down. The man sitting down next to her stood up and embraced her with one arm taking the microphone from her with the other. "I'm Jamie's dad," he said, his voice choked. "He drowned in Australia."

"He wants you to stop worrying, he's safe now. He wants you to move on. This is a message for you, Maureen. He said give his belongings to charity, you don't need them anymore."

"Thank you, Aaron," Jamie's dad said.

"The message isn't from me, sir, it's from your son. Please let's thank these lovely people," Aaron concluded, encouraging the audience to clap as he moved backwards to the centre of the stage. "I've got a woman coming through, she's guiding me over here," he said walking to the area where Ashley and Tasha sat.

Here we go, Ashley thought as he stopped dead in front of her.

"She's scared, she docsn't know what happened. She can't understand why nobody can see her. She can't pass over until something is settled . . . Ashley," he called. "She wants to connect with Ashley."

Ashley's back stiffened against her chair as the camera once again scanned the room, this time focusing on her area.

"If you are out there, Ashley, Melissa wants to talk to you," he said. "Don't be frightened."

Ashley could feel Tasha staring at her, but she kept her face looking forward.

"She wants you to know that she will always be with you, like you both had planned—though she is not with you in person she will always be by your side. Does this not relate to anyone here?" he asked.

When there was no response he moved to the back of the stage. "Sometimes people are too scared to respond when spirits comes through."

"Was he talking about you, Ashley?" Tasha asked frowning.

"I've heard what I needed to. Do you mind if we leave?"

"Not at all, I find him a bit creepy if I'm honest."

They quietly left their seats and headed towards the exit.

"Do you fancy going for a drink?" Ashley asked

nodding towards a bar across the street.

"Yes I think I need one."

The bar was spacious with cream coloured walls and dark hardwood floors. Wooden tables and red upholstered seating were scattered around the room in no particular order. Parents and their boisterous small children ate in a separate section from where lone men stood at the bar drinking.

"What you having?"

"A dry white wine, please," Tasha said taking a seat while Ashley went to the bar. She returned moments later with a glass of wine and an orange juice for herself.

"I don't want to pry," Tasha said when Ashley had sat down. "And you can tell me to mind my own business, but was that message for you?"

"It would seem that way," she said taking a mouthful of juice.

"I'm sorry, I didn't know."

"It's okay."

"Do you mind me asking what happened?"

Ashley leaned back in her chair and thought it through for a few moments. "My partner, Melissa, was killed in a car crash four years ago."

"I'm so sorry, Ashley," Tasha said covering her hand with hers. "That must have been dreadful."

"It was. A drunk driver came out of nowhere. She didn't have a chance, she died at the scene. I walked away without so much as a scratch."

"I'm sorry if I sound insensitive, but doesn't that make you believe him more?"

"No, not at all."

"But he told you about Melissa. How could he

have known?"

"That's the thing, he didn't know—the night she died we were on our way home from a counselling session. We had reached the end of our relationship. Realistically, we should have split years earlier but we just dragged it out. She had just bought Muffin, despite me not wanting a dog, not that I didn't love him, but the hours we both worked, I just thought it wasn't fair on him. But like everything else in our relationship she just steamrolled ahead—the dog was the final straw for me."

Whenever Ashley recalled that night, which seemed so long ago now, she experienced varying emotions following each other in rapid succession. First, the relief that she had felt when she realised she hadn't been hurt. Then her surprise that Melissa hadn't answered her when she asked her if she was okay. And then came the horror when she realised Melissa was dying. She had held her in her arms as she had looked up at her and said, "This is not goodbye, Ash, I'll see you later." And then she was gone.

"But he knew about the crash?"

"It was in the local papers. When I went to interview him the first time he tried to spook me by telling me her dying words. But I found out that one of the other drivers who came to help, heard her say it and told the press. At the time I never read any of the reports but I went over them a few days ago. I knew he must have found it out from somewhere. It was also a big story when it went to court—had he known that we weren't together anymore I would have held my hands up and given him full credit but now I know he's talking bullshit."

"How would he have known you would be there today?"

"I booked the tickets through his website in my name. He obviously has access to the listings. He was probably expecting me to turn up at some point— what with all the pressure we've been putting on him."

"Oh, my God, that's dreadful."

"There's more to it than that. He has a forum on his website where loads of people discuss their personal problems and talk about what shows they are going to attend. I'm not saying it's the be all and end all of what he does but it's starting to make sense. How he's doing what he's doing. Hailey Campbell booked her ticket through his website the same way I did, that's how he knew she was going to be there."

"But that still doesn't give you the answer that you need."

"I know, but it's a start. I know he has inside information, it's just about getting it out—" Ashley stopped mid sentence, sinking back into her chair as a memory popped up out of nowhere.

"What?"

"I've just remembered something. I'm really sorry to have cut our night short again but I need to check it out."

***

Having dropped Tasha at the tube station, Ashley drove towards Hailey's house in Hampstead. As she passed through Camden she recognised Bender's bar—it had a tinted glass frontage which made it look like a sleazy adult sex shop. Pulling into the only space available, Ashley made her way into the bar. *I must be getting old*, she thought, wincing as the bass of the music pounded her ears. She fought through the crowd and headed towards the neon signed bar.

"What can I get you?" a barmaid covered in tattoos asked.

She leaned over and raised her voice above its normal level. "I'm looking for a couple of women—Claire and Louise—I think they're partners."

She nodded her head towards the toilets and walked off to serve a paying customer. Ashley reached the toilet door, waiting a few seconds before pushing it open and finding the two women talking animatedly amongst themselves.

"Can anyone join this party?"

"If you've got the money," one of them said sliding up to Ashley like a snake on heat.

"What you got?"

"What haven't we got?" she said and laughed for no reason. "What you after?"

"Coke would be good."

"Coke it is," she said, withdrawing a small bag from underneath her skirt.

"I'd think twice before offering it to me," Ashley said, flashing her ID.

Claire recoiled away from her. "Is this some kind of shake down?"

"No, it's more like a friendly warning. You know a woman called Charlotte?"

"Might do—so what?"

"I'll come straight to the point. You need to drop

her company —sharpish, because if I have to come and see you again I won't be coming alone. Do you get my drift?"

"Did her goody two shoes friend send you here?"

"The only thing that matters is that you take my advice. Let me see some ID."

"What for?"

"Do you want me to open your bag and get it myself because if I do I will arrest you."

"I'll make that bitch pay for this," Claire said, rummaging through her bag and taking out her driver's licence.

Ashley made a note of her details in her notebook and handed it back to her. "You mess with her and you'll be dealing directly with me and believe me it won't be in here."

***

The following morning, Ashley and Dale were in an early meeting with Colleen.

"Uniforms went to pick up Roger Collins this morning and found he left yesterday soon after you went to see him," Colleen said.

"He's on the run?" Ashley asked.

"It seems so. I've put out an APW. I think we may well have found our man."

"Do we know of any connection between him and Aaron Davies?" Dale asked.

"Not yet. I have a number of the other DCs looking into it now. What did you find out last night, Ashley?"

"From what I can gather, Davies knew Hailey

would be attending his show because he saw her details when she bought a ticket from his website. I went to see Hailey last night about how his show came to her attention. When I first interviewed her she said she had received a flyer through her door, which struck me as odd at the time but I didn't think anything of it," Ashley said.

"But the whole street would have received one?" Colleen said.

"This is where I come into it," Dale said. "McCoy had me canvassing the block surrounding Hailey's house last night. We knocked on doors with his leaflet, asking if they had been left one. Although some couldn't remember, a lot said they hadn't and they were quite adamant."

"Why's that?"

"Because they recycle all paper and said they would have remembered the flamboyant flyer with a man claiming he spoke to spirit guides. I mean, it's not the sort of thing you normally have posted through your door.

"As well as this, Hailey's home is at least six miles from the venue. Nobody in their right mind would deliver flyers that far out, they normally concentrate on the immediate area which means someone deliberately put it through her door."

"Okay, say your theory is right, Dale. What's the reason behind it? Why bring it to our attention now? It's been so long since these women have been missing."

"Guilt?" Dale hazarded a guess. "Or he thought he could use this as a way to create publicity for his failing career. Come on, think about it—this case has been a godsend to him. He's selling out every night."

"Okay, we'll go with this and see where it leads. Go and see Amber's parents, see if they've got anything new to add to the picture."

Their conversation was interrupted by the sound of a tap on the door.

"Come in," Colleen called out.

A handsome young police officer with jet black hair and vivid blue eyes walked in looking as if he belonged in a pop group not the police service. "Sorry to barge in, Ma'am, I have a message for Detective McCoy," he said in a rich deep voice as he turned to her. "Someone called Tasha is urgently trying to reach you. She said your phone's switched off."

"Did she say what it was about?" Ashley asked, a wave of concern colouring her voice.

"Yeah, your dog's been in an accident!"

Within twenty minutes, Ashley was pushing through the door of Natterjacks Vets. The first person she saw was Tasha, her head in her hands bent over. She hurried to her, touching her shoulder.

Jerking up, she looked shocked.

"Is Muffin okay?" Ashley asked.

Tasha nodded, her puffy eyes making her vulnerable and girlish. "I'm so sorry, Ashley, he just sprinted across the road chasing that Husky and a car just came out of nowhere."

"Is he badly hurt?" Ashley fought to stay calm.

"He's just had an X-ray, he's got a broken leg and a few swollen ribs. The vet will be out in a minute."

Ashley sighed with relief and sat down beside

her and took her hand. Surprising it felt like the most natural thing to do in the world. "Hey, come on, it wasn't your fault."

"It was. I should have held on tighter."

"If you had then I might have been coming to see you in a morgue," she said gently. "Come on stop crying, I'm sure he'll be fine."

"I suppose you wouldn't feel safe me walking him again. I wouldn't blame you."

"Don't be silly, Tasha. I'm just glad you're both still alive." She had never said a truer word.

"I've spoken to Polly and all of your vet bills will be covered under the company's insurance."

"That's the last thing on my mind."

"I know, but I don't want to add extra pressure. I know how these bills can run into the thousands," Tasha said.

The door swung open and a tall thin man with short fluffy hair walked over to them. "Hello, Ashley, I think it's best you don't see him at the moment, he's under sedation."

Ashley stood. "How is he, George?"

"Doing a lot better than your friend here," he said smiling as he looked down at Tasha. "His front leg is fractured in several places. I'm going to put it in a cast. He's going to have to stay inside for six to eight weeks, I'm afraid, during which time he's going to need someone to keep a close eye on him for the first week as his leg will swell about then. A lot of care is going to be needed during these next couple of months. Do you have someone at home that can give him his meds three times a day?"

Ashley's heart sank—this could not have come

at a worse time. She was in the middle of a murder enquiry and her mother had gone to her sister's in the south of France with her dad and they wouldn't be back for a couple of days. There wasn't any way Nathan could get time off work.

Tasha stood up. "It's okay, I'll be there with him."

"Tasha, I couldn't ask you to do that."

"I know you wouldn't but he was my responsibility. Please, Ashley, it's the least I can do."

"That's sorted then," George said. "I'll give you a list of how to care for him when I've got him ready, and please— Tasha is it?"

She nodded.

"Don't blame yourself, these things happen to the best of us. Getting him here as fast as you did meant he wouldn't have been in pain for very long."

"Thank you."

"No problem. Why don't you both grab a drink and I'll see you in a couple of hours. I'll arrange for the animal ambulance to take him home. I don't think he'd find the car too comfortable."

"Thanks, George," Ashley said as he walked back through the door. She turned to Tasha. "How exactly did you get him here?"

"I flagged down a car and the lady was kind enough to drive us here."

"Hearing something like that always restores my faith in human nature," Ashley said, grateful such a person just happened to be travelling along that stretch of road. "Tasha, I don't want you to feel obligated to look after him."

"I don't—"

"If you're absolutely sure, I'd be very grateful. My mum will be back from her sister's in a couple of days then she can come over and see to him."

"I'm glad that's settled. Do you think it would be for the best if I stayed at yours until then? That way I can be with him all the time. I know you're working late."

"Won't your aunt miss you?"

"Ashley, I'm twenty six years old and my aunt's in her late seventies, I don't think she'd even realise I'm gone."

"Brilliant," Ashley said, glancing down at her watch. She was meant to be going to see Amber's parents and by the looks of it was going tomorrow instead.

"Ashley, if you've got somewhere to be it's fine."

"Are you sure? It's just that I have to go and see the parents of the woman whose body was found yesterday."

"Yes, now go. Don't worry about Muffin, he'll be fine with me—I promise."

"You're a star, Tasha," Ashley said, reaching over and kissing her on the cheek.

"I'll see you later at home."

The sound of those words was like sweet music to Ashley's ears—Tasha waiting at home for her.

Chapter 24

Graham Brooks walked along the short hallway with his arm wrapped around the trembling body of his wife, rubbing her back as she whimpered as though in severe pain. Every few seconds he whispered to her words of comfort and encouragement to help her hold onto a faith that had long faded from his own life. The police had called him earlier that morning in relation to their missing daughter, Amber—it had been twenty five years since he had last seen his only child. Twenty five years when the pain began and had never stopped. How many times had he closed his eyes and prayed to God never to open them again.

Each night since she had gone missing he'd had the same dream of Amber dying in his arms and now that dream was coming to fruition. Only now she had died somewhere else and he hadn't been there to protect her. He fought the urge to burst out and cry— he needed to be strong for Kim, he was all that she was going to have left now, once they came and told them that their hopes had all been for nothing.

"I need to get some air," he said as he slowly removed his arm away from his wife and went out into the garden. They were going to be there any minute, the ones who were going to finally put an end to it all. The ones who were going to tell him Amber wasn't coming back. How did a parent prepare themselves for this? There wasn't a self-help guide on how to cope when your child is murdered. *Maybe I should write one myself,* he thought, but then he shook his head, *what would be the point? I'd have no words to fill it with.* He sat down on the bench and lit a cigarette, drawing so deeply on it, the lining of his throat burnt in the process.

He heard the soft footsteps of his wife, stopping directly behind him before placing a baseball cap over his head. "You'll burn yourself sitting out here and then what will Amber say," she said, her face tear stricken.

"Stop it, Kim! We both know that she is dead. We can't deny it anymore, she's dead, she's not coming back, not now not ever!"

"But the police didn't exactly say that did they, Graham, they have only told us they found remains. It doesn't mean it's Amber."

He patted her hand with his. "Yes, darling, you're right," he said, locking his cry inside his heart.

Ashley's felt her chest clogging up with sadness as she waited for the door to open. Two sets of parents in one week was something new to her. Dale stood quietly, his head down, his foot toying with a grey stone on the paved floor.

Finally, the door opened and they came face to face with Mr Brooks. Though their social status may have been substantially different than the Campbell and Carver's, the look of grief on his face was just the same. Someone had to break the awkward silence. Ashley started, "May we come inside Mr Brooks?"

"It wasn't her was it? She's still alive isn't she?" Kim interrupted, quickly walking up the hallway to stand by her husband's side. Ashley couldn't find the words to speak to her after seeing the expectation in her eyes. She could tell by the half slumped way Mr Brooks stood that he knew what they had come to tell them, but his wife—denial was written all over her face which made it even harder to break the news.

Relief flooded her when Dale began to speak. "It would be better if we stepped inside."

"No, I want to hear what you've got to say now."

Dale inhaled deeply. "We're sorry to have to tell you, Mr and Mrs Brooks, but the remains have been identified as your daughter's. That is all the information we can provide right now. We are very sorry for your loss." He spoke the words like a cardboard actor, his tone monotone all the way through, relaying bad news to parents was not his forte.

Kim turned towards her husband weeping. She reached out to clutch his hand. He held it briefly before letting it fall away. Ashley could see he was struggling to find the right words to say.

"I think it's best if we go inside Mr Brooks. We have a few questions we need to ask you," Dale said.

They slowly moved into the living room. The walls and tables were crammed with framed photographs of Amber, from childhood to her late teens—presumably up until she had disappeared.

"Mr Brooks, please don't interpret my need for information as being insensitive to your grief but if we're going to find the person that did this we need some answers," Ashley said.

"I know, I understand."

"Thank you. Now did Amber have a boyfriend?"

Graham shook his head.

"Were you strict about her seeing boys?"

"If you mean 'would she have gone behind our backs to see boys' the answer is no, she was a good girl, who loved her art and poetry, that's what meant the world to her," Kim Brooks said, glancing towards a picture of Amber smiling demurely into the camera.

"Okay," Ashley said. She had heard the same lines from other parents who wanted to believe that their children were still the innocent little beings that hadn't changed since birth. She herself had escaped down the drainpipe many a time when she was a teenager to see someone her parents didn't approve of. Only then it had been girls instead of boys. "On the day of her disappearance what plans had she made?"

"The same as every day. She went to college in the morning and she should have been home by tea time. When she wasn't, Graham went looking for her at the college. When he couldn't find her we went to the police."

Graham added, "They were convinced she was out with friends or with her boyfriend. They didn't believe us when we told them it was out of character for Amber not to come home. After a few days they started to take our claim more seriously."

"Have you still got any belongings of Amber's?"

"Only her books, all the rest of her stuff we eventually gave to charity."

"What types of books were they?"

"Poetry and art books."

"May I have a look?" Ashley asked.

"I don't know what you think you'll find in them, the police didn't bother before." Graham gave a quick glance at Kim who now sat quietly, hands in her lap.

"Well, I'm interested. Would you mind?" Ashley insisted.

"No, of course not, I'll go and get them," Graham said standing unsteadily. "Can I get you a cold drink or something?"

They both declined.

"Okay," he said, leaving the room.

Moments later he brought back a sealed brown box and lay it down in front of Ashley.

"Have you read these books?" Ashley asked, using the letter opener he handed her to slice open the tape.

"No, we could never understand any of that poetry business. It didn't make much sense to us," Kim replied.

Ashley smiled. "I know what you mean," she said as she brought four books out and handed them to Dale before dipping her hand back in to get some more. As she looked down she saw a handmade book.

"This is very pretty," she said, her fingers skirting over the top.

"Ah, that one is Amber's own poetry." Graham caught himself quickly. "I mean was Amber's."

"Do you mind if I read it?"

"It doesn't matter now does it," he said, turning away and sitting back down next to his wife.

Ashley turned the delicate pages of Amber's handwritten poetry book. Although she could never claim to be a literary critic, she knew quality work when she saw it. Amber was indeed a gifted writer. As she opened the next page something fell from it onto her lap—a dried rose. Picking it up, she looked intently at the old rose. On the page that it had fallen from she read the poem:

The forest green surrounding
Drowns beneath your gaze
I feel your heat
Stirring my soul from its dreamy haze
Power ripples across your skin
As you come to me and extend your hand
A perfect rose
To place my heart in your command,
And though we have only just met,
I feel as if I know you.
Even now, I ponder the ways
My fragile heart could show you
Just how much I love you
Beyond what words could ever explain.
The wild beat within my chest
Is now forever yours to tame.
This secret burns inside me
As I try to hide my yearning,
For no one yet can know
The way my soul is burning
With the need to be yours
And only yours.

Ashley closed the book gently and waited a few moments before she spoke. "Mr and Mrs Brooks, are you absolutely sure that Amber wasn't seeing anyone?"

"Absolutely," they replied in unison.

Ashley clamped her jaw together. Who wanted

to be the one to tell grieving parents their daughter had been keeping secrets from them. "I may be wrong," she said pausing carefully before choosing her words, "but according to this poem she'd met someone she'd fallen in love with."

"I don't understand," Graham said in a puzzled uncertain voice.

"In her poem she talks of meeting someone that she has basically lost her heart to." Ashley lifted the rose. "It seems this was a gift from him."

They remained silent, as if another blow would knock them right over.

"Look, I need to look into it as a possibility. Do you mind if I take Amber's book with me? I promise I will return it safely during the week," she said.

"Yes, by all means. Do you think this boy or man she was seeing had something to do with her murder?" Graham asked.

"I honestly couldn't tell you, Mr Brooks, but it's a start," Ashley said, slipping a card from the side of her jacket as she stood. "This has my direct number on it—please make sure you use it if you can think of anything."

***

"Man this sucks," Dale said, slamming his hand against the steering wheel. "Were those lazy bastards asleep on the job or what?" His face turned red.

"I know, Dale," Ashley said, shaking her head, agreeing with his frustration.

"First they search in the wrong place, then they miss valuable information. I mean why didn't anyone go through her writings? Surely that would have been one of the first things they would have done."

"I know, the way the whole investigation was run seems a little bit strange." Ashley made a mental note to check Amber's case file to see whether she had actually attended college that day. She was sure that the officers who were originally on the case would have done so but after the mess up with looking in the wrong place for Esther she wanted to double check.

"Well it's good to see things haven't changed. Those incompetent bastards are still at it today." Dale took a deep breath.

"You know there's nothing we can do about it, Dale, our hands are tied."

"That's where you're wrong."

"What'd you mean?"

"I'm leaving, Ash."

"What do you mean you're leaving? Leaving what?"

"The job—I've had it. I had a job interview as head of security at a West End hotel, I told them I'm taking it."

"Whoa, let's back peddle here a bit. You've already told them yes? And I'm just hearing about this now?"

"I'm sorry, Ash, this was really hard for me. Well quitting wasn't, telling *you* was. I stayed this long because of you, after . . . well you know what happened, but the way things are going down lately, it sort of pushed me over the edge."

"I've got to admit, I never saw this one coming." Ashley let out a deep sigh.

"I'm sorry."

"Don't be silly, I'm happy for you," Ashley said gently nudging him. "It's just a bit of a shock that's all. So have you handed your notice in yet?"

"I was waiting until next week. When things are a bit more settled with this case, but by the looks of it, nothing's going to change."

She leaned over and kissed his smooth cheek causing him to blush slightly.

"What's that for?"

"Just for being you."

Chapter 25

With her mind still on Dale's sudden announcement, Ashley slowly made her way up the path. She would miss him—he had been like her right arm since they started working together so many years ago, it would be like losing a brother. But she only wanted what was best for him and she would always support any decision he made. She pushed her front door open. *This is becoming quite a habit,* she thought as the fragrance of cooking hit her senses. She refrained from calling out as she didn't want Muffin to come rushing to her, which she knew he would, regardless if he was taking his last breath. Seeing the living room was empty she headed straight to the kitchen and found Tasha at the cooker with multiple pans on the go.

"Whatever you're cooking smells great," Ashley said as she neared her.

"I didn't hear you come in," Tasha replied, turning to her with a smile.

"I'm not surprised, cooking with that many pans must take a lot of concentration." For some reason Ashley felt like kissing her—the sort of action one normally did when they arrived home from work and found their partner looking irresistible. Dressed in a light blue summer dress and barefooted, she looked like she naturally belonged in her house.

"Here, taste it." Tasha spooned some of the red wine sauce and put it up to Ashley's mouth.

She leaned forward opening her mouth until the spoon disappeared inside. Ashley raised her eyebrows. "Hmm, that taste's delicious. Did you make it yourself?"

"I'd like to say yes but you've got Marks and Spencer's to thank, I'm afraid."

"It's the thought that counts," Ashley said remaining close to her. She didn't want to move away, they were so close yet so far away. "How's Muffin?"

"He's doing really well, he's asleep on the decking. The vet said he'd be quite sleepy for the rest of the day."

"I won't bother him then," she said, moving away and taking off her jacket.

"Would you like a drink?"

"I'd love one." Ashley placed the jacket on the door knob then took a seat on the stall.

"I hope you don't think I'm being forward but," Tasha said, moving towards the worktop and a slick looking silver machine, "I bought you a juicer."

"You did!" Ashley said, slipping off the stall and going to her side. She hadn't even noticed it, her eyes had been glued on Tasha. "Thank you," she said, resting her hand on her lower back and leaning in to kiss her cheek.

"My pleasure. I've filled your fridge up with lots of different fruits for you to try—I was hoping you'd replace your morning coffee with a juice."

Keeping her hand in place Ashley said, "I will. I always kept meaning to buy one but just never got 'round to it."

"I'll make one for you now if you like, unless you'd prefer a beer?"

"No, a juice would be great, thanks, Tasha."

"Okay, dinner will be ready in half an hour. I

hope you're hungry."

"Famished, I'll just go and get changed." Ashley reluctantly made her way upstairs to her room. Taking off her suit, she thought how wonderful life would be if she could come home to Tasha every day. She knew, though, there was no point wasting her thoughts on something that could never be. Tasha had firm commitments which had been in place long before she had ever met her and she would never ask her to change them. She just had to accept that they had met at the wrong time in their lives. As she headed to the shower her phone rang, she flipped it open.

"Hi, Mum how are things?" Ashley listened whilst her mum told her of all the activities her and her father had been up to. "Yes, everything's fine here and no we still haven't caught him. Yes, I'm eating very well, actually Tasha is just making dinner as we speak. Listen, can I ask you a favour? Muffin had a bit of an accident today. No, don't worry, he's fine, he's got a fractured leg. Could you look after him for a while at least until this case is over when I can get some time off? You just need to pop in for a few hours a day. That's brilliant, thanks, Mum. Okay, I'll see you in a few days." She finished the call and snapped the phone shut.

Feeling refreshed and sitting in the garden having finished her meal she sat back feeling satisfied.

"That was a very good selection of dishes you put together," Ashley said.

"You're such a charmer aren't you?"

"Oh, I forgot to tell you. My mum said she is

happy to take over looking after muffin when she gets back."

"Are you sure? I really don't mind."

"I'm positive. I'm sure you've got more important things to be doing than dog sitting."

"Okay, but if you need me for anything, let me know."

"I know we've only known each other a short time but you've done more for me than you'll ever know."

"The feeling is mutual, Ashley. It's crazy but I feel like we've known each other forever. Do you believe in reincarnation? Maybe we know each other from a previous life."

"It's just another one of those things that we'll never know the answer to." Ashley let out a little laugh.

"If it's true, I'm sure in my previous life I was my father's servant and he's come back to reclaim me in this lifetime."

"Is he still bothering you?"

"Yep," Tasha said, standing and clearing the table.

"Leave that I'll do it," Ashley said half rising in her seat.

"No you will not," Tasha said pressing her back down. "I've only got to put the plates in the dish washer."

"Okay, thank you."

Rinsing the plates before she put them in the rack, Tasha bit her bottom lip. As the days drew closer, the more unhappy she was becoming. If she hadn't made an excuse to leave the table she knew she would have cracked and told Ashley how she felt about her but she knew it wasn't fair on either of them. She was falling in love with Ashley—it was hard not to. She had found in her everything that she had desired in a woman and she was going to lose it all because of family commitments that had unwittingly been bestowed on her. She looked through the French doors at Ashley sitting beside Muffin, gently stroking his face. Their features lit by the subtle light of the candles. What she wouldn't give to change places with him, though without the fractured leg. When Ashley stood so close to her earlier, she had fought so hard not to touch her. She could never have imagined someone could have such an effect on her, but Ashley had—from the first day she'd laid eyes on her. She couldn't imagine her life without her now.

"Do you need any help?" Tasha heard Ashley call to her.

"No, I'm just finishing up," she called back, closing the door and making her way back to the garden and sitting on the floor opposite Ashley.

"He's going to get so spoilt by all this attention," Ashley said as Tasha began stroking him.

"Like he's not already," she said smiling.

Ashley eyes rose to meet hers, there was something unreadable in them. She opened her mouth as if to say something then stopped as if thinking better of it.

"How's your case coming along?" Tasha asked to fill the silence.

"I think we may have made a little progress. We

have a prime suspect who is on the run. And it seems like one of the victims may have been romantically involved with the killer. We've got officers interviewing her friends as we speak. Hopefully someone will have seen him and at least be able to give us a name. If it matches our suspect then it's over."

"That sounds promising."

"It's the first real break we've had in the case."

"I'm glad to hear it. Hey, listen I was wondering. I don't know if you'll have the time—what with everything but if you're not busy on Saturday, I've got a free pass for Newmarket. My aunt is a bit of a racing fanatic."

Ashley thought for a second—she had never been to a racetrack before and maybe the change of scenery would do her the world of good. "Sure, why not."

"Great, I'll let my aunt know."

As the time drew nearer to midnight the women decided to call it a night. They had spent the evening playing scrabble and just enjoying each other's company.

"I take it you'll be having the yellow room again," Ashley asked, with a laugh.

"Seeing as I've never been a creature of habit, I think I'll take the other one," Tasha said as they slowly walked along the hall together, their bare arms touching slightly. They stopped at Ashley's door.

"Goodnight then," Tasha said. "Don't worry about Muffin. I'll go down in a couple of hours to check he's okay."

"Thank you," Ashley said reaching out to her as

Tasha stepped towards her, stopping a foot away from her. Their eyes revealing everything their voices couldn't.

"Goodnight, Tasha," Ashley said softly as she leaned towards her and kissed her lips. Tasha remained still, her arms rising to Ashley's waist.

"We can't do this," Tasha said. "It's bad enough as it is, if we cross that line I don't think I'd be able to cope."

"I know," Ashley said drawing her into an embrace. "I know."

They held onto each other, neither wanting to let go but not having the strength to go any further. *At least we both know where we stand now,* Ashley thought as she released her and Tasha walked to her room.

***

The next few days went by in a flurry. Nobody knew or had seen Amber's love interest and Roger Collins was nowhere to be found. Although calls from the public were coming in thick and fast they were of no use to the investigation. It seemed once again the case had hit a dead end. Ashley's mum had taken over caring for Muffin the day before—she didn't realise how much she missed Tasha until she walked through the door and she wasn't there.

She was relieved when Saturday came around and the sun had shied away the clouds which had been threatening to cause a bleak day at the races. She'd met Tasha at the entrance to the track and was taken aback at how stunning she was. Dressed in a silk, free flowing dress with thin straps showing her toned shoulders, her tousled hair draping past her shoulders. She couldn't take her eyes off her.

Tasha led Ashley up to Riley Mile executive box—telling her it was a place her aunt always hired whenever she attended Newmarket and that she herself loved it for its unrivalled view of the Rowley Mile course. Champagne in silver ice buckets graced the white linen table cloths of the six circular tables that were set out in a row of two. Tasha's aunt's guests sat on the wooden chairs with blue upholstered padding, laughing and cracking jokes with each other in a friendly and familiar manner.

Tasha pushed open the door and Ashley raised her eyebrows. "When you said a day at the races, I was under the impression we were going to be in the paddock eating fish and chips out of newspaper wrappings."

Tasha laughed. "Thankfully, things have moved on from those days," she said as she put her arm through Ashley's and guided her towards the balcony. "I can't wait for you to meet my Aunt B."

Ashley picked out the woman at once—her resemblance to Tasha was so uncanny she could have been mistaken for being her mother and she definitely didn't look seventy five. Dressed simply in a flower patterned dress and low heels, she could have easily passed for someone twenty years younger. She turned when she heard Tasha's voice, her face beaming as though she was greeting a long lost relative. Ashley stood back while they embraced.

"Aunt B, I want you to meet Ashley."

Ashley stepped forward and held out her hand. "It's very nice to meet you, Ms Bleak, Tasha has told me so much about you."

"Likewise," she said giving her a warm welcoming smile. "Though I think Tasha talks way more about you than she could ever of me."

"Aunt B," Tasha said chidingly.

"Well, it's true and I can see why." Beryl glanced an appreciative eye over Ashley. Dressed in a white linen suit, she looked like she had just stepped from the pages of a magazine.

Ashley laughed. "Well, I hope it was all good."

"Oh yes, of course. Now, Tasha, go and get Ashley a drink while I show her how to pick a few winners." She took Ashley by the arm and walked her to her table at the front of the balcony.

"What an amazing view," Ashley said looking down.

"Yes it is. I've been coming here for over fifty years and it still excites me. There's nothing better than the thrill of horse racing and I mean nothing, if you get my drift," she said, nodding at Ashley knowingly.

Ashley smiled at her as she brought a pair of binoculars to her eyes and began to trace the movements of the horses.

"Come on, Sheila's Gal, come on," Beryl roared as the runners galloped towards the winning post. The crowds shouted below in delight as their Sheila's Gal passed the post first.

"That's my first winner of the day," Beryl said, smiling with a twinkle in her eye.

"Tasha was telling me, you're quite good at picking winners."

"I should be, I was a trainer for forty seven

years. Though I never had horses like Denman or Red Rum, my stable gave a lot of the big-money-men a run for their money."

"Here we go," Tasha said, handing Ashley a glass of bubbling champagne.

"Thank you," she said taking it. She was so glad she had said yes to coming out. She felt more relaxed than she had done in years and she had taken an instant liking to Tasha's aunt. *She seems to live life to the max*, Ashley thought as she watched her studying the form in her paper with the same intensity she herself did when going over case files. *Enough*, she rebuked herself firmly—there are seasoned officers working on the case, they have everything under control, she just needed to let go. After a few sips of champagne, that's exactly what she did.

"It's so nice to see you without a worried look on your face," Tasha said to Ashley after her aunt went to converse with friends.

"Are you saying I frown a lot?"

"No, not at all." Tasha placed her hand over Ashley's—they both looked down but neither removed their hand. "What I mean is, you just seem carefree at the moment."

"That's because I am," Ashley said lowering her gaze.

"Good, I'm glad."

"If I was your—" Tasha stopped abruptly and put her hand over her mouth.

"If you were my what?" Ashley asked.

"Nothing, I wasn't going to say anything. I think the mixture of the sun and alcohol are messing with my brain." Tasha raised her hand off Ashley's and took another sip of her drink.

"I'd really like to know what your messed up brain was thinking."

"Do you really?" Tasha asked, looking at her seriously.

"Yes, I think I do."

"If I was your partner, I would make sure you were carefree every day."

"That would be near enough impossible."

"Why's that?"

"Because you'd be thousands of miles away and that would only bring me sadness," Ashley said, breaking eye contact with her and looking down into her glass.

"Come on, you two. You're meant to be having fun, not sitting there moping about," Beryl said, bringing back a large plate filled with an assortment of canapés.

"Thank you," Ashley said as she took one filled with prawns and a seafood sauce. Sinking her teeth into it she groaned with pleasure. "Mmm, that is delicious," she said reaching over and offering Tasha a bite.

Opening her mouth and locking eyes with her, she bit into it.

"Mmm, you're right. I'll get the recipe and make them for you one day."

"Ashley, as much as I love my niece I would not recommend her culinary skills."

Ashley laughed. "I think she's got a good eye for dishes that go well together."

"Only because I used pre-packed food."

"Talking of which, Tasha, Angela has just

informed me that she won't be using her room at the The Old Mill hotel this evening and she asked me to ask you if you want it for the night—it's all paid for."

Tasha turned to Ashley. "Oh, Ashley you must say yes, the rooms there are amazing."

"I can vouch for that—you'll never experience a hotel like it again. You should both go and enjoy yourselves," Beryl confirmed.

"In that case, yes," Ashley said with a smile.

"Good, I'll phone Angela and let her know," Beryl said tucking into her bag retrieving her phone. "Please excuse me," she said, standing and wandered off to the end of the balcony to make a call.

"You don't feel pressured to stay the night do you?"

"Of course not. If it's as good as you say, I'd be a fool not to take advantage of it."

"Don't worry about the sleeping arrangements, there are two rooms."

"Who said I was worried?"

***

The Old Mill hotel was tastefully decorated with modern features but still managed to maintain the old charm of the century old building. Tasha excitedly showed Ashley around the suite—from the luxury walk-in shower room decked with marble tiles to the master bedroom with exposed wooden beams and a four poster to the king-sized bed draped in white linen.

"And this is to die for," Tasha said, sliding back a glass door in the living room and stepping out onto a secluded balcony with views of stately swans sailing along a river.

"Wow," Ashley said joining her and admiring the serene scene. "This really is something. The whole place is amazing."

"I'm glad you like it. I love staying here, it's so peaceful and so close to nature," Tasha said inhaling deeply.

"You're very lucky."

"I'm glad you're here to share it with me," she said turning to her.

"So am I."

"So," Tasha said clasping her hands together and leaning back against the rail, "what do you fancy to drink? Or would you prefer something to eat?"

"Oh, god no, I'm stuffed. I think I'll still be digesting all the food I ate today for a week. An ice cool wine would go down a treat, though."

"One white wine, coming right up. Take a seat." Tasha nodded towards the three-seater wicker chair.

Tasha popped inside leaving Ashley alone. For the first time in a long while she'd totally been at ease all day. She'd enjoyed Tasha's company immensely as well as her aunt's and coming back to such a beautiful hotel had been the icing on the cake. Not only was the room spectacular, she got to spend more time with Tasha. Returning with a bottle of wine and two glasses, Tasha flopped down beside Ashley, carelessly kicking off her sandals and bringing her legs to rest underneath her.

Ashley watched her as she poured the wine. She adored her carefree nature. She felt so close to her but sadness was always looming close by—it wasn't long now before Tasha would be getting on a plane, going to start a new life. One that she wasn't going to be a part of.

"Are you okay?" Tasha asked, frowning as she passed her a glass.

"Never better." Ashley smiled, brushing aside her depressing thoughts and taking a sip.

"You looked sad."

"Oh, it's nothing, some things just aren't meant to be," she said leaning over to rest the glass on the small table in front of them.

"That doesn't sound good. Are you thinking about work?"

"Nope," she said smiling, and it was the truth. Work had barely entered her mind all day which was a first for her. She was so caught up in the day she had felt like that other side of her didn't exist.

"I'm prying again, aren't I?"

"No you're not and I promise there's nothing wrong. Everything is . . . perfect."

"Good, I'm glad."

"Now, tell me all about your aunt and how she got her uncanny way of picking so many winners," Ashley said, changing the subject.

"Well, that's a long story," Tasha said. She talked about the extraordinary life her aunt had, rearing horses and also what a wonderful role model she had been in her life, replacing her mother in so many ways.

Hours later, with the hot summer evening drawing to a close, the sound of water flapping against the banks was at its faintest. Both women stared ahead at the crescent moon far in the distance.

"When my friend Charlotte and I used to stay

here when we were teenagers, we would sit out here all night, telling each other our fantasies," Tasha said.

"And you were surprised when she introduced you to swingers?"

Tasha laughed. "Well that was one fantasy that she never told."

"So what were yours?"

"Oh, just the usual, falling in love and how it would be the first time I had sex."

"Did it live up to your expectations?"

"Not really. We ended up on a single bed trying our hardest not to let her parents hear us in the room next door. It wasn't that exciting, if I'm honest. I wanted to do it in the open air."

"Really?"

"Yes, there's a sense of naughtiness about it—the thrill of being seen."

"You do know if I ever caught you, I would have to arrest you for indecent exposure."

"What if I was being indecent with you?" Tasha said, turning to her with a seductive smile.

Ashley felt her inhibitions disintegrate as she leant forward and pressed her lips to Tasha's. She could no longer contain herself as the weeks of sexual tension exploded inside her. They kissed deeply before Tasha drew up her silk dress to her waist and straddled her, trapping her between her legs.

"I've wanted to do this since the first day I met you," Tasha said, adjusting herself on the seat.

Ashley's arousal was evident in her face, as she pressed her lips against Tasha's throat, gently caressing her skin with the tip of her tongue. A delicate perfume of rose and pear water assailed her senses.

Pressing Ashley's shoulders back against the chair, Tasha looked at her with a strange mixture of fear and desire. "Are you sure you want this?" she asked, her face hovering inches away.

Ashley met her gaze unwaveringly. "Yes," she whispered as she tightened her grip around her waist, *it's too late to stop now*, she thought, her breath catching in her throat as she pulled her nearer, covering her mouth greedily and hungrily with her own and gently easing her lips apart with the tip of her tongue.

Tasha wrapped her arms around her neck drawing her closer until their bodies moulded into one. Ashley let out a sigh of pleasure as she felt Tasha's taut nipples pressing against her chest—the sensation she felt throughout her body made her even more eager to get closer to her—she could barely stand the agonising wait until their bodies would be together, skin to skin. That this moment had arrived filled her with a drunken excitement that made her senses whirl.

She entangled her fingers in Tasha's hair as their kiss deepened, the blood in their lips rushed and swollen.

Reluctantly breaking the kiss, Ashley asked, "Are you sure you want to stay out here?"

"Yes," Tasha answered, as her delicate fingers peeled away the thin straps from her shoulders in a slow and seductive manner until she revealed her nakedness.

"Touch me," she whispered, her breath hot against her ear.

She answered Tasha's need by slowly gliding her hand underneath her dress. The blood coursed through her veins and her hands trembled as Tasha rose up on her knees, her upper body rhythmically shifting up and down as she built up a momentum, their movements perfectly synchronised. Closing her eyes, Tasha gripped Ashley's shoulders, her back arching. The chair creaked beneath as Tasha's body began to convulse as a succession of spasms gripped her.

Tasha let out a cry before her head fell against her shoulder.

Ashley reached up and wiped away the damp hair plastered against her forehead.

"Well that's one of your fantasies accomplished. Do you have anymore?"

"Yes, to make love with you."

"That can easily be arranged, seeing as the bed is only a few feet away," Ashley said smiling.

"I wasn't talking about in bed," Tasha said with a faint smile playing on her lips.

"Where then?" Ashley asked, her voice faltering. She hoped Tasha wasn't going to drag her into the woods—there were certain things she would draw the line at— bugs and creepy crawlies did absolutely nothing for her, apart from make her scream.

Tasha stood up, taking Ashley's hand, guiding her to the bathroom. Ashley let out a sigh of relief—sex in the shower was something she could handle.

***

As dawn broke on a new day, both women lay naked in rumpled sheets.

"This feels so right," Tasha said, encircling in Ashley's arms.

"I know," Ashley said burying her face in the nape of neck.

"These past few hours have been perfect."

"In every way possible."

"Do you think we sound like a clichéd couple out of a romance story?"

"Who cares," Ashley said turning Tasha towards her. "It's true. I've never felt like this about anyone before."

Tasha looked up at her, examining her attentively before saying, "Me neither, I wish we could stay like this forever." She pulled her closer, her arms tightening around her waist.

"You have the stamina of an athlete," Ashley said, laughing as she bent her head to kiss her for the thousandth time. "It's going to be hard to say goodbye." She felt Tasha's body stiffen beneath her.

"Let's not talk about that," Tasha said, tears welling in her eyes.

"Hey," Ashley said, kissing away her tears. "I'm sorry. How about we do something nice today. What do you fancy? Anything you want."

"Anything?" she asked smiling through her tears.

"Yes, anything."

"How about we start off with going back to yours and spending some time in the hot tub."

"I can think of nothing I'd enjoy more. I'll call my mum before we leave here and tell her to make herself scarce," she said, wondering to herself if she was going to have the emotional strength to let Tasha go.

Chapter 26

"Something looks different about you," Dale said as Ashley jumped into the seat beside him.

"Really? I don't know what that could be," she said smiling.

He narrowed his eyes. "You've got like this—love glow thing going on. Did you have a good weekend?"

"Yes, yourself?" she said still smiling.

"It was alright. I watched a bit of tennis in the pub, went for a curry with the lads. What did you get up to?" He began to drive.

"I went to Newmarket racecourse."

"Really? I didn't know you liked racing."

"It's not somewhere I'd normally go, but the invitation was there so I took it."

"Who did you go with?"

"You remember Tasha?"

"I knew it. I knew it was only a matter of time. Oh my god—about she's only your dog walker," he said with a wide grin on his face.

"She was, is."

"Isn't this blurring the line a bit, you know employer and employee?" he playfully said, teasing her, "she might sue you for sexual harassment."

"That's highly unlikely."

"It was that good, huh," he said moving his eyebrows up and down.

"A lady doesn't tell, Dale, you should know that."

"Come on, Ash, I tell you about my"— he cleared his throat— "rendezvous."

Jade Winters

"Yes you do and not because I ask about them, you boast about them to anyone that will listen. Anyway I've been thinking."

"I'm surprised you had the time," he said cajolingly, as he turned the car onto the A10, heading towards the station.

As they walked into their office they barely had time to remove their jackets before Colleen burst in. Her normally composed features had a strained look.

"You are not going to believe this," she said.

"What's wrong?" Ashley replied.

"Uniform pulled over Roger Collins on a routine stop yesterday and brought him in. It seems he had good reason to run, his DNA came up as a match for a rape eight years ago."

"What about the Epping murders?"

She looked at her in dismay. "He's not our killer—the bastard is still out there."

***

With their number one suspect now off the list, they were back to square one. Ashley sighed as she settled back at her desk after the latest briefing. Everyone felt demoralised with the investigation, once again at a standstill. She switched her mobile phone back on—six missed calls from her mum.

"Hi, Mum is everything okay?"

"Yes, nothing to worry about, well not now anyway. I just popped round to yours to drop off your present and found poor Muffin locked in the living room in a frantic state. He's done a pee and number two. Wasn't he meant to have been taken out for a walk today?"

"Yes he was," Ashley said frowning. She didn't know what to make of it. When she'd left Tasha everything had been fine between them. Had she got cold feet?

"I'll call you back in a minute, Mum."

"Okay, love, make that half hour. We're going to take Muffin to the park for a run."

"Thanks, Mum, I appreciate it."

"I know you do, darling. I hope everything's okay with Tasha."

So do I, Ashley thought, but said, "I'm sure there's a reasonable explanation. There must have been an emergency." She hung up. *But wouldn't she have called me?* she thought as she dialled Tasha's mobile number. The phone went straight to voicemail. She didn't have her home number and the last thing she wanted to do was worry her aunt. If she'd had second thoughts about their relationship she was big enough to take the blow.

She dialled the number for Barking Mad and Polly picked up after the first ring.

"Hi, Polly, this is Ashley McCoy—"

"Ms McCoy, how are things? I hope you are happy with our service."

"Yes, very happy." *In more ways than one,* she thought.

"How can I help you today?"

"I was just wondering if you had heard from Tasha Hudson today."

"No—have you had a problem with her?"

"No not at all, she's fantastic. Has she been on her other rounds today?"

"Other rounds?" Polly said sounding confused.

"Tasha only walks your dog now, Ms McCoy. She has scaled back on her employment here as she is leaving in a couple of weeks. She thought it best that she gave up her rounds so we could have somebody trained and ready to replace her when she goes. Didn't she turn up to you today?"

"Yes she did, but I missed her, early start and everything. I just needed to clarify something with her about, um, another dog in the park. Okay, not to worry, thank you." Ashley hung up before Polly could ask any more questions. She let out a sigh. *This is why being single is for the best, no mind games.*

Picking up the phone again she dialled a number she knew off by heart. "Deborah, how are things?"

"Hey, Ashley, good, how about you?"

"Things are still hectic here as usual."

"I didn't ask about the job, I'm more interested in your well being."

"I'm doing fine, Debs, so there's no need to worry."

"You know, I'm always here to help you know. I know how hard things can be when—"

"Sorry, Debs, but I'm really pushed for time. The reason I'm calling has to do with an elderly lady I met during the course of a case. She's living on the 5th floor of a block of flats without a lift. She isn't in the best of health and the other day her neighbour, the one person she could rely on, has died. Is there any way of getting her moved?"

"Does she want to?"

"Yes, desperately but she doesn't think the council will help her. She thinks nobody cares about her."

"Email me her details, I'm sure I can arrange something for her. I'll pop round to see her and if she agrees I'll open a case for her. We can opt to get her moved on health grounds."

"That would be fantastic." It was not the first time Deborah had gone out of her way to help the vulnerable people Ashley came across in her job. As a senior social worker for the local council she was in the position to make things happen—and she did.

"So when are we meeting up? I haven't seen you in months."

"I know, we'll sort something out soon."

"You've got to stop blaming yourself, Ashley, it wasn't your fault."

"Yeah, I know. Look, I've got to dash, keep me updated about Mrs Baker, please."

"Okay, Ashley, I get the hint—just know that I'm here when you're ready."

She'd be waiting a long time if that was the case, Ashley couldn't envision a time when she'd ever be ready to discuss the Coleman case.

She tidied up her desk. There was nothing left to do at the office, she would just have to wait until she saw Aaron again and see if she could force a lead out of him.

Chapter 27

"It's lovely thank you, mum," Ashley said holding the large sundial her mother had brought her from the garden centre.

"I thought it would look lovely in the garden."

"I hear your dog walker's gone AWOL," Nathan said, biting into a burger, tomato sauce escaping from the sides and running down his mouth.

"No she hasn't, she had a family emergency. Here wipe your mouth," Ashley said handing him a napkin.

"Oh, so you heard from her then, that's good," Sandra said.

"Do you want a beer, Ash?" Nathan asked as he rested his burger on his plate and strolled into the kitchen.

"No, but can you pour me a large glass of wine, please."

"What's the matter, darling? You only ever drink wine when you're depressed."

"It's nothing."

"Don't give me that, young lady."

"Leave the girl alone, Sandra, she doesn't want to talk," Ray said from underneath the hat he had pulled over his face.

"You're a man, darling you don't understand women's issues. Now come on, Ashley, is this about that ghastly case you're working on at the moment?"

"No."

"Because if it is, you should ask them to give it to someone else. Honestly, expecting you to solve a case that's nearly the same age as you."

Ashley laughed. "Mum, it's nothing, I promise."

"Ash," Nathan called out from the kitchen.

"Yeah."

"Why's there a mobile phone in the bin?"

"Aye?"

"Look," Nathan said, stepping out into the garden handing her a glass of wine and a phone. It was Tasha's phone with its unique dog paw print patterned cover, with what looked like droplets of blood.

"Nathan!" Ashley shouted jumping up. "Get me a sandwich bag out of the drawer and don't touch anything in the kitchen, nothing! Just come straight out here!"

"Why?" he asked frowning.

"Just get it and do what I ask!"

Nathan hurried into the kitchen and brought back the bag.

"Open it."

He did as she asked and he gently tossed the phone into the bag.

"Ashley, what is it? Whose phone is it?" Sandra asked.

"Tasha's." Ashley clutched the phone in the bag as a wave of nausea hit her. Had Tasha been attacked in her home? Was she still upstairs? She had gone straight to the garden when she had arrived home from work, she hadn't checked upstairs. Why would she? She'd thought Tasha had gone home. "Nobody go back into the house," Ashley stated as she threw herself into action, almost falling over Muffin who lay contented on the floor. As she ran up the stairs, taking two steps at a time, she reached the outside of her bedroom in less than thirty seconds. "Tasha!" she called out loudly as she pushed open the door. She froze when she noted that the bed was still unmade and Tasha's clothes were in the exact position on the floor where they had been the night before. She was alert enough to remember that she might be standing in the middle of a crime scene and was careful not to touch anything as she crossed over to the built in wardrobes and nudged them open with her foot. A short flood of relief ran through her when they still contained her clothes. *Where the hell is she?* Ashley thought as she hurried into the hallway, throwing open the doors to the other bedrooms and bathroom. They were all tidy and looked untouched. What could have happened to her? Did she have an accident downstairs? Had she banged her head and was now walking about lost and confused? But why would she have thrown her mobile in the bin? It didn't make sense. Had she been caught up in the middle of a burglary? Her blood ran cold. Someone had been here and for whatever reason, they had taken Tasha and right from under her nose.

Minutes later she was out of her house and driving along the deserted road. She pushed her foot down harder on the accelerator, willing the car to go faster. She had just spoken to her friend Nelson at the forensics lab, he was waiting for her so he could check the phone for prints. Ashley had called Colleen who was on her way home when she heard her frantic call for help. She'd swerved her car around and headed back to the station. She had arranged for forensics to go over to Ashley's house and look for evidence. Dale was already on his way to meet her at the lab. Ashley cursed herself. Why hadn't she double checked the lock on the back door before she left for work? She had been so caught up in the rosy coloured affects of the weekend her guard had been down. She had not been paying attention. She, more than anyone, knew what happened when one took their eye off the ball—anything could happen and it had.

The Forensic Services Laboratory was housed in a large non-descript building next to the police station. Dale's silver car pulled up beside her as she switched off her car engine. She jumped out of the car, picking up the mobile phone gently as though she were handling a new born child. Within seconds Dale was by her side and they were walking towards the large glass door of the building.

"Now tell me what happened again?" he said as he held the door open for her.

"I left Tasha in bed this morning. Everything was fine. I'd not been able to reach her all day so I thought maybe she had second thoughts about things. I didn't really read too much into it." She pushed open the swing doors. "Nathan found her phone in the bin. I stayed down stairs when I got home from work so I didn't know that her clothes were still on the floor where she'd left them."

"Were any items missing?"

"My white dressing gown, and that's it, her shoes are still there as well."

"Was your house locked up?"

"Yes . . . no. I don't know or remember. We were in the garden last night, I can't remember if I locked the back door. Why would someone randomly break into my house and take Tasha with them? It doesn't make sense. What if they hurt her and they took her to hide the body?"

"Come on, Ash, let's not get ahead of ourselves. You need to pull yourself together, you're not going to be able to help her if you're running around like a headless chicken."

Nelson was waiting at the door for them. Ashley thrust the bag into his hand. "Wait here, I've set the machine up, go and grab a coffee. I'll find you when I've finished," Nelson said.

"I have an idea where she might be—I'll be back as soon as I can," Ashley said, as she ran to her car, jumped in and opened the glove compartment. Taking out a slip of paper, she punched the address into her sat nav, put the car in gear and sped away.

***

Ashley turned the car at high speed into a side street where most of the houses looked as though they were decaying—crumbling brick work, tileless roofs, broken windows and graffiti littered doors was the common theme amongst them all. She felt as if she had left civilisation and wandered into no man's land. She brought her car to a screeching halt outside one of the dilapidated houses and was out of the car in seconds, climbing the fragile stairs two at a time. Reaching the door, she rapped her knuckles against the thin plywood that threatened to engulf her hand if she applied any more force.

"Open up," she yelled upon hearing muffled footsteps behind the door. "Police!"

The door opened a crack and a young woman, who couldn't have been more than eighteen, with large dilated pupils, stared mindlessly into Ashley's eyes. "Where's the fire?" she asked, her words coming out as though they were being forcibly dragged out one by one.

"Where's Claire Smith?"

"Who?" she said with a drawl.

Ashley had a faint notion that she would be there all day trying to get any sense out of the woman. Pushing past her she stepped into what looked like a disaster zone. The piles of rubbish and debris were so overwhelming she had to inch her way in to get to the first door which she presumed would have been the living room. The floor was covered with free-basing paraphernalia, broken glass, beers cans, wine bottles, cigarette butts and several bodies which looked like they had slept wherever they had passed out.

"Tasha!" Ashley shouted at the top of her voice waiting a few seconds for any form of movement before moving onto the next room where the scene was more of the same.

"Hey, what's with all the noise?" Claire called out, running down the stairs, oblivious to the fact that she was naked, her red hair swaying over her breasts.

"Where's Tasha?" Ashley asked her in a frenzy as she reached the ground floor, spinning her round by the shoulders and pinning her against the wall.

"What the fuck are you on about? How would I know?"

The anger hung in the air between them like an invisible dagger.

"Don't fuck with me, Claire. Where is she?"

"I don't know, I swear," she cried.

"I'm Tasha's friend. What's happened to her?"

Charlotte asked appearing at the top of the stairs.

Ashley slowly took her eyes off Claire and trained them onto Charlotte. "Charlotte, is she here?"

Her eyes held the expression of a startled fawn. "No, why, what's happened?"

"She's missing." Ashley's expression was pained, as though just saying the words wounded her.

Claire's features twisted into a maddening leer. "Well, she isn't here, check the whole god damn place if you don't believe me."

"You threatened her."

"Jesus, you took that seriously. What do I look like, the mafia? It was an empty threat, you know, something that's said in the heat of the moment."

Ashley loosened the pressure on her chest as Charlotte came to stand beside her. "She's telling the truth, we've all been here all night. I wouldn't lie to you, Tasha's my friend, too."

"Is she? You could have fooled me. If this is what you traded your friendship in for, then God help you. Look around you, can't you see she was trying to help you from making the biggest mistake of your life. Can't you see they're using you?"

"We don't even want her here, she's more trouble than she's worth. She's the one always begging to come round."

"Not anymore," Charlotte said as if coming to her senses at long last. "Does Aunt B know she's missing?"

"No."

"I'll tell her and stay with her until you find out where Tasha's gone."

"I'm sure she would appreciate that, Charlotte."

Turning back to Claire Ashley sneered. "If I find out—"

The sound of her mobile preceded her next words. "Dale, anything?"

"Get back here we'll have the results in half an hour."

After what seemed an age, Nelson walked out from the lab, a piece of paper in his hand.

"Did you lift any prints?" Ashley demanded.

He nodded. "Three sets, two are unidentified and one," he said, handing her the sheet of paper, "matched the prints of the woodlands killer."

Chapter 28

The man cursed himself. *How could I have made such a stupid mistake?* He leaned over to look at the unconscious body of the young woman he had in his backseat. He'd got the wrong one. After all the meticulous planning he'd totally messed up. He didn't quite understand how he'd missed the detective. Her car was still parked outside her house and he had only been gone five minutes max to relieve himself up against a wall around the corner. Getting into the house had been easy. It never failed to amaze him how stupid people were. It was as if the sun made them lose their sense of awareness. That they had the misconception that people only broke into their homes in the winter. That's when they barricaded their houses. In the summer, they left their backdoors and windows open like they didn't have a care in the world.

He grew angrier as he recalled his failed plan. His intention was to take the police woman. He hadn't realised his mistake until it was too late. She'd had her back to him when he entered the bedroom. She'd turned around before he'd reached her, which was a big mistake on her behalf—she'd seen his face which meant she was then a liability. He had grabbed her and she had bitten him with such ferocity he'd had to let go. She managed to run past him and get to the kitchen where she picked up her phone from the counter and started to dial but he was too quick for her. One sucker-punch to the face was all it had taken to knock her out cold. Her blood had squirted from her nose onto the floor which he'd had to clean. When she'd started to mumble something incoherent he made a split decision. Whoever she was he couldn't leave her there, she'd be able to identify him and he'd be locked away. There was no way he was going to prison, he'd rather be dead. Besides he wanted to have a bit of fun with her—she wasn't the detective but she'd do. He started to regret throwing her phone in the bin now but he'd been worried they'd be able to track her signal.

He heard her let out a painful moan, she'd be coming round soon. He felt a deep hatred run through him for the man who had been responsible for all of this—for bringing him back out of hiding. He'd put his past behind him, trying to live a normal life. It hadn't been easy, the demons still beckoned him but he had fought it—until now. He knelt on his seat and stared down at the side of the woman's face, his eyes travelling down to her neck noticing her throbbing vein. The sight ignited in him a flame that he thought he'd extinguished years ago.

Chapter 29

For the first time in her life Ashley needed someone to lean on. Her legs were limp, her vision blurred. It was as if someone had dealt a blow to her head with a hammer.

"He's going to kill her, isn't he?" was her sole question to Dale as they crossed the car park.

"We don't know that." But his voice didn't relay confidence.

"What am I going to do?"

"You need to go home, Ash, you're in no fit state to work."

"I can't go back there, I feel like this is all my fault. I need to be doing something."

Dale stopped walking and took her firmly by the shoulders. "Listen to me, Ashley," he said sternly. When she failed to meet his gaze he tilted her chin up and noticed the tears in her eyes. "Nobody is going to be killed, least not Tasha. Do you hear me? You need to let us get on with trying to find her. You need to step back and get your head in order—you're not helping her like this."

"If anything happens to her it will be my fault!" she cried impulsively. "How could I have let this happen!" Breaking away from him, she leaned against the car resting her elbows on the roof, gripping her hair in her hands.

Dale stood idly by her side for a few moments before encircling her waist and guiding her around to the driver's side of the car. "Nothing's going to happen to her—we need to come up with a plan to move forward."

Ashley nodded as she wiped the tears away from her eyes. "You're right. I think we need to search the forest—you never know, he might be stupid enough to take her there. I'm going to go and see Aaron then I'm going to go home for a few hours in case the bastard rings me. He might call me and let me know what he wants."

"Do you want me to come with you?"

"No, you speak to Colleen about the search. I need to speak to Aaron alone. Maybe he'll be a bit more cooperative."

"Alright, I'll call you the minute I hear anything."

"Thanks, Dale."

He leaned forward and held her tightly. "Don't lose faith," he said in a choked voice, before releasing her and hurrying off to his car.

***

"I'm coming, I'm coming," Aaron called out in response to Ashley's incessant banging on his front door. "I hope no one else has been found."

"We need to talk," she said, pushing her way past him.

"Do come in," he said talking to her back as she passed him.

"So, what can I help you with now, Detective? Has another body been found?"

Ashley fought to control herself. "Aaron, please listen to me."

"I'm listening," he said sitting on the arm of the chair.

"The person"—she struggled with the words—"who is responsible for the remains we found, has been to my house and taken someone very special to me."

"What!" Aaron leapt up from his chair. "What do you mean taken her?"

"Exactly what I said. Her bloody phone was found dumped in my bin and the clothes she was wearing were still at my place. He has her somewhere and she's only wearing my dressing gown."

"When did this happen?" Aaron said moving to stand in front of her.

"A couple of hours ago, the fingerprints were matched off her phone to his."

"Oh, my God," he said swirling round. "This is very unfortunate for you and for her."

"Please, Aaron I'm begging you, if you know where he's taken her, please tell me!"

He studied her intently, his expression unreadable.

"Please don't tell me you don't know who it is, this has gone far enough—he will kill her, Aaron. Do you want her blood on your hands?"

"How can it be my fault? I told you from the beginning, Ashley, spirits talk to me, not the killers. I'm sorry but there's nothing I can do for you."

"You're really going to let him get away with this, aren't you."

"Ashley, I think I have proved myself to be a reliable source. Not only have I brought to your attention the whereabouts of two bodies I also brought a message from someone you once loved."

"Don't start all that again."

"Look, I'm sorry, if I could help you believe me I would, but I swear to you I have no idea who is responsible for the killings or who has taken your friend."

"I will get you for this, Aaron, mark my words."

She drove home on autopilot, an endless stream of tears forming like puddles at the bottom of her eyes, rendering it difficult to see more than a few feet ahead of her. The pain she felt emotionally was almost unendurable. She barely managed to get to her front door her legs felt so weak. What a difference a few hours could make. Just yesterday she had been the happiest she'd ever been in a long time and now—now she was at her lowest. The house was quiet, forensics had left, Muffin was with her mum and she was all alone. She had never felt this way before not even after Melissa had died.

She heard a sound coming from the living room. Her body straightened, her eyes alert as she crept towards the room. The door opened and Nathan walked straight into her letting out a scream as he saw her.

"Oh, my God, I didn't hear you come in," he said, placing a hand over his chest.

"I'm sorry," Ashley said dully. "What are you still doing here? I thought you went home with Mum and Dad."

"And leave my big sis? Never." Nathan enveloped her within his arms.

"Thanks, Nat," she said, sounding muffled against his chest.

He held her at arm's length. "Come into the kitchen," he said brightly.

She followed him and sat on a stool.

"Do you remember when we were kids and

Mum used to make us the best hot chocolate in the world when we were upset about something?"

Ashley nodded. "With extra marshmallows."

Nathan laughed. "And I always used to pinch yours when you weren't looking."

Ashley half heartedly laughed at the memory.

"Well," he said, opening the cupboard and taking down a jar of chocolate and two large mugs, "I'm playing Mum today and I come with a full supply of marshmallows." He shook the bag of marshmallows.

"I don't think I've got any milk."

"Yes, you have," he said, opening the fridge door which was stocked with food. "I'd like to take credit for it but Mum and Dad went shopping, but I unpacked it all." Nathan grinned.

"I always did tell you that you had hidden talents."

"And a lot more, sis, with your help and encouragement I'm the man I am today," he said seriously. "And I'm going to be here until she walks through that door, and I have no doubt that she will, because my sister is the best detective around and if anyone will find Tasha, it's you."

"Thanks, Nat," she said her eyes welling up again.

"This is not the time to be mushy, sis, you need to drink this then get some sleep. You need to be on top of your game tomorrow—every second is going to count."

Chapter 30

"Have you got a minute?" DCS Ripley asked.

"Sure, come in," Colleen said, closing the file she was reading. "Is anything wrong?"

"I'll get straight to the point, shall I?"

"Of course."

"It's about McCoy."

"What about her?"

"What about her? I've just heard that the missing woman has been linked to her . . . romantically. Not only that but she was taken from McCoy's house."

"With all due respect, sir, I don't see what bearing that has on Ashley."

"Well, you must have a very short memory, Colleen. Shall I jog it for you?"

"I don't think that's nec—"

He spoke over her. "If I recall, not so long ago, McCoy was involved in another case where she let her emotions get the better of her and she nearly brought this office down with her."

"Actually," Colleen said standing, "that's not true. If *I* recall rightly, she nearly brought *you* down, we were just following orders that you gave us."

He turned suddenly, his face reddening. "Orders I believed were the right ones. I had a decision to make and I made it. I would do it again if I had to," he said, slightly raising his voice. "And I have not come here to resolve any guilt, I've come to talk to you about one of your officers *again*." He walked over to her desk, placing his palms flat on the table and leaned inwards. "Let's get one thing straight. McCoy is a loose cannon, she always has been. The only reason she hasn't been kicked off the force is because she has been under your wing, but no more, no more, do you hear me? I want her off this case, off it immediately!"

"Or what?"

"What do you mean 'or what'?"

"What are you going to do if . . . when I *don't* remove her?"

"Well, we'll just have to see about that, won't we," he said straightening up and adjusting his tie.

"*Ian*," Colleen said moving around her desk and standing beneath his skinny frame, "you don't scare me and I don't appreciate you coming into *my office* and making idle threats. You think you've got clout, think again. You stand for nothing. I would rather have Ashley watching my back than a thousand of you. Now, if you don't mind, *sir,* I have got work to do."

He stood motionless as though he were glued to the spot. "This is not the last you're going to hear of this."

She smiled. "Somehow I think it is and it's the last I want to hear of you regarding Ashley," she said side stepping him and walking to the door and opening it. "And if you know what's good for you, you'll leave her well alone. You really don't want to have the past raked up again. I don't think your reputation could withstand such tight scrutiny."

"You wouldn't?"

"Do you want to bet on it?"

"But you would be committing a career suicide."

"I would rather go down than have this team involved in another mess of your making—the choice is yours."

"You're a fool, a bloody fool. That woman will break you one day. You just mark my words."

"What, like we nearly broke her?" Colleen asked sadly as he whisked past her.

Chapter 31

Two hours later, Ashley was still staring at the ceiling. Hugging the pillow to her chest, she could still smell Tasha's scent. All of Tasha's clothes and the bedding had been removed by forensics. She knew what they were looking for and she prayed to God they wouldn't find it. She felt like she was in a bad dream where she would wake up any minute, tell Tasha all about it and they would laugh it off as being improbable. She tried to still her over active mind but it wouldn't let her rest. *This is what it must be like when an addict needs their fix*, she thought as the questions kept prodding at her. *Why had this happened? Why Tasha?* She had nothing to do with the case, she didn't seem to fit the profile of the victims who had been murdered so far. They had been young girls—teenagers. Tasha was a grown woman and she had been taken from her house, not from the street. How would he have even known who she was? Was she even his intended victim? She shot up in her bed—*my God did he think she was me?*

Ashley swung her legs over the bed and headed for the shower, her heart beating fast. She saw a glimmer of hope—maybe he wasn't going to harm Tasha. It was time for the other part of her—the trained detective, to take control. It was the only way she was going to save her.

Twenty minutes later she quietly let herself out of the house, not wanting to wake Nathan. He would only try and persuade her to get a few more hours rest. Within minutes she was speeding towards her office, her mind alert and focused—she had missed something, she was sure of it, she didn't know what but she knew she would not rest until she found it.

She stood at the doors threshold watching Dale study a file he held within his hands. She felt a lump rising in her throat. He was still wearing the same clothes from the previous day and looked exhausted. He looked up startled, taking a second look as if he was seeing a vision.

"Ash, what are you doing here?" he said, standing up.

"I need to be here."

"What if he calls?"

"I've diverted my calls to my mobile. Have you found anything?"

He shook his head. "No, not yet."

"What files are you reading?"

"Colleen thought it would be a good idea to go through all of the tipoffs that have been called in."

"Colleen? Where is she?"

"In the incident room. She's been here all night."

"Are you kidding?"

"No, she's really worried about you, we both are."

"You've got nothing to worry about. Tasha is going to be fine, I'm sure of it. I think he came looking for me—there's no reason for him to harm her, not yet anyway."

"Come on, let's go and see Colleen, fill her in with what you think."

They walked quickly through a set of white swing doors and into the incident room, which was buzzing with activity. The large space resembled a conference room. A large oval table, which could seat at least sixteen people, was in the middle of the room. The few empty chairs around revealed blue soft padded upholstery. Colleen made a beeline towards her.

"I wondered how long it would take for you to come in. Are you feeling okay?" she said in a tone that carried sympathy.

"Not really, but my mind is clearer."

"That's the most important thing," she said squeezing her arm. "I'm going to do everything in my power to help you get through this and bring Tasha home alive. I'm not going to let you down again."

"What about Ripley?"

"Fuck, Ripley!"

"Thanks, Colleen, I appreciate it."

"The last time, I—" Colleen paused briefly. "I want you to know that I was powerless to do anything."

"I know."

She sighed deeply. "I know now I should have done more. I should have stood up to Ripley and I should have stood up for you."

"It doesn't matter now. It's all water under the bridge."

"Is it?"

"I can't think about that at the moment." Ashley glanced to the floor.

"Okay, so have you thought anymore about yesterday?"

"I've done nothing but think about it."

"Was there anything out of the ordinary? Any unfamiliar cars parked near your house?"

Ashley squeezed her eyes shut before shaking

her head. "Nothing." She hadn't seen the dark car again after the first sighting.

"Okay," Colleen said. "We need all hands on deck. Grab yourself some files and take them back to your office where you can concentrate. We've had over two hundred tips—it's proving a slow process getting through them all."

"I'll get right on it," Ashley said, giving Colleen a faint smile before grabbing a box of papers and heading back to her office.

Chapter 32

Tasha came to in a chilly darkness. The foul stench of rotting wood and damp soil permeated the room and nauseated her with every breath. Her face throbbed in rhythm with her pounding heart. Quickly moving her hand in an attempt to touch her face, she felt the coarse texture of rope around her wrist tugging it back to where she lay.

As the realisation hit her she frantically pulled against her bindings, her back scraping against a splintered surface through the dressing gown she wore, only serving to increase her discomfort. She tried to scream but her cries were muffled by the tape fixed across her mouth. She desperately fought to suck in the dank air through her nostrils as fear gripped her.

Calm down, she thought, *panicking is only going to make it worse.*

Managing to slow her breathing, she turned her head sideways—her eyes darting around the room searching for any glimpse of light—anything to give her an inkling of where she was. She saw daylight barely streaming beneath what appeared to be a door. Shadowy movements eclipsed the pale glow, again intensifying the terror within her.

Who is he? Why would he do this? Tears welled in her eyes as she yanked more aggressively against her restraints. A feeling of elation overcame her as she managed to free one of her feet.

Come on, come on. You can do this!

Using her free foot, she worked hard to loosen the tie on the other foot. Adrenaline took over as she fought through the pain and finally broke free.

Yes!

She brought her knees up to her chest and took a deep breath in through her nose, trying to relax herself after the exertion. As the pain subsided she lowered her legs and began working on freeing her hands. After what seemed a lifetime, she managed to slip free of one binding and then the other. She ripped the tape from across her mouth and gasped deeply. Slowly, she eased herself off what appeared to be a table and onto a wooden floor. She moved a step at a time, gingerly reaching out with her arms outstretched in front of her, as she crept towards the door, careful to not make a sound with her feet. She touched the door tentatively and then placed her ear against it. A draft of cold air blew from underneath, briefly stinging her injured ankles. She strained to hear any noise—nothing, there was not a sound. She hesitated—what if it was a trick? What if someone was waiting outside the door? As a precaution she stooped down and peered through the gap under the door. She could see nothing. Confident there was no one out there, she slowly turned the door knob and finding the door unlocked, opened it slightly. Light filtered into the room, illuminating the wooden table to which she'd been tied and a stack of logs next to it. Outside, dense woodland surrounded the small shed, to her right she noticed a larger cabin with a car parked in front of it.

He must be in there, she thought as she moved stealthily towards the car in the hope that the keys were still in it. Keeping low to the floor, she reached out for the driver's side door, gently easing it open. Hanging from the ignition, were a set of keys.

Thank God! Tasha thought, before feeling a large hand clamp onto her shoulder.

Chapter 33

"It seems Aaron David has set a precedent," Ashley said as she set aside a statement from another helpful do-gooder who claimed he could talk to the dead. "Apparently this one wants to see the autopsy pictures so he can get a better feel for the victim."

"There are some weirdos out there," Dale said looking up at her.

"Tell me about it."

"Well, my box is done—nothing stands out. Most are claiming an ex killed a couple of the victims."

"Are they worth checking out?" Ashley asked.

"No," he said, yawning and rubbing his hand over his face.

"Why don't you go home and get some sleep, Dale, you look like you're about to drop."

He shook his head. "I won't be able to sleep. I'll just kip in my chair for an hour then have a coffee."

"Are you sure?"

"Yep, you carry on reading. Wake me if you find anything."

Ashley felt despondent, she was near the bottom of the files and there had been nothing—two hundred calls with no fresh leads. But she couldn't lose hope. She dipped her hand in the box and brought out another sheet. As she began to read her heart skipped a beat. "Dale," she said quietly. "Dale."

He jerked up, dazed. "What is it? What have you found?"

"This," she said thrusting the paper at him. "Someone's daughter called in two days ago. She said her mother called the hotline when Esther first disappeared in '84, she said she saw her the day she went missing."

"So, lots of people said that."

"Dale, this woman claims Esther spent an hour in her mother's house."

"Which means? I'm either thick or too tired to follow where you're going with this."

"Her call was never followed up. Nobody even went to talk to her. If she was the last person that saw Esther alive, she may have told her something."

"Let's go," Dale said jumping out of his chair. "Where does she live?"

"Ten minutes from Epping Forest."

Ashley smiled her first real smile of the day as they waited for Mrs Patterson to open the door. It was seven thirty in the morning and she had called down from her bedroom window to say she had to make herself decent first.

"I've got a good feeling about this," she told Dale as she moved from foot to foot on the doorstep.

"You'd better calm down, we both look like we're high on something."

The door opened and a tall woman in her late seventies stood in a pair of black trousers and a lemon coloured blouse. "I hope I didn't keep you waiting too long."

"Not at all," Ashley said.

"Please come in."

She walked them through to a sunny living room which overlooked a well maintained garden. "Can I get you both something to drink?"

"No, thank you. Now, Mrs Patterson, it's very important that you tell me everything that you can remember about the day you last saw Esther Campbell."

"Of course, dear, if somebody would have turned up twenty five years ago I could have told them then."

Ashley and Dale took a seat on the floral print sofa.

"Well, now, where to begin. Yes, I'd just returned home from hospital not long, I'd been in an accident and broke my leg," she began. "I was walking home from the shops, struggling with a few shopping bags when a young woman approached me and asked if I needed some help, well of course I said yes, nobody else had offered. So she walked me home and came in for a cup of tea."

"Okay," Ashley said, trying her hardest to remain patient. "So what did you talk about?"

"Well, it was her doing most of the talking, seemed she lived a very interesting life and she had met a very handsome young man that she said she was going to marry. I can't remember his name now. What was it?"

"That's okay, so what else did she say?"

"That she was on her way to Epping Forest for the afternoon."

"Did she mention if she was going to meet anybody there?"

"No, if I remember rightly she had some decisions to make. I remember her vividly, like it was yesterday, such a pretty little thing she was."

Ashley's heart sank—this didn't seem to be leading anywhere. "Do you have any children, Mrs Patterson?"

She shook her head. "Sadly me and Alfie were never blessed with any. Mind you, even without them we had a good marriage. God bless him, salt of the earth he was, married fifty years, lost him this year."

"I'm sorry to hear that," Ashley said, meaning it. "So was there anything else you can think of that stood out to you?"

"No, I'm afraid not."

Ashley suppressed a sigh as she stood. "I take it the information wasn't much use to you then."

"Yes it was, at least we know where she was in the hours before she went missing." Ashley closed her notepad—she had written nothing.

"Nice garden," Dale said as they left the room.

"Thank you. That's one thing my Alfie never minded spending money on was the garden, everything had to be the best, from the soil to the flowers. He even vetted the gardeners to make sure they were the best," Mrs Patterson said opening the door for them.

"Well, thanks again."

As they stepped through the door she called out to them. "I suppose it's nothing, dear, but when I was making the tea I overheard her talking to my gardener, Miles, about her love of trees, especially the Silver Birch."

Chapter 34

The deeply lined face of the man with thick lips and a face tanned and roughened by exposure to the outdoor elements loomed over her, the dim light behind making him look even more sinister. "So, you thought you could get away from me did you?" he said, roughly pushing her down on the wooden table, his steely eyes roaming over her legs when the dressing gown fell to the side.

"Who are you? What do you want with me?" Tasha blurted out as she felt splinters sticking into her back as she wriggled trying to escape his grip. With one hand he effortlessly pinned her to the table by her neck, squeezing on her windpipe with powerful thick fingers. She clawed at them, trying desperately to release the pressure so she could breathe, her legs flailing in the air.

"Will you shut up if I remove my hand?" he asked.

With what neck movement she could manage Tasha tried to signal yes. Gasping for breath as her throat became free he wasted no time quickly tying her hands.

"There will be time for questions later on but for now I want answers," he said as he tightened the last piece of rope to her wrist.

She grimaced. "Anything, just please don't hurt me." She decided to play the hapless victim—she was terrified and didn't want to antagonise him any further.

"What's your name, little lady?"

Her throat felt sore and as dry as sandpaper.

"Tasha."

"Tasha, and how old are you?"

"Twenty six." She choked.

"Hmmm, now tell me what were you doing at that house?" he asked oblivious to the pain he had caused her.

"I . . . I was visiting—" Her brain stalled. Should she tell him the truth? That she was with the woman she loved. She decided against it, for all she knew he could be a maniac with a hatred for gays. "A friend," she finally said when her brain reengaged.

"So is McCoy a close friend would you say?"

"Yes."

"So she would have told you all about me, yes?"

"No," Tasha said tearfully. "I don't know who you are." A tingling shiver ran up her arms as he looked intently into her eyes.

"Please don't insult my intelligence," he said, withdrawing a knife from behind his back and holding it up to the light for her to see. "Are you saying she hasn't told you about the woodlands killer?"

The moment felt surreal. She could just imagine her conversation with Charlotte if she made it out of there alive. *How's your week been? Oh just excellent, couldn't have been better. I was held hostage in a cabin by a madman who didn't care much for housekeeping, oh and he had a fetish for knives and . . . my blood.* She almost laughed at the ridiculousness of it all. One minute she was the happiest she had ever been in her life and the next she was wondering if she had much of a life span left.

"I . . . yes, I've heard of you, but I didn't know you were him, I swear, Ashley doesn't know who you are either, the police haven't a clue." Her chest rose heavily as she felt the gnaw of fear again ripple through her.

"I believe you, Tasha, but that poses a problem for you because you're the only one that knows what I look like."

"But I wouldn't tell anybody, I promise, you don't have to kill me. I'm meant to be going back to Australia shortly I wouldn't even be in the country," Tasha said pleadingly as tears welled in her eyes.

"You know, Tasha, killing someone is the easy part. It's the clean up that's the problem."

He hovered over her—so close she could smell his sour breath. She rolled her head to the side, recoiling from him as if he were a dangerous snake.

"Are you frightened?" he asked as he traced the knife lightly along the outline of her face.

Tasha nodded, a single tear rolling down the side of her face. Fear gripping her heart like an ice cold hand.

"Good." He sneered. "It would all be worthless if you wasn't."

She heard the sound of heavy footsteps approaching. As they neared her heart raced—had Ashley found her? She looked up into the man's steely blue eyes as they darted towards the door. He'd heard the noise as well.

"Make one sound and I will kill you in a second," he whispered menacingly, as he tiptoed towards the door.

The handle rattled then seconds later the door slowly opened. Light spilled in as Tasha turned her head to see if she could make out who it was but her attacker blocked her view.

"What are you doing here?" her abductor said to the man, relief evident in his voice.

"I could ask you the same thing, you bloody idiot. What are you playing at?"

"Just trying to clean up the mess you started." He growled.

"Have you killed her?"

"Not yet."

"Come outside," the newcomer said.

The closing of the door momentarily stilled her hammering heart. She could hear them in a heated argument with insults being traded between them. Their voices rose for a few minutes—she could hear her name being mentioned as well as Ashley's. There was a thud and then the sound of something being dragged away from the door. Footsteps headed back towards the door, the sound of the handle rattled as the door was pushed wide open and the man who had been splattered all over the newspapers walked in— Aaron Davies.

"I'm so sorry you had to get caught up in all of this, Tasha," he said, closing the door behind him. "I really am, but this is what happens when you deal with people with less than average intelligence."

She squirmed on the table. "Where is he? Please let me go."

He sighed. "I should think he's gone to the other side by now, not the heavenly place where you're going to, more like down there," he said tilting the knife down towards the floor as he took a step forward.

"Why are you doing this? I thought you were the

good guy in all this."

"The good guy." Aaron laughed. "You're kidding me, right. Do you think having been through my childhood that I could have remained untouched, untainted?"

"I don't understand? What happened to you?"

He looked at her, and for a moment she thought she glimpsed a melting in his hostility.

He glanced down at the knife he held and ran his finger along the blade. Leaning against the pile of logs as if contemplating, he looked up at her and said, "I was ten. Can you believe it? Ten years old and my father wanted to teach me some work ethic. The lazy bastard never worked a day in his life, yet he wanted to teach me how to be a man." He let out a bitter laugh. "He was friends with Miles—you know, your friendly attacker—and told me I could earn my pocket money going on jobs with him during the summer holidays, gathering leaves— that sort of thing." He took a deep breath then shook his head before continuing. "We were at a job in Epping when he asked me if instead of going home I wanted to play hide and seek in the forest—obviously I said yes. We were there about ten minutes when I couldn't find him. I heard a noise nearby and went to investigate and then I saw him, on the floor with this pretty young girl. I vividly remember that I stepped on a dry twig—I can still hear the cracking sound it made . . . and the girl, she sort of like turned towards me. I doubt she saw me, her eyes were covered with her own blood and then they just slowly closed. I felt really bad for her, because I knew her as we did jobs at her parents' house. We'd also just seen her at another job we were doing. She was kind to me, whenever I went to her house, she'd give me an ice cream."

"So you didn't kill her! Then why can't you just let me go? You did nothing wrong, you were just a child."

"Tasha, Tasha, if only it were that simple. You scc, I wasn't involved in the first one no—but then things changed. I was actually pleased when he killed the second one—I didn't like her. She was asking for money and said rude things to me when I tried to warn her. I told her to run away. She pushed me onto the floor and started laughing at me. Well, she wasn't laughing for much longer," Aaron said, a wry smile crossing his face.

Tasha looked into his eyes and saw a cold emptiness. *He's going to kill me, he's insane.*

"Miles said killing made him feel powerful. I wanted to feel what it was like for myself." He shook his head and let out a little laugh. "I thought he was going to be so pleased with me when I showed him that I could be as powerful as him. I don't know if you know but Amber was Miles' girlfriend. She'd never been to the forest with both of us before so I thought—"

Tasha held her breath, she tried to prepare herself for what she knew was coming.

"That he'd brought her there you know, to kill her. While he went to the van to get his fags, I saw the knife sticking out from his jacket. So . . . I took it . . . and I"—he rubbed his hand over his chin—"stabbed her in the neck. I'll never forget the way she looked at me—I have never seen such fear and that's when I knew what Miles meant, about having power. I felt like God." He stood up straight and then began to pace the room. "Well, you can imagine Miles' face when he came back and found us both covered in blood and her choking on the floor. For a minute, by the look on his face, I thought he was going to kill me. He did hit me though, really hard in the face, my mum wouldn't let me go out with him again after he took me home with a big bruise on my face." He smiled as though remembering fond childhood memories. "He did try to save her but it was too late," Aaron said as he walked towards Tasha. "I never thought they'd find her body."

"Aaron, you were only a child. No one has to know about this. I'll tell the police you saved me, you'll be like a local hero, all of your shows will be a sell-out—you'll be world famous." Tasha grappled with the first thing that came to her mouth, anything to try and stop him from getting closer but the more she spoke the closer he got. "Aaron, you won't get away with it if you kill me, Ashley will find out the truth."

He stopped in his tracks. "Ahh, Ashley, with you dead she won't have any proof—and I, my dear, will be far away on the other side of the world—my ticket is booked for tonight, they'll have no reason to track me down."

If you can hear me, Ashley, I love you so much, was Tasha's last thought as she heard Aaron cry out, "God forgive me!" and felt the knife piercing through her skin.

It took little more than a few seconds before images of her life swam before her eyes.

Chapter 35

Ashley did all she could while waiting for Dale to hand her box after box down from the attic. She prayed, long and hard that the gardener's details would be somewhere amongst all of the papers. She had asked Mrs Patterson to make them a cup of tea as her incessant talking was making her more on edge. She needed silence, space to think. Dale handed her the last box and made his way down the loft ladder. Opening the first box by her foot she reached in and grabbed the folders. "Mrs Patterson said there's one with gardening on it," she said as she flicked through the wad she held. Nothing. She tried again. Still nothing. There was everything else but nothing about the gardening.

"Ash, I've got it," Dale said, waving the folder in his hand.

She grabbed it from him and opened it. Miles Fisher, 44, Campsite road, Enfield.

She checked the date on the receipt—1984. "Dale, call this in and get someone to run a check to see if he's still at that address. Tell Colleen we're on our way."

She nearly knocked Mrs Patterson down as she bumped into her when she reached the ground floor.

"I take it you found what you were looking for."

"Yes, I'm sorry, Mrs Patterson. I will send an officer round later today to put all of your boxes back."

"Has Miles done something bad?" she asked.

"Yes, I think he's done something very bad," Ashley said as she rushed through the door and into the waiting car.

Dale had already got the confirmation back that Miles' address was the same by the time Ashley reached the car—within seconds he had put the address details in the sat nav and was swerving round corners like his life depended on it.

It took them twenty five minutes to reach the middle house terrace on a quiet street. Outside were several squad cars. Ashley leapt out of the car and ran to the first officer she saw. Flashing her ID she asked him, "Is Miles Fisher at home?"

"No but his missus is."

Dread flooded her, as she mounted the four steps and entered the small house. She found Mrs Fisher still in a flimsy negligee looking visibly distressed.

"I've told you a thousand times he didn't come home last night," she said looking relieved to see a female officer. "Please tell these gentlemen, I'd like to get dressed."

"It's alright I'll take it from here," Ashley said showing her ID to the two officers that were hovering over her. She glanced around the room as the officers left. Her attention was drawn to a large family photograph of Miles and his wife; his tanned smiling face, the buff body in a tight fitting T-shirt. For some reason his face looked really familiar to her. She tried to place it, filtering through of the thousands of images she had stored in her memory. Then she made a hit—he was the gardener that she had seen when she'd gone to see the Campbells, the man she had seen cutting the hedge and felt sorry for.

She closed the door behind them. "Please, Mrs Fisher," Ashley said kneeling down beside her. "This is a matter of life and death. If you know where your husband is, you need to tell me now."

"Like I told—"

"No, you need to think! Where does he go to spend his time? Who does he see?"

"Well, he goes to play darts, but he's never not come home before and not let me know."

"Does he have any other hobbies?"

"Well, he used to go shooting pheasants at his cabin but he hasn't been there for years since he got fined for poaching."

Ashley stood—her adrenaline pumping. "Mrs Fisher, where is the cabin?"

Chapter 36

The air was thick with noise from siren wails. As their car sped down a long winding dirt road in the vast foreboding forest, Ashley gripped the slippery steering wheel tightly as she fought to keep the car under control as it swerved and swayed against the oppressive foliage on the uneven ground. She'd torn up the country lanes enough in the past hour to strip the tread bare—all for Tasha. After what seemed like a lifetime, the trail bent off on a sharp right and there, a hundred feet ahead of her stood two structures, shielded by kelly-green vegetation. The dilapidation around the place made her cringe inside, hoping Tasha was holding up her usual fighting spirit within its bowels, long enough for her to get squarely inside. She held her breath, saying a silent prayer to God that she wasn't too late.

Seconds later she brought the car to a screeching halt outside the timber cabin—both herself and Dale exiting with the engine still running.

"I'll go check out the large cabin, you look in the shed," Dale whispered.

Ashley nodded and approached the shed entrance, wary of anyone inside that might be on the lookout for intruders. *I'm probably going to have to go around the side window in order to get in*, she thought. But as soon as she tested the handle she was surprised to find it open; sometimes the most obvious things are hidden in plain sight and she knew that most criminals recognise that fact. She paused and thought for a moment that an unlocked door could mean Tasha wasn't actually there, or worse. . . No sooner had the door creaked on its oily hinges, spilling sunlight into the darkened front room did she see a crumpled body—Tasha's body she was sure.

Losing all adherence to the usual protocol, Ashley dived towards her body, oblivious to her surroundings. The killer could be anywhere, but the mixture of blind fury and passion that welled up within her chest and expressed themselves as salty tears, made her abandon all else other than that moment; it was in this spare freeze-frame of time that two distinct possibilities simultaneously existed: she was alive; she was dead. Hitting the floor next to her as she screamed out her name, she wasn't sure she could handle the truth in either circumstance. What if she were still alive but wracked for life with emotional scars?

As she grasped her limp form between her tense arms, she could smell the coppery tang of blood wafting through the air and noticed her bloodied left-side. She was listless, eyes shut, unaware of her presence. She felt for a pulse and felt the greatest wash of relief she'd ever experienced. As adrenaline coursed through her veins, causing the moment before her to strobe like a primitive picture show, she tugged at her white gown to check on the damage underneath. Gnats swirled through the beams of sunlight in the dank abode; for all she knew the would-be killer would barge in at any moment, but all that mattered now was making sure she was safe enough to move out of the place.

Ashley sighed as he examined the gash— a knife wound. As Tasha's head lolled she became sickened at the heavy scent of mould in the cabin air, she tightened her reassuring grip on her right shoulder. "It's me! I'm here now . . . we're going to get you out of here! Can you hear me? Tasha, it's gonna be alright!" She had to choke out the last part through clenched teeth and another wave of briny-warm tears of relief, confusion, anger and regret; mostly regret that she could have let this happen to the woman she loved.

"Over here quickly," Ashley shouted as she twisted around at the sound of heavy footsteps rushing through the door. "You're going to be okay," she said, whispering in Tasha's ear as a male paramedic knelt down opposite her with a large green bag open at the seams and bursting with medical equipment.

"She's got a weak pulse."

"Please make some space," Bill said resting his hand on Ashley's shoulder.

She turned away and stood up—she couldn't bear to hear them talking in their medical codes.

"I want to come with her," she shouted above the noise.

"It's best if you follow us, detective. I'm going to have to work on her en-route. She's being taken to the Princess Alexandra. I'd get there sooner rather than later," he said dismally.

She stood and stared as if in a trance as she watched Tasha being wheeled away on the stretcher to the ambulance. She knew what he meant by what he said. How many times had she used those very words to relatives of victims who were at deaths door? She was going to lose her so soon after just finding her.

"Ash, we found a male body round the back," Dale said, his broad frame filling the doorway as his gaze followed the ambulance.

"Is he dead?"

Dale nodded his head. "There's no way he could have survived injuries like that. How's Tasha?"

She looked away. "Alive." Just barely but she had to hold on to a glimmer of hope.

"Go be with her, Ash. After I've assessed the crime scene I'll catch up with you at the hospital."

Before the last word had left his lips, Ashley was running towards her car. As a police officer it was a necessity for her to be hardened to every type of situation she came across and she had been, up until now. Even when she had held Melissa in her arms there was still some kind of reserve which enabled her to comfort her in her last seconds of need and not break down, but with Tasha it had sent her over the edge and she didn't think she could climb back from it if Tasha. . . She couldn't bring herself to even think the word, all she could hear were the words from the medic: *Get there sooner than later.*

Ashley ran as fast as her legs would carry her through the long fluorescent lit corridor, her feet slipping and sliding on the polished floor as she turned a corner and headed towards the sign which read Intensive Care. She sidestepped the elderly and infirm who walked ahead of her—*she had to get to her*. Suddenly a scene from the past hit her like a bolt of lightning. The memory was so overpowering, it nearly stopped her in her tracks. Could it have only been a year ago that she was running down a similar corridor, to another intensive care unit? Only then it had been a child she was rushing to see—a child whose mother she had promised she would bring back home—safe and alive. But she had failed. Though everyone said she had done her best, to Ashley her best just wasn't good enough. The case had been a kidnapping of two pre-teen children; Laura from a wealthy family and La Tia, from a family where the mother was a prostitute and the father was nowhere to be seen. The then DSI Ripley had been in charge of the case, calling all the shots and revelling in the press coverage he got as the spokesperson for the force.

The case was going nowhere fast as the children had just vanished out of thin air. No one had any clues as to where they had gone and there was no link between the children themselves. It was after painstakingly going over all the evidence that she'd noticed a discrepancy in the father's alibi that brought new blood to the case. Had Ripley listened to her and taken divisive action when she'd brought it to his attention, La Tia could have been saved. Instead, he had chosen to believe the father, who it later turned out went to the same golf club as him but all of that was quietly swept under the carpet as Ripley was promoted to a higher rank when the case was solved. One girl dead, the other traumatised for life by a father who had used her as bait to entice La Tia into his car. It was up to Ashley to find her limp body which had been dumped in a lay-by following a tip off. And it had been left to Ashley to tell La Tia's grief stricken mother that she had failed her. Colleen had tried her best to bring it to the attention of officers higher up but her requests were ignored—

she just didn't have the clout Ripley did. Every detail of that case was stored in her mind. The guilt hung over her like a dark storm cloud, ready to shower her at any minute with terrifying visions.

She slowed down as she approached the light oak coloured door to the accident and emergency unit waiting room ahead of her. She wiped away the perspiration with the back of her hand and stood before the door. She needed to get her act together. Behaving like a headless chicken wasn't going to get her anywhere. With her breathing resuming its natural rhythm, she pushed open the heavy door with one hand, leaning her weight up against it. Running straight to the receptionist, she asked where Tasha was. Finding out she had been taken straight into surgery, she walked to a free chair and slumped down in a daze.

An hour later she heard a voice talking to her, but couldn't comprehend it.

"Ashley?"

Looking up she saw Tasha's Aunt B. She looked like a completely different woman, racked with worry. Ashley attempted to struggle to her feet but desisted after a moment of hopeless effort and sank back into her chair. There was no exaggeration in her action. The shock of what had happened seemed to have rendered her so weak that she was simply unable to stand. Tasha's aunt was by her side in an instant. Ashley moistened her lips before attempting to speak, but found no words to say.

"I know, I know, it's alright, Ashley," Aunt B said patting her hand. "She knows you're here, that will make her strong. She'll get though this, she's a fighter."

Her words went straight to Ashley's heart. This great woman who was sat before her, whose only niece was near death was more concerned about her surviving for Ashley's sake.

A doctor walked through the door with a sombre look on his face. He looked at Ashley first then to Beryl. "I'm sorry," he said clearing his throat. "There's no easy way to tell you this, but Ms Hudson has lost a lot of blood—we've given her a blood transfusion and stopped the bleeding, we've done as much as we can. We'll just have to wait and see if she can pull through."

"Can we see her?" Ashley asked hopefully.

"Of course."

Chapter 37

Aaron closed his front door and ran into the kitchen and immediately began to strip, putting all of his clothes and shoes in a black bag. He made his way up to the bathroom, switching the shower on full heat and scrubbed himself until he was red raw.

He planned to dump his clothes in a rubbish bin at the airport, he couldn't risk leaving any forensic evidence at his house or even the local dump—he wanted to make sure he left no trace of himself. Everything had turned out for the best in the end. Though he hadn't ever intended to kill Tasha, she'd just become one of life's hiccups that needed to be dealt with. It didn't matter now, it was all over. Tasha was dead and she wouldn't be able to identify him, there wasn't any way that anything could be pinned on him now. He'd covered his tracks well, no one would suspect anyone else was involved.

He made his way through to his bedroom and quickly dressed in one of his many black suits. He relaxed now—he was in no rush. His flight wasn't for another eight hours, he had all the time in the world. Dragging out a large suitcase from the wardrobe, he began filling it up. He whistled as he thought about the new life he would be living in America. He fancied himself as the next Dave Morrell, a superstar psychic who was rich beyond belief. He had the skill and the know how to make it anywhere. He'd find himself a good team of people when he arrived then he'd be back in business.

Once packed, he dragged his case down the stairs and left it by the door before going into the kitchen to prepare himself dinner. He glanced up at the clock—*not long now*, he told himself as he opened the fridge and took out a bottle of wine and some steak.

***

Dale stood sheepishly in the doorway. "I'm sorry to intrude, but I need to speak with you, Ash."

Ashley looked at Beryl who smiled at her. "Don't worry nothing's going to happen."

"Can I get you both a tea?" Dale asked.

"Yes, that would be lovely, thank you," Beryl said squeezing Ashley's hand as she walked past to greet Dale.

They exited the unit and headed to the foyer. "How is she?" Dale said.

"She's not looking too good. They've given her a fifty percent chance of pulling through. It's down to her really."

"This place brings back some bad memories."

"I know," she said linking his arm. "So what have you got for me?"

"Looks like Tasha and Miles were caught up in some kind of fight together. They're both covered in each other's blood, looks like she was struck first and somehow she managed to get the knife off him and stab him straight in the heart. He stumbled out the cabin and collapsed and died 'round the back where we found him."

"There wasn't any evidence of a third person?"

"None whatsoever, unless they were a ghost. All families have been informed the killer has been found."

"We still never figured out how Aaron or Peter were involved."

"It was most probably what you said. Aaron overheard someone talking and decided he could capitalise on it with his show. Maybe Peter did stumble across Esther's murder and blackmail Miles. Top brass aren't interested, Aaron was ten at the time and Peter's dead. They don't want the publicity—they are just basking in their own glory that they've solved some twenty five year old cold cases."

"Is that bastard Ripley about?"

"Funnily enough, I haven't seen him about these past few days."

"That's got to be a good thing."

Ashley put the coins into the machine and waited whilst it dripped out the tea.

"You look like you need something to eat."

"I don't think anything will pass through my throat, it feels like a brick is lodged there."

"Come here," Dale said pulling her into a bear hug. "Just thought you'd like to know I'm not resigning."

She drew herself back, her eyes opened wide. "You're not! How come?"

"It's days like today that remind me why I became a cop in the first place."

"I'm glad, I would have missed you."

"Not as much as I would have missed you," he said.

As they walked through the intensive care unit door she saw Beryl sitting with her hands over her face sobbing. Without speaking to her she ran to Tasha's room just in time to see them taking all of the equipment away from her still form.

Chapter 38

At precisely eight on the dot, Aaron's doorbell rung. He stood, draining the last drops of wine from his glass and looked around the room for the last time. He had left a letter for the cleaning lady asking her to pack up all his belongings and put them in storage for him, giving her a hefty bonus for her trouble. Once he was settled in America, he would contact an estate agent to put the house on the market. He switched off the light and made his way to the front door. The driver hadn't waited to help him with his luggage—*there goes his tip,* he thought as he dragged the case out and double locked the door behind him. With some difficulty he managed to get the case to the car's open boot. He was going to call the cab station when he arrived at the airport and report the shoddy behaviour of the driver. Slamming the boot shut he slipped into the backseat, with his head down, checking he had his passport. "Heathrow," he said.

"I'm afraid you won't be going anywhere near Heathrow airport for a very long time," Ashley said, turning around in her seat to face a wide eyed Aaron.

"What is going on?" he asked trying to open the car door.

"Don't waste your time," Dale said from the driver's seat. "It's security locked."

Dale began driving.

"Where are you taking me?" Aaron said raising his voice.

"Don't you know? Haven't you been speaking to your spirit buddies lately?"

"I'm going to call my solicitor and have you both charged with harassment and kidnapping."

"You can call them as soon as you get to the station."

"Am I under arrest?"

"Yes you are—for the attempted murder of Tasha Hudson."

"Attempted?" he asked confused.

"Yes, attempted. She said to say hi."

Chapter 39

"Well, I can't say I'm not glad that this case is over," Colleen said, letting out a sigh of relief.

"Tell me about it. And to think that if Tasha had died, Aaron could have gotten away with it scot free—"

"I'll be honest with you, I didn't think he was going to roll over so easily."

"There was no easy way out for him—he actually had his bloody clothes in his suitcase. I'm sure once we get the DNA results they'll match Miles Fisher and Tasha's blood. Once he found Tasha had survived he knew the game was over."

"So tell me, Dale, honestly, did you ever believe that he could talk to the dead?" Colleen asked, taking a bottle of whiskey out of her drawer and pouring two shots into glasses.

Dale knocked his back in one gulp. "I'll admit I was taken in at the beginning, I mean what's the likelihood of that happening?"

"Yeah, he had me going as well—let's not ever admit that to Ashley. She'd never let us live it down," Colleen said refilling his glass. "So when you charged him, did he say why he brought it out into the open?"

"Yeah, I wish I could tell you it was all about the families and giving them closure but it wasn't, it was all about him. Ashley was spot on. All he wanted was to make a name for himself here so he could take the states by storm. Moving into the big league with the likes of Jonathan Edwards. The worst thing is that he nearly succeeded. Can you believe that he's angry at her for blowing his chances?"

"Nothing surprises me anymore, Dale."

"Is Ashley at the hospital?"

He smiled. "Yep, like glue. I don't think we'll be seeing her around for the next few days until she's convinced Tasha is on the mend properly."

"Good, she deserves a break. You both do, you did a great job . . . as always."

"Thanks," Dale said standing. "Er, you know that resignation letter I gave you. . . "

"What letter?"

He gave her a grateful smile. "Thanks, Colleen, see you tomorrow."

Chapter 40

Tasha stirred and opened her eyes.

"Hello, gorgeous. How're you feeling?" Ashley asked as she leaned over and kissed Tasha on the lips.

"Very sore."

"Don't worry. When you come home, I'll look after you round the clock with tender loving care."

"Did you get him?"

Ashley nodded. "He confessed to everything. The worst thing is that it was all so pointless."

"Hello, Tasha," a male voice said from the door.

Tasha moved her head slowly towards the voice. "Mark! What are you doing here?"

"Is that any way to greet your big brother?" he asked, moving towards the bed.

"I'm sorry, but I thought you were in Bali."

"Aunt B called me and told me what happened. I got on the first flight out." He leaned over and kissed her forehead. "And you must be Ashley?" he said out stretching his hand. "Thank you for saving my sister's life."

"Think nothing of it, was all in a day's work."

"Don't be so modest. Aunt B told me you were instrumental in bringing her home alive."

"On that note, I think I'll leave you two to catch up." Ashley took Tasha's hand and squeezed it. "I'll see you later and Mark, it was nice to meet you."

"Likewise."

When Ashley had left Mark took a seat next to the bed.

"So how have you been?" Tasha asked him, rolling her head to the side.

"Living the dream, as they say. I didn't come here to talk about me, Tasha. I came here for you."

"I'll be alright, Mark, the doctor said I'm as strong as an ox."

"I know you are—you always have been." He let out a deep sigh. "While I've been a coward."

"Don't say that, you've done nothing wrong."

"Haven't I? I left you alone with Dad didn't I? After knowing what he tried to do with my life."

"I'm a big girl, you know. I don't need looking after."

"No, but you need support, especially when it comes to Dad and that's why I'm here— I'm going to go back to the business."

"Mark, you can't, you'll go insane."

"It will only be for a while, until he's, you know, gone. This has been a massive wake up call to me. You're my little sister. I know I haven't always been there for you but I'd like to make it up to you, if you'll let me."

She reached out her hand for his. "Thank you."

"It should be me for thanking you—for showing me the light."

"Why don't you go to Aunt B's and get some sleep, you look exhausted."

"I am, but I just needed to see you first," Mark said standing. "I'll send Ashley back in. So are you two an item?"

"It seems that way," Tasha said.

"She seems really nice, I look forward to welcoming her to the family properly—you should both come over to the hotel for a long break when you're up for travelling."

"We will," she said as he turned and left the room.

"So what did your brother have to say?" Ashley said as she sat down beside her.

"My dad's on his way to England."

"He doesn't think you're fit enough to travel does he?"

"I don't care what he thinks. I'm not going back."

"You're not? Does that mean what I think that means?"

"Yes, Mark has decided he's going to go back into the business so you're stuck with me."

"I can think of worse things," Ashley said.

"I've been thinking."

"Yes."

"I'm going to write a book about this."

"Really?"

Tasha nodded. "I think it might help me to come to terms with what happened."

"Well, it beats sitting with a therapist, so when it comes to writing my character," Ashley said clearing her throat, "I hope she's going to be this beautiful, intelligent, leggy blonde who despite it all saves the day and she and her lady live happily ever after."

"Obviously—you know what they say—the truth is sometimes stranger than fiction."

***

"Shut that racket, Davies or I'll come in there and make you," the prison guard shouted outside the metallic door.

Aaron banged on the door with the palm of his hand. "It's important you listen to me— you have to warn Detective Ashley McCoy."

"What are you on about now," the officer asked opening the flap in the door.

"You've got to tell her I had a vision—tell her to watch out for a dark car—she's in danger."

10851191R00177

Printed in Great Britain
by Amazon.co.uk, Ltd.,
Marston Gate.